The Phoenix Plan

Sarah & Simon, Book 1

Terri Selting David

Spiderdust Studios

To Marc, the love of my life and my greatest support.

CONTENTS

PROLOGUE: INTO DARKNESS

They only bring him out when it's dark.

He can smell their fear. He breathes it in when they open the door. Massive muscles ripple as he lumbers out of the small, white room.

They pull away as he approaches.

The air outside smells like pine trees and sky. He stops, just for a minute, and closes his eyes, turning his face to the wind, nostrils flaring. He knows he's not supposed to stop, but he does anyway.

Huddling behind the door, a man yells for him to keep moving and waves a small, rectangular object at him. It's dark and sleek with buttons that glow under the man's fingers. He wants to grind that object, and the arm holding it, into the dirt. To crush them beneath his fists. His eyes narrow in rebellion as he plants his feet, every muscle in his body tense, refusing to move.

The man presses a button. A red light blinks on his wrist and the pain starts. It's like a swarm of invisible hornets stinging him from the inside out. Biting and crawling their way from the red light up into his brain. He shakes his head but the flickering pain overrides his senses. Light dances in front of his eyes, ringing fills his ears, and the imaginary hornets swarm over his body.

He'll do anything to make it stop.

He'll even do what they want.

Ahead, a truck idles with an impatient rumble. He climbs into his cage in the back and the pain stops. The vehicle shoots away, throwing him backward. He grabs the bars with powerful hands, tasting the wind as it rushes past.

They travel further than on any previous night. By the time they shutter to a stop, the air feels cooler. The musty smell of earth and rotting food fills his nostrils. Rats scuttle around somewhere, but the people who brought him here can't hear them. Their ears are weak, and their arguing is too loud. One of them waves a piece of paper at the other.

He wants to smash their shrill voices into silence. A low growl reverberates in his throat as he shuffles towards them. Then the pain starts again. Controlling him. The man holding the shiny object sneers at him while pressing another button.

They pretend to be strong, but he's the strong one and they know it. He savors their fear, drinking it like fresh water.

Nearby, a building looms in the moonlight. Beyond the building stretches open space. Quiet. Trees. And far below, a sea of lights twinkles.

The people walk toward the building, dropping the now-forgotten paper. He grabs it as he follows them. It's a photograph they've shown him before, a mountainside full of trees and freedom, where he could disappear forever. It's familiar, comforting.

They open a door and motion him inside. It's a cave, deep and dark. Suffocatingly dark. He hesitates and the hornets return, crawling like fire through his body. He steps inside and dank earth envelops him. The air itself tastes stale.

Behind him, the door slams shut. He takes one slow step along the passage, then another, and the pain drifts away. He moves further and further down the tunnel until he's completely blind.

His nose twitches. They want him to embrace the blackness. To get comfortable using his other senses in the smothering dark. If he doesn't go deeper, they'll hurt him again. The musky smell of rats guides him, their sharp claws scraping the stone as they navigate the darkness. He follows. His mouth opens to taste the bitter ammonia trail they leave behind in the air. One hand trails along the cave wall, and the other clutches the reassuring presence of the picture.

Cavern after cavern, turn after turn. Suddenly, his hands hit solid stone. He slides it to the side only to find more stone. It's everywhere. The cave has swallowed him whole. There is no way forward, and he can't find the way back. The picture falls, forgotten, as he reaches out desperately into the blackness. Where is the way out?

He's lost and blind, drowning in hard darkness and the sharp smell of rats. With the force of desperation, he hurls his body against the encasing rock, forward, backward, to the sides, but escape eludes him; there is no way out. His muscles throb. Blood thunders in his ears. He can't breathe. He wants air and trees, the moon, even the white room. Anywhere but here. Icy fear spreads through him.

Then furious rage replaces the fear. A rage more powerful than even the pain from the man's object.

His scream echoes throughout the cave, doubling in

volume, tripling in power. Rats scamper away, their terror awakening a power inside him. The power focuses his mind with sizzling clarity and he roars again, listening to them scatter. Their terror brings him a feeling of control. He wants to crush them beneath his feet like the gravel he walks on.

Then, one of his fists finds the opening. A way out! He squeezes through and the tunnel opens up again, but the powerful rage still flows through him like water.

Thump-thump, thump-thump.

His feet hammer like a heartbeat, filling the darkness of the cave as he thunders towards the exit.

A dim light appears ahead. A beacon, an open door. He breaks through it into the fresh air. Alone. No one waits for him. No one is here for him to rip apart. But the power still boils within him. It whispers only one thing, over and over. Destroy. Destroy.

Beyond the building, posts as tall as trees criss-cross with ropes, like a spiderweb. Like the ropes they bind him with. Muscles bulging with inhuman strength, he throws himself at the structure. The ropes squeal and snap. He falls. With lightning reflexes, he catches another rope and swings out over the edge. The structure hangs off the side of a cliff. The ground falls away, hundreds of feet beneath him. His muscles flex. Wood splinters.

It feels good to destroy.

He pauses at the top of the structure's carcass, and surveys his surroundings, breath coming fast and harsh, chest heaving. He knows he needs to find his way back to the small white room or the pain will return, worse than ever. But for now, he throws his head back and roars at the open sky. He wants the stars themselves to hear how strong he is.

Nearby, a camera on top of a tall metal pole watches him. He knows what it is because it's just like the one that watches him in the small white room.

Everyone watches him. While he sleeps, while he eats. They're always watching.

Screaming again, he launches his massive body through the air, muscles straining with raw power. Arms as thick as tree limbs grab the pole and smash the camera in a single movement. Then he slides to the ground, the rage finally spent, flowing out of him. His mind clears.

He pauses near the wreckage, just a shadow in the night. Compared to the cave, it's bright as day. A shock of hornets blossoms from his arm. A warning. He may be outside and alone, but he's not free. The air is just better out here.

With a grunt, he melts into the trees to find his way back to the men waiting for him and the cold, white room.

1: SARAH, FALLING INTO A VOLCANO

The volcano isn't quite exploding.

It belches toxic orange clouds that glow from the molten lava deep inside. A fast-moving shadow, silhouetted against those clouds, circles the volcano's crater. Twilight deepens the sky. Even in the light of day, this swift figure would be impossible to identify because it's clad head to toe in a fitted tactical suit, face and hair covered entirely by a smooth black mask.

That's me. In the suit.

Exactly one hundred and seventy-two and a third feet away, a rocky outcropping conceals our stolen helicopter. The landform probably has some kind of fancy name, but I don't know what it is. I'm not a geologist, I'm a spy. At least I'm supposed to be.

I can shimmy through an air duct faster than a trained rat, fling myself off a cliff in nothing but a wingsuit, maneuver a car with severed brakes down a twisty mountain path, or run an entire black bag operation based only on chicken feed, pass off my intel to a dead drop, and be home in time for pancakes. I can, in theory, kill a man with my pinky toe.

What I can't do is leave this stupid island.

From up here, I can see the whole island stretch out

beneath me. The setting sun paints purples and oranges across the limitless ocean and the Island's thick jungle, white sand beaches, and a bay protected by a coral reef. It's paradise from the active volcano I'm circling on my off-road skateboard to the extinct volcano on the other side; the dead one that houses our secret headquarters. Everyone thinks this place is a tropical vacation, a playground of natural wonders. An absolute utopia.

Idiots.

They aren't stuck here. They have lives and friends and jobs to go back to. My brother and I are here because this is home. Not the home you return to at the end of a long day, but the home you're stuck at because no one will give you a ride anywhere else. The kids brought here for safe-keeping are all the children of important adults. We aren't anyone's children. We belong to DAAAD.

But I'm not here to complain and I'm not here for the view. I've got a job to do.

Tonight, we're filming footage for our YouTube channel, Crazystuntz. (Don't laugh, we named it when we were, like, twelve.) It's got a pretty good following. No, it's not battling an oppressive regime, but at least we get to use our well-honed spy skills.

My little brother Simon and I are ready to go out and bust some bad guy butt. But does DAAAD trust us to actually go out on a mission? No. No, they do not. They treat us like children. What's the use of having amazing skills if we can't get out there, right? All we do is train. We're like circus animals, performing inside a show ring.

But not tonight.

Tonight it's just me, my little brother, my tricked-out skateboard, and the active volcano we call Mount Explody McBoom. Happy seventeenth birthday.

(Also, just so you know, Mount Explody McBoom is not the volcano's official name. We made it up. Simon and I are the closest thing the Island has to a native population, therefore we get to name everything.)

DAAAD, the Disinformation Assessment and Administration Department, knows all about Crazystuntz. I mean, they're spies, too. That's why we have to wear these really sweaty outfits. Seriously, we have to cover every inch. DAAAD didn't spend all that money raising us as untraceable agents from birth in order to have our identifiable features plastered all over YouTube.

Simon thinks we look cool in these things. I think we look like henchmen in a cheesy movie. Seriously, it's embarrassing.

I get it. Duty and all that. The sacrifices you make on the road to greatness. You don't become a spy for the fame; you do it to save the world. A good spy disappears like tears in the rain, like an octopus on the sandy ocean bottom, like a taco in my stomach.

At least I have Simon. There's no one I'd rather be raised in a secret government facility with.

Please don't tell him I said that.

My skateboard's adapted wheels crunch gravel as I get close enough to peek into the volcano's crater. The vent extends a little over forty-three and a half feet down from the rim into a thickly bubbling lake of molten rock. It's satisfyingly deadly down there. If I fall over the edge, every bone in my body will break on impact before bursting into flame. Without my respirator mask, the toxic vapor would sizzle my lungs on the way down, too.

But falling into the volcano isn't my plan.

My plan is to nail an Impossible, one of the hardest skateboarding tricks ever, with red volcanic smoke spewing behind me at sunset. It's gonna be epic.

Simon stands nearby, wearing a suit and mask identical to my own. (We're totally henchmen.) A green light blinks on his shoulder, showing that the camera mounted there is recording. This is the last footage we'll get until the next time we sneak away. It's my job to make it good.

An Impossible is where you jump up and spin your plank end over end, like flipping a bo staff over your hand. It's not just hard, it almost defies the laws of physics, especially on an off-road board with its elevated trucks and giant rubber wheels. How can that not go viral? And at this point going viral is a matter of honor. We have to get more views than that stupid pooping cat video.

In our latest Crazystuntz post, Simon swam through the coral reef surrounding the Island and punched a shark. It should have been internet gold, but it didn't get as many views as this one cat sitting on a toilet. Which, apparently, is hilarious. Simon wants to do something spectacular to knock that cat off its throne. Figuratively. I don't know why he's so competitive about Crazystuntz, but I'm here for him. I'd do anything for my little brother.

I plant my back foot near the board's tail, slide my front foot to the center, and jump just as I move into the frame. The skateboard spins around my back foot as I pull my front foot out of the way, textbook perfect. Take that, pooping cat.

Suddenly, my toe snags on one of the extra-large wheels. The board flies out of control. It tangles in my feet and I bail ungracefully.

My plank and I skitter across the ground toward the rim of the volcano's vent. The skateboard tips up in a salute as first the wheels, then the entire board slips over the edge.

It plunges towards the lava where, as expected, it shatters and bursts into flames. I watch in horror, sliding right behind my board, scrabbling wildly for something to hang on to. Heat blasts my legs as they slip over the rim. Gravel rattles alongside me, sounding like popcorn being poured into a popper. I grab frantically for a handhold and find a tiny one just as I follow it over the edge, leaving me dangling there by one hand.

Twenty-nine and a quarter feet below, molten rock waits patiently to melt my face. The small circle of flames dancing on the lava winks out as they finish devouring my board. Spies aren't supposed to get attached to things, but I'll miss that plank. RIP, buddy. At least your end was spectacular.

"Sarah!"

A rope smacks against the rock next to me, a gift from my little brother. Never call him that, though. Remember, he's a trained operative, and for some reason the fact that I'm older really bothers him. He seems to think that being twins makes us the same age, but we're both perfectly aware that he's nine entire minutes younger than me. That may not sound like a big difference, but a lot can change in nine minutes. Don't believe me? I'll show you.

Start the clock—

- *Situation assessment:*

- o *I hang from one hand 29.25 feet from the lip of the vent shaft*
- o *A rope, 8 millimeters in diameter, is 33 centimeters from my left hand*
- o *Reaching for the rope will shift my balance. I might lose my grip, which is kind of important since it's keeping me from dying.*
- o *My right hand's flexor muscles have about 3.5 minutes tops before they give out*
- o *The toxic cloud of sulfur dioxide stinks in an "I'll kill you" kind of way, even through my mask*
    - ▪ *I don't like being thankful for DAAAD's regulations, but here we are*
- • *Conclusion:*
  - o *Chance of grabbing the rope 93.8%*
  - o *Chance of losing my grip 73%*
- • *Let's do this*
- • ***Time of Analysis: 14.8 seconds***

Here we go.

I brace my feet against the vent's wall, tighten my grip, and reach for the rope. My gripping hand already aches. Don't judge, it was a long day even before I fell into a volcano. But I only have to hang on long enough to grab the rope taunting me just out of reach of my wiggling fingers.

Sweat tickles my face. I'm sweating everywhere. It's hot this close to the lava, especially in this stupid outfit. Once again, I'm secretly thankful for DAAAD's regulations, because these dumb sweaty gloves have traction pads that keep me from slipping off my handhold. My outstretched fingers close over the rope. Almost there.

Suddenly, a bubble of magma pops below me. A jet of fiery gas shoots up, fogging my visor completely. The gust blows the rope just as my fingers close.

I'm left holding literally nothing.

My weight shifts. I squeeze the handhold tighter and my muscles whine. *Please don't cramp up. Please don't cramp up, please don't cramp up.*

They cramp up.

I don't even have time to roll my eyes before I plunge towards the lava. My brain flatlines, which is just sloppy. But all I can think is: *I wanted to eat a street taco before I died.*

I plummet, flapping my empty hands around. Great. Not only am I going to die, I'm going to look stupid doing it. On camera.

Then something hits my palm. I grab it, and my arm almost rips out of its socket as I yank to a stop. Momentum swings me out over the lava and sends me crashing back towards the wall. Pain explodes in my shoulder. That's going to leave a bruise, but at least I'm still alive for now.

- *Elapsed time: 21.96 seconds*

See that? Almost twenty-two seconds is more than enough time to kill a well trained-spy before she's even been to Paris.

I dangle over the lava like a—umm—I don't know, something that dangles on the end of a string? I don't have time to be poetic, I'm on the clock.

- *Time wasted trying to be poetic: 9 seconds*

I wipe my visor against my sleeve and take in the view. Cool night air and a brilliant moon beckon through the small stone circle of the volcano's throat.

The silhouette of a head stares down next to a blinking green light. I assume the silhouette is my little brother, and the light is his camera.

- *Goal:*
    1. *Get out of the volcano*
    2. *Don't embarrass myself on film any more than I already have*
- *Options:*
    1. *Die (this one is suboptimal)*
    2. *Gym-Class technique rope climbing; relies on arm strength, looks dorky*
        a. *Refer to Goal #2*
    3. *S-Wrap technique; super secure, but slow*
    4. *J-Hook technique; fast, but a less secure than the S-Wrap*
- *Conclusion:*
    o *Let's go with option 3*

I kick my leg around the rope and lock it in place with my other foot. I straighten my legs, reposition my hands, grip, lift, re-wrap the leg. Up and up, s-wrap by s-wrap. Safe may be boring, but if anything happened to me, who would take care of Simon?

- **Elapsed time: 52.3 seconds**

I finally make it to the top and peek over the rim. Simon leans back against the rope, counterbalancing me. He slouches expertly, so his camera keeps me in focus. As a tall teenage boy, slouching comes naturally to him. He braced the rope behind him, wrapped around and wedged under a boulder. Nice and sturdy. Good job Simon, you get a gold star.

Now comes the tricky part; letting go of the rope in

order to claw my way out. I pull my legs up as high as I can, wrap the rope around, and swing it over my foot twice this time, trapping it in its coils. Tugging my body over the rim, I clomp the rope-entangled foot beside me, and flip onto my back.

I rip off the respirator, breathing in fresh air. We'll just edit my face out later. This air is too delicious.

- *Result:*
    - *Fiery flaming death AVERTED! Yay!*
- **Total elapsed time: 1 minute, 31.4 seconds**

In about a minute and a half, I saved myself from certain doom. Just imagine how much I must have accomplished in the nine minutes between my entering the world, and when my little brother joined me. *Nine.* It boggles the mind.

The sky has grown totally dark. I lie on my back breathing heavily, staring into the endless void of night as the adrenaline melts away. I'm left feeling as empty as the sky above me (not counting all the stars. If there's one good thing about living in the literal middle of nowhere, it's the lack of light pollution.) The Milky Way galaxy glows in the endless black canopy, every constellation bright and clear.

I try to stop my brain from automatically identifying each group of stars, to just enjoy the artistic beauty the universe has laid out before my eyes. I fail. The glittering points of light automatically name themselves in my head. Constellations come together like—something poetic. Except they aren't poetry. They should be poetry or art, or something. But to me the beautiful night sky reads like a textbook. With a little more effort, I could probably identify my approximate latitude and longitude, the day of the year, maybe even what time it is. But it's my day off so I just glance at my watch.

An insistent red light blinks on its side. I sigh.

You sit around in your super-secret spy base all day, and nobody calls. The second you leave to go climb a volcano, suddenly everybody wants to chat, right? And now we'll probably get in extra trouble for not responding immediately, despite the amazingness of what I just accomplished. Nobody appreciates me.

"Hey little bro," I call to Simon, who's busy coiling the climbing rope around his arm. "We got a summons. We'd better get back to HQ lickity-split."

"Yeah," He replies. "I've been trying to tell you. While you've been messing around, Agent Zero pinged us like forty times."

We head towards the waiting helicopter. Agent Zero certainly won't be throwing us a birthday party. It's time to face our punishment.

"On the upside," Simon grins, "The footage of your bail and fail is killer. We'll finally beat that pooping cat."

"You better hope so," I say, frowning at the word 'fail.' Agents like me don't fail. We just succeed with an unexpected twist. "Happy birthday, Simon. Let's go see what Agent Zero has in store for us."

The smile melts off Simon's face. "We'd probably be safer inside the volcano."

2: SIMON FACES THE MUSIC

Chopper blades *whupp-whupp-whupp* above the circle of light that is helipad three. My sister swings our tail around for a landing.

The downward thrust from the blades flings leaves, vines, and a few small reptiles up into the air in a swirling dance of biological confetti. I watch a lizard drop to the ground, flip itself upright, and tango away into the darkness. Our six-and-a-half-ton Sikorsky Jayhawk touches down as lightly as a hummingbird.

The helipad is near the top of the extinct volcano we call home. Engineers carved through it like industrious little ants to sculpt our high-tech base, HQ Mountain (not its official name).

Sarah yells something above the chopper's loud din but it's just noise to me. I'm alone in my head with only my slowly fraying nerves to keep me company. My wristwatch keeps flashing red. With every blink, I can sense Agent Zero's disapproval.

What did we think would happen? Taking a helicopter without sign-off, sneaking into an off-limits area. What a dumb idea.

We're adults now, Simon, Sarah had told me. *We deserve more responsibility. Training with Agent*

Abernathy was three times more dangerous, and we did that when we were fourteen. Also, it's our birthday.

They'd seemed like reasonable arguments. They always do. But all our well-thought-out rationale will seem ridiculous under the head of the Department's icy gaze.

> *Wind whirls in the night*
> *Hummingbird or hurricane?*
> *The dark holds secrets*

Hello, my name is Simon, and I'm a poet. I'm also a spy. And yes, I'm Sarah's younger brother. Only nine minutes younger, but never forget it. If you do, even for a second, she'll remind you. Trust me.

We don't have any birth certificates in any database anywhere, but there's no reason to doubt what we've been told about our birth. I mean, we're obviously twins; the same thick, dark hair, the same brown eyes, the same long, straight noses and wide chins, and the same olive-toned skin.

We're not sure how we ended up being raised by DAAAD, and if anyone else knows they won't tell us. After years of fruitless searching and digging and prying and sneaking files into our rooms for late night perusal under the cover of darkness, Sarah and I finally gave up trying to find out who our parents are. For all we know, they might have artificially created us in a lab. The important thing, to me anyway, is that I have Sarah. Sarah, who lives her life like she's the star of an action movie. Sarah, who never fails at anything. Sarah, who would throw herself on top of a grenade for me, but won't share her sandwich. We've always been together and always will be. I'd follow her anywhere.

Sarah hops out of the helicopter, crouches under the still-spinning blades and heads towards the giant metal doors that lead into HQ. She doesn't look back. She doesn't have to. I grab our gear and slouch after her.

A concrete frame surrounds metal bunker-style doors, illuminated by a single light. There aren't any guards. The only threats on the Island are vicious plants, a few snakes, and the occasional wild boar, and they certainly aren't interested in what's beyond those doors.

Sarah slaps her hand against a flat glass plate embedded in the concrete frame. A bar of blue light slides beneath it. As I wait next to her, she throws an arm across my shoulders (which is getting harder for her to do as I get taller.)

"Let's go face the music, little bro," she laughs. "Find out how much trouble your clever idea got us into this time."

"It was your idea," I snap. Obviously, she doesn't understand how much trouble we're in. She thinks she's bulletproof. "Besides, you're the one who got sloppy. We'd have been back here before they'd even noticed we were gone if you'd been more careful."

"Which delayed us by what? Way less than nine minutes," She grins. "Sounds like you're admitting that nine minutes really matters."

I sigh as the doors whoosh open.

The brightness of the small elevator temporarily blinds me as we step inside. Next to the doors are a long row of buttons. The top button says "ZERO" spelled out in letters. All the other buttons are numbers. Sarah smashes that top button without enthusiasm but with a lot of attitude. I hope she doesn't say anything stupid when we get up there. It's been known to happen.

The elevator trembles as it rises. I don't get motion sickness, but I feel like I'm going to throw up. Unfortunately, that's been known to happen too.

Stop acting like a little kid, I tell myself. *If you can face off against a shark, you can stand up to Agent Zero. Look at Sarah. She's not scared.*

I reach for my sister's hand. She gives mine a squeeze and steps closer to me. I lean against her and she stands steady as a rock. The doors slide open. She drops my hand, takes a deep breath, lifts her chin, and enters Agent Zero's office. I linger for a moment, then force myself to follow.

We stand in a familiar, cavernous room high atop the volcano's cone. The elevator doors whisper closed, plunging us into a soft darkness that fades into the black of the night sky, visible through the floor-to-ceiling windows wrapping around the entire space. We become one with the luminous moon and stars out there. It's like the boundary between us and the sky has dissolved, like I've stepped into a poem. I melt into the moment and my fear drifts away.

In the light of day, the windows offer an excellent view of the Island and the surrounding ocean. Sight lines to the horizon. From up here, you could spot an air or sea invasion ten miles away.

The sparse furnishings in the room give it great visibility, while being sturdy enough to act as cover from random gunfire or flying glass if someone smashed the windows. They wouldn't break if you threw a chair at them or anything, but five or six bullets in a tight grouping might create a weak point.

I mean, I never expect to be in a shootout in Agent

Zero's office, but after a lifetime of training, my brain does what it does.

An immense conference table lurks in the shadows to our right. To our left, a fireplace full of dancing flames brings warm light and a possible source of ignition to the room. It's in front of a cozy seating area with two overstuffed armchairs and a sofa with removable pillows, good for sitting comfortably or for anything from cushioning a fall to acting as a make-shift silencer. Teetering piles of files and loose papers sprinkle across a polished concrete coffee table between them. An unfamiliar, brightly colored cardboard box struggles to be noticed in the middle of the piles, like a flamboyant party clown slogging through sheets of white paper snow.

As I step out of the elevator, I don't look at any of it. We keep our eyes straight ahead, where a large U-shaped desk greets us. It's buried under more papers, laptops, glowing monitors, and three important-looking red phones. A small woman's head peeks out from under the clutter.

Even with my trained eye, I've never been able to pin down a national origin for the woman sitting behind the desk. Her dark skin could indicate Mediterranean, Malaysian, or perhaps Middle Eastern descent, but her facial features imply African, or maybe Polynesian ancestry, while the texture of her hair, a grey-streaked black, suggests the Americas.

"Welcome back. You've had a busy day." The woman speaks with crisp precision, in flawless, unaccented, news-reporter American English. I've also heard her speak British English like the Queen, and Liverpool-region English like a Beatle, not to mention Parisian

French as if she were born there. I wonder how she keeps up with modern foreign slang when she never leaves the Island.

Sarah stands at attention next to me, upright as a wooden soldier. Her voice is more confident than I feel. "Reporting as requested, Agent Zero."

Agent Zero shifts a few stacks of paper to the side and closes her laptop, setting it next to her desktop computer. She doesn't reply immediately. I steel myself for another epic lecture.

Instead, she says, "Join me on the couch."

She sounds almost wistful. I throw a questioning glance at Sarah, who shrugs so only I can see. Where are the expertly crafted words of concern, dripping with disappointment? The hours-long diatribe on responsibility? An immediate five laps around the Island?

But Agent Zero just grabs a few folders from her desk and leads us across the room and sits in one of the overstuffed chairs. She motions towards the couch. I eye it suspiciously.

Maybe it's a test. Am I supposed to refuse? Admit that we snuck off again and borrowed a helicopter and stoically accept our punishment? Is this some kind of trick?

"I appreciate your caution Simon," Agent Zero grins, as if reading my thoughts. "But it's unnecessary. I won't be betraying you today. In fact, I think you both might like what I have to show you."

We sit. Agent Zero sweeps piles of folders away from the bright box in the center of the table.

One paper, folded in thirds like a letter, falls out of a folder. For an instant, moonlight from behind it illuminates the writing on the other side. I don't mean to look, but it's what they trained me to do. The image embeds itself into my brain, backward and upside down. It spins around in my head and in an instant, without effort, I know exactly what it says. Snippets anyway. "The agents are not ready for deployment," "experiment," "expense," and "justify." Red ink in the margin declares, "Deploy agents. Confirm." I don't recognize the handwriting, but it's not Agent Zero's. My eyes dart away.

Agent Zero stuffs the paper back into its folder and sets it on top of the rest of the pile. Then she places one hand on each side of the colorful box, smiles at us, and lifts it. There is no bottom, it's just a cover hiding a small cake.

A real, actual birthday cake. It even has our names on it, surrounded by seventeen candles. Agent Zero lights them one by one.

"This is a big day for you both," she says as the candles flicker to life. "I'm sorry we couldn't celebrate earlier. But you know how it is. After all, you're not children anymore, are you?"

Most agents are afraid of her, but Zero has watched over us, disciplined us, rewarded us, and sometimes even answered our questions all our lives. She was the one we brought our little treasures to when we were little. She'd hold us on her lap and ooh and ahh over an unusual leaf or a colorful shell we'd collected during training. When Agent Bartholomew was too rough a few years back and I refused to talk about it, Agent Zero was the one Sarah told. The next day Agent Bartholomew was gone.

But no one, not even Agent Zero, has ever celebrated

our birthday before.

Birthday cakes, much like taco trucks, girlfriends, and single-family homes, are mythical things. They belong to characters on TV shows and movies. Not in real life. Not for us. Yet Agent Zero pulls out plates, forks, three glasses of already poured milk, and a wicked-looking knife from a small cabinet nearby.

"Go on, make a wish," She urges. "Blow them out."

"Do you want to do it?" Sarah offers.

I can see the longing in her eyes. Somewhere in there, under all the training and talk about duty and responsibility, a little girl sits on Agent Zero's lap on this very couch, showing her a rock just because it's pretty and wanting to blow out candles on a birthday cake, just like they do in the movies.

"You're the oldest, that's your job," I say, and her smile warms my heart.

Sarah closes her eyes and a dreamy look spreads over her face. I know exactly what she's wishing for. She's dreaming of her first assignment. I hope that if she gets her wish, they'll send me with her. Somebody has to watch her back.

Then she blows out the candles and Agent Zero slices the cake. It's red velvet, my favorite. She remembered. She hands us each a piece, along with a glass of milk.

"I thought you said we aren't children anymore." Sarah holds up the milk and raises an eyebrow.

"Some things are just delicious together, Sarah." Agent Zero scoops a forkful of cake into her mouth and washes it down with her own glass of milk. "No matter how old you are."

I laugh. I've never had a better birthday.

The one small moment

Dreams drifting in a milk glass
Melting in liquid

"But you're right, you're not children." Agent Zero sets her fork down with a sigh. "As of this morning, you are no longer wards of the Department. And now we must decide what to do with you."

Sarah opens her mouth, but Agent Zero holds up a hand. Sarah fills her mouth with another forkful of cake instead.

"As you know, DAAAD has invested a considerable sum and no small amount of effort to develop your highly specialized skills." Agent Zero sets her plate aside. "But the world has changed in the last seventeen years. As technology evolves, today's nuanced art of online influence and propaganda creates a different challenge than we could have predicted when you were acquired."

"Acquired?" Sarah blinks.

"Excuse the jargon. Occupational hazard," Agent Zero apologizes. "I mean since you came under our protection. DAAAD has plenty of hackers and coders and geniuses in the arts of electronic surveillance, and more are emerging every day. What we don't have many of are field operatives like you. Especially ones without birth certificates, social security numbers, or any other records. Not everyone understands the need to have boots on the ground in this electronic age, but I do. We can't foil every plot from behind our keyboards."

Agent Zero stacks our plates and sets them on top of the cabinet, and I steal a glance at Sarah. She stares intently at the head of DAAAD.

"The decision has been made to expand your training to include undercover work. And the best way to do that is to put you in the field."

She puts the box back over the remains of the cake and moves to the couch next to me. With a wistful smile, she reaches across and runs her hand over Sarah's cheek. Sarah leans into her touch. Just slightly, but I notice.

"I may not have prepared you sufficiently for the world outside," she continues. "I know living here isn't always easy, but it's not all dance parties and taco trucks out there either. It's not always like what you see in movies. The modern world takes a lot of subtly, and we didn't train you to be subtle. I never envisioned you having to go undercover."

Agent Zero shuffles through the folders again. She opens one with a surveillance photo of a gigantic man I instantly recognize. His muscles fill a well-tailored, expensive-looking suit. He's bald but sports a sculpted beard and mustache that look like they could beat the crap out of any razor dumb enough to try to shave them.

"Dr. Dinkelmeyer," Sarah frowns.

"Yes." Agent Zero glances at the photo and sets it aside, continuing to look through folders. "Dr. Dinkelmeyer and his team are stirring up trouble—"

"And you want us to hunt him down." Sarah reaches for the paper with a serious nod.

Agent Zero plucks the photo from Sarah's hand. "Yes, I'm assigning two untested teenagers to hunt down one of the most notorious criminals in the world. Dinkelmeyer's mysterious organization continues to topple governments around the world and destabilize entire regions with his carefully placed disinformation. He's slaughtering thousands by stoking civil wars with his rumors and lies. We don't know how he's funding his operations, what his motivation is, or where he'll strike next. My entire covert agency has been working on the case for over a decade, but surely you plucky kids will succeed where many seasoned agents have failed."

Sarah's face flushes bright pink. Dr. Dinkelmeyer is seriously evil, not exactly beginner-level.

"So what is the mission, then?" I ask, with a quick squeeze of Sarah's hand.

"DAAAD has red-flagged some internet chatter in a town in mainland America. Colorado," Agent Zero finds the folder she wants and points to a map of the United States inside it. A red line circles a city on the front range of the Rocky Mountains. "Here in Colorado Springs."

"Colorado Springs? What's that?" Sarah asks. "Some kind of spa?"

"Unfortunately, no." Agent Zero pulls out some blurry pictures that look like they're from a security camera. They're horrible photos showing a single figure that looks vaguely, but not entirely, human. "If this were just some random town in the middle of nowhere or a fancy spa, I doubt anyone would care. But El Paso County, where Colorado Springs is located, is the only county in the nation that houses five military commands, some of them highly secure: Fort Carson, Peterson Air Force Base, the United States Air Force Academy, Schriever Air Force Base, and Cheyenne Mountain. It's also the home of NORAD, the North American Aerospace Defense Command, and the current home of the U.S. Space Force."

She pauses to let the information sink in.

"There are also several aerospace and defense companies, an Olympic training facility, and a large tech presence. Even the environmental tech group Pareto has a large workforce there. Because of this conglomeration, the location is a fertile breeding ground for conspiracy theories. As you can imagine, since our department assesses and handles disinformation, DAAAD keeps a close eye on this region. I'm sure it's been in some of your briefings."

"Now that you're explaining it, I do remember," Sarah nods.

"Someone or something is causing disturbances around town and the same mysterious figure keeps popping up, a massively muscled person who doesn't look like an ordinary man. Rumors are flying." Zero fans out a collection of photographs and online chatter.

I look at one photo more closely. "Why is the image resolution so bad?"

"Most of the world doesn't run on state-of-the-art technology, Simon. That photo is from a night-vision camera at a tourist area called the Cave of the Winds. Blurry as it is, it's the best we have, which is another part of the problem. With blurry photos, top secret military bases, and a massive, muscled man no one can get a good look at, you can see how it all might lead to chatter about secret government tests and escaped military supersoldier experiments."

"And that's not what's going on?" I ask. "The government isn't doing any experiments like that?"

"Not in this location. Not right now." Agent Zero shakes her head. "Your mission is simple. Find out who this mysterious person is and neutralize this conspiracy before it grows any bigger. These military bases are essential to the security of America. Even something as ridiculous as a supersoldier rumor could provoke conspiracy theorists to break into any of these bases, trying to expose something that isn't there. When they don't find anything, it will only fuel their conspiracies and who knows what other classified information they might dig up. It'll be Roswell all over again. We want to nip this thing in the bud. It's a matter of national security. Your success on this mission will determine your future with DAAAD and what happens to you now that you're no longer our wards. Sarah and Simon, you are now officially junior agents."

Agent Zero's phone buzzes. Without a word of explanation, she holds the phone to her ear and walks away.

Sarah leans over to me and whispers, "Is this for real?"

"I know, right?" I grin. What a day. It's everything we'd ever hoped for. A birthday cake, our first mission. Sarah must be as thrilled as I am. "Get ready to dispense some justice! OH! That should be our secret catchphrase."

Sarah's mouth drops open. "You actually sound happy about this mess."

I'm not sure what she means, so I ignore the tone.

"Are you kidding me? Look at this," I point to the map. "Colorado Springs. It sounds enchanting! Exotic! What a first destination!"

But Sarah doesn't sound happy at all. "Don't you get it? This is a softball assignment. Some chatter and a few blurry photos? Agent Zero doesn't think we're ready for any kind of actual mission. She doesn't appreciate how good we are."

I pause, confused. "This is what you wished for, isn't it?"

"No. I mean, yes I wanted an assignment. But, this is just another training exercise, just, you know, in a different location." Sarah frowns. "I want to do something important."

"It sounds important to me."

"You are so naïve." Sarah's face hardens. "She's just talking it up. It's a nothing assignment. We're going to get pigeonholed. The clean-up crew. The odd job guys. No one will ever take us seriously."

"Do you think so?" I hadn't even considered that. But she sounds so certain, and Sarah usually figures this kind of stuff out faster than I do. Still, I mean, it's our first mission. It's not like we'll be going after Dr. Dinkelmeyer.

Sarah leans back, sullen and quiet.

Agent Zero reappears, carrying two bright red boxes. "I have a gift for each of you. They'll come in useful for your first mission. Unfortunately, there's a crisis in Albania. I'd love to watch you open them, but you'll just have to know that they come from my heart. Be on the tarmac at o-eight-hundred tomorrow. I expect frequent updates. Good luck."

She hands us each a present and pushes the elevator's call button. Our party is over.

3: SARAH'S GIFT

The elevator descends into the mountain with a comforting purr as I try to convince myself I'm happy about this stupid assignment, too.

"You're right," I mumble to Simon. "We have to start somewhere, and this mission is totally in DAAAD's wheelhouse."

"It is," he agrees.

DAAAD exists to combat disinformation and conspiracy, the biggest threats in today's world. Disinformation is just another word for lies. Carefully crafted, plausible, well-placed lies and half-truths meant to manipulate people and cause violence, riots, insurrections, and assassinations. Lies turn people against each other. Conspiracies separate societies into Us and Them. They spread through news and social media like a virus, just truthful enough to believe, and virulent enough to eat away at a nation's soul.

Agents a lot smarter than me hack databases, track sources, and are savvy enough to tell which conspiracies on social media need to be shut down and which ones aren't worth the effort. If the pen is mightier than the sword, they are the pen.

Simon and I are the sword.

I mean that figuratively. We don't have a license to kill and frankly, I don't want one. We aren't assassins, we're the good guys, the people who get out there and find the hidden documents, infiltrate secret lairs and listen in on clandestine meetings, extract hostages, or bring down the data centers supporting the dark web. Important stuff.

"It's just—we're supposed to be special, Simon. An elite surgical strike force, you know? Getting the job done, then disappearing, untraceable, into the wind. We've worked hard to be the best." I grit my teeth. "This mission isn't just boring, it's beneath us. It's insulting. How will Agent Zero ever see what we're capable of if we don't get a chance to show her? How can we prove we've been worth her time and investment with a stupid low-level grunt work? How will I ever be able to make her proud of me? Of us, I mean. Do you want to be a junior agent forever?"

Simon shrugs. "I dunno. I'm just excited to get out there."

"You would be." I roll my eyes. "Well, I'm not excited or happy about it. I want to hit something."

"Hmmm." He sets a hand on my shoulder. "Dealing with feelings like that will take deep introspection and significant personal evaluation, Sarah."

"You're right," I reply. "Sounds like a job for a burrito."

The elevator counts up as we move down into the mountain, like negative numbers. Four, five, six. The doors slide open at the seventh floor down from Agent Zero's office. I step from the glaring light of the elevator into a dark, curving hallway, recessed lights mimicking the night sky as if it were lit by the moon and stars on a warm summer evening.

It's a tactical weak point. It takes three and a half seconds for my eyes to adapt to the lower levels of illumination. I think it's a poor design feature, but the interior lighting is supposed to keep our circadian rhythms balanced. I guess no one ever told the elevator that.

I stomp down the hall past doorways that dot the right side. They lead to bedrooms facing the outside of the mountain, each with its own giant window looking out over paradise. Mine has an expansive view of the bay.

On the left side, facing the interior of the volcano, an archway opens up into a spacious room. It's empty at this time of night. A dozen tables have chairs flipped upside-down on their tops. The room smells like citrus with an undercurrent of nothing at all. No sweat, no stuffiness, no food cooking. A clean smell. A counter divides the room. Appliances stand at attention against the back wall. A giant mural of a garden integrates a few doors along the walls. The painting covers the walls and extends onto the ceiling with a fake sky. During the day, full-spectrum lights hidden in that sky masquerade as sunlight.

Simon thinks it's pretty. Form and function shaking hands. You feel like you're dining on a patio in Tuscany or Provence with a light breeze provided by the air circulators. The engineers scientifically designed the cafe to fade from day to night to, like the lights in the hallway, match our circadian rhythms. Right now the room twinkles in pretend starlight. It's always the perfect temperature, always perfect weather on this imitation patio, even when it's monsoon season outside. Beautifully perfect, totally fake.

I ignore it all and head straight for the freezer, slipping around the counter and not even looking at an electronic pad embedded in its surface. The freezer bathes me in light and cold air as soon as I open the door to liberate two frozen burritos. Behind me, I hear Simon take down the chairs from one table with a whispering swish.

Suddenly, a wedge of light shoots into the room from an opening doorway, illuminating me like a spotlight. I slam the freezer closed and spin around, clutching the frosty food to my chest protectively. A silhouette looms large against the glowing doorway rectangle.

"Go back to bed, Gus," I sigh. "We're sorry we woke you."

I do not know how we woke Gus. The guy seems to have a sixth sense. There's a rumor that he was once an agent himself, but I don't know if I believe it. The man bears a profound resemblance to a dumpling, round and doughy. He shuffles towards me in his pajamas. At least I assume they're his pajamas. You never know with Gus. They're flannel and have little hedgehogs all over them. Plus, he's wearing fuzzy brown slippers. His smooth head glistens and his ears stick out just enough to be a notable feature.

"Sarah! Simon! You weren't at Third Meal. You must be hungry." He grabs an apron, ties it on, and plucks my frozen bounty from my hands. Like all the best chefs, Gus has a slight French accent. It's probably part of the qualifications when making fancy meals is your job. "Let me make you some proper food."

He tosses the burritos on the counter with a clatter and waves his hand over the embedded electric screen in the counter. It flares to life.

A list appears, and he picks my name from it, reviewing my whole regimented meal plan, optimizing my nutrition and caloric intake based on my individual chemistry and exercise plan. Then he does the same for Simon. "*Mon Dieu*, you haven't logged your–nevermind, I'll take care of it."

I can almost see the gears spinning in his shiny round dome as he considers our individual needs, and computes the acceptable options. How much protein have we had today? Fiber? Vitamin B6? What's in the pantry that can check off those boxes on the electronic pad's little food chart? It only takes him a moment. Next thing I know, he's lumbering towards the refrigerator.

"What would you like? There's some leftover fish. I could whip you up a salmon wellington and add some... let's see... ricotta shells?"

"We just want those burritos, Gus," I say, feeling gastronomically rebellious. Who cares about optimal nutrition? Seriously, I could just eat chips forever and be perfectly happy. I've seen people do it on YouTube. "Why do you have to make everything so complicated?"

"It's no trouble at all. Duck leg confit? Coq au Vin? I could pull together a mushroom risotto if you're not in the mood for meat tonight."

Simon and I have this dream involving a lot of junk food. Here on the Island, though, clandestine frozen burritos are the closest thing we have to junk food.

Gus waves a plate of duck legs at me, but I glare back at him. He sighs and sets the duck legs back in the refrigerator. With a disapproving shake of his head, he tosses the rock-hard burritos onto some delicate china plates and shoves them into the microwave.

The smell of rebellion and cheese wafts out of the whirring machine. It's a minor victory, but I'll take it. I join my little brother at the table.

"Can you imagine if we could just walk up to the

window of a taco truck and get some hot taco goodness without logging in, without adjusting our caloric intake? Just living on tacos and chips?" Simon whispers.

I glance at Gus shuffling around behind the counter and keep my voice low. "Don't let Gus hear you say that. You'd break his squishy little heart."

A look of fondness washes over Simon's face as his eyes dart towards our friend. "Of course not. But I'm not wrong, right?"

"OMG so right," I chuckle, hiding my face from Gus with my hand. Gus looks our way, and I quickly point to the boxes in front of us to change the subject. "Hey look! Birthday presents."

"Did you notice mine is bigger than yours?" Simon points out, setting the boxes next to each other.

"Hey, it matches your giant head. But you know, size isn't as important as speed."

It's a challenge, and Simon knows it. Our eyes meet. My hands dart to my box, first on the draw, but Simon has a longer reach. We both rip the paper off our presents as fast as we can. Red scraps fly out in a frenzied tornado until a naked box stands in front of each of us, but neither of us open the actual boxes yet. I slam my hands on the table a split second before Simon does.

"I win!"

"We both win," Simon shrugs. "We both have a present."

"What good is winning if nobody loses?" I pout.

"It's not about beating someone else, Sarah." Gus calls to us from inside the refrigerator, where he's sticking his bald head. "Winning is about personal satisfaction. Your motivation should come from within."

I'm not in the mood for one of the long, philosophical conversations we usually get into with Gus. He may be our closest friend, but that's never kept him from lectures on life's lessons. "Okay, but the purpose of DAAAD is helping other people. Our motivation comes from sacrificing for the greater good."

Gus's voice takes on a serious tone. "You don't know what it's like out there, Sarah. People don't appreciate your sacrifices. No one cares about what you do for them. They only care about themselves."

He's wrong. I do know what it's like out there. I've been watching shows and movies and YouTube and reading books my whole life. People care. I see it in the last ten minutes of every show, the last twenty pages of every book. But frankly, even if they didn't care or even know, we spies are just trying to make the world a better place.

Gus suddenly appears at our table, carrying steaming hot food. It smells delicious and for a moment I forget everything else. He grins with his usual tranquil smile as he sets the plates in front of us. Each burrito has a sprig of parsley on it. I guess he couldn't help himself.

"What have you got there?" He points to the gift boxes and pulls up his own chair to join us.

"Birthday presents from Agent Zero," says Simon.

He reaches inside his box and pulls out a camera. A small sheet of paper flutters out, covered in Agent Zero's scrawling handwriting. Gus grabs the paper before it hits the floor, but Simon doesn't notice. His eyes widen and he lets out a soft gasp, holding up the gift. I can't figure out why he's so happy.

"Oh, a camera," I raise an eyebrow. "In case you don't feel like using your much smaller and more portable phone to take pictures."

Simon delicately rotates the camera to take in every angle. It's encased in black rubber and looks like it could survive a fall from a three-story building, so his delicate handling is probably overkill.

"This isn't some cell phone camera, Sarah. This puppy can hold dozens of hours of video, it's got thermal and infra-red vision, and network connectivity. Look at this zoom!" He points it over my shoulder and rotates a lever.

"A set of shiny new throwing knives might have been a better gift on the eve of our first mission," I point out. No one on this Island (or off it) can throw a knife like my little brother.

"I like the knives I already have," he replies, pointing to the one that's always in his boot. "Just think of the footage I can get with this!"

"He's right. You kids might find more opportunities to gather intel than to throw knives at things on this assignment," Gus hands him the paper.

"Wait, how do you know about our mission?" I ask.

Gus ignores me. "Apparently the camera links to the Department's network through a dedicated satellite hookup. Whatever you film or photograph gets streamed directly here where our analysts can evaluate it immediately. And you can also edit your footage on the camera itself. That's handy. Plus a few more minor features. It's all in the note there."

"It also says DAAAD will give us our own cell phones. You know, the ones that work almost anywhere on the planet and have battery life for days?" Simon's eyes glow with excitement as he digs his teeth into his burrito. "We'll get those and a hard copy of our mission brief on the plane. That's in just a few hours, Sarah!"

I ignore him and plunge my hand into my own box. I feel something small and metallic. A knife? That's really Simon's thing, but I wouldn't say no to a nice new blade.

It's a necklace. Not what I was expecting.

A rope-like chain disappears into both sides of a large, stylized pendant. The pendant is about five inches long, two inches wide and half an inch thick. It's not heavy, but has a tangible weight. It's an iridescent black, curved like a scimitar. Colors slide over the surface like on an oil slick. It's beautiful and unique, but I don't understand. Jewelry is useful for undercover assignments, but it's not good for most ops. You don't want to snag a bracelet on the hinge of a safe you're cracking, or accidentally leave behind trace DNA on an earring that got pulled out when fighting your way out of a headlock.

I run my fingers over the pendant's length, feeling its cool smoothness. It IS beautiful. Would Agent Zero really give me something purely decorative? Still, she said it came from her heart. Is it possible that in her heart, maybe Agent Zero, I dunno, maybe she sometimes thinks of me as more than a spy? No, that's ridiculous. She said our gifts would help us on our mission. I dig inside my box for my note.

> *Dear Sarah,*
> *This bit of jewelry reminds me of you. Its understated beauty hides an amazing ability to get the job done. A strength you'd never suspect from just looking at it. They made the pendant and chain from a type of graphene developed in our labs. It's one of the strongest materials in the world. You'll find a button on the side. Hold the pendant away from anything else when you*

press it. I think you'll find it as interesting as I did. Best
of luck on your mission.
    Agent Zero

I point the pendant away from us and press the button. With a tiny click, three delicate hooks pop out, like the claw of some elegant, deadly beast and it separates into two pieces, connected by a chain. As I pull the pieces apart, the chain grows, whirring out of its casing. The chain retracts as I bring the piece with the claw closer to the other section, which has a clip on it, staying taut between the two pieces.

Suddenly I get it. "It's a grappling hook!"

Before Simon or Gus can react, I throw the hook end at a table across the room. It soars gracefully through the air going *fffffwipp* and catches on the leg of an overturned chair. Both the hook and the chain look so thin I'm afraid they'll break, but I clip the bottom to my belt and push another button.

The chain retracts with a lovely whirring sound. It tugs at my belt, but since I'm heavier than the chair, it crashes down, clanging deafeningly against the stone floor. The grappled chair screeches across the room at high speed as the chain retracts. Straight toward us. I tug the approaching chair's trajectory away from Gus and Simon, and flick my wrist to unhook the grapple from the chair's leg, stepping clear.

The four-legged projectile hits another table like a bowling ball. The table and all its stacked chairs tumble to the floor with yet another ear-splitting crash.

Maybe Agent Zero was right about us not being subtle.

I snap the grappling hook closed and fasten it around my neck with a giant goofy smile plastered on my face. I plop back into my chair and nonchalantly take a bite of burrito. It's still warm.

"Whoops," I say around a delicious mouthful. "Sorry Gus."

Gus stares at the destruction. He drops his face into his hands without a word. Simon catches my eye, and we both burst out laughing.

"We'll help you clean that up," Simon chuckles, not actually moving to help clean up.

Gus just sighs.

"You go get some sleep. You have a plane to catch in a few hours." He grabs our plates, empty now except for the parsley, and heads for the back. "Why does no one eat the parsley? Do you even know how many vitamins parsley has? But no, it's green. Why would anyone eat nice healthy greens?"

His voice fades as he disappears into the janitor's closet.

"Love you, buddy," I call after him. Then I sigh. "He's right, we should get what sleep we can so we can get this stupid assignment over with and move on to more important things."

Simon leans towards me. "Don't worry, Sarah. I'm sure this mission is important. I have a good feeling about it."

"I hope so." My hand slides over my new necklace. "I want all our training to mean something, to show everyone, especially Agent Zero, what we're capable of. We are so much better than a clean-up crew."

"We'll get more opportunities." He places a hand on mine. It's warm and comforting. "And who knows, maybe these sightings aren't as simple as they seem. Maybe something big is going on after all."

4: SIMON VISITS AN EXOTIC LOCALE

It feels weird not to jump out of the plane.

We aren't even *flying* the plane. We're just, you know, passengers. Weird. I keep expecting the pilot to call back that we've reached altitude, waiting to be pushed out the door with a wingsuit and a prayer. (our lab is developing a wingsuit that transforms from regular clothing, and we're not even field-testing *that*.)

Instead, Sarah and I stretch out in the plush leather interior of our private government aircraft like some sort of VIPs. The Rocky Mountains rise and fall below us, an undulating sea of green. Mountaintops peek up above the treeline like Agent Sterling's balding head, barely visible from our cruising altitude of 41,000 feet.

> *Patient, unchanging*
> *Time, wind, and snow rise and fall*
> *Earth beneath the trees*

Poetry is words that draw pictures in your mind, and haiku is my favorite form. Poetry and other forms of visual arts, like photography and all my film work, help me process things. My feelings and emotions, anything I can't express by just talking about it. When you think in pictures, like I do, poetry can say what pages and pages of prose can't. It's how I cope when waves of emotion crash into me. I've been known to dabble in acrostics, limericks, and the occasional sonnet if the mood takes me, but good old-fashioned haiku is like breathing. What can I say? For a modern spy, I'm an old-fashioned guy.

Hey, that rhymed.

Images and words continue their dance inside my head as I watch the splendor unfold beneath us. Sarah, on the other hand, is sleeping. I get it, a good spy conserves their energy and sleeps when they can. You never know when you'll have to go days without a chance to rest. But, it's so beautiful down there. How can anyone sleep with the entire world stretched out below?

It's not like it's our first time on a plane of course. We've been up in plenty of them, both to jump out of them and to rack up our pilot certification hours. I've seen waves sparkle to the horizon across the sapphire ocean, soared above clouds, below clouds, and inside clouds. I've targeted the Island and all the little baby islands huddled around it for emergency landing drills. But I've never seen land stretch beneath me with no ocean in sight. The Rocky Mountains make our volcanoes look downright dinky. Peak after peak, a great herd of mountains stretching in a long road like a chain of migrating whales.

In the bright, clear sun of this morning, I had said goodbye to the Island for the first time in my life. It shrank smaller and smaller until it became a deep green dot amid the endless sea. Then, sooner than I would have expected, the Island disappeared entirely. Goodbye.

Glistening blue

*O*cean, spreading
*O*ut forever
*D*rifting like
*B*irds flowing
*Y*onder into
*E*ternity

Sarah doesn't do goodbye. She only looks forward. To her, this plane ride is just transportation. Once aboard, once we realized no one had any tasks for us, she had simply reclined her soft leather seat flat, stretched out, and snored.

Now, hours later, I'm sitting at a little table on the other side of the fuselage, trying to tear my eyes from the window long enough to analyze our case file before we crest the Rockies and make our descent into Colorado Springs Municipal Airport. Shiny new DAAAD issued cell phones sit next to the stack of documents. They may look like regular smartphones, but they're really more like genius phones. Teams of brilliant tech people make sure agents using them never lose reception while out in the field, and a full battery should last them more than a week.

I sort through the documents. Sarah and I each have a new alias. I've seen the movies and no, agents don't really carry around five different passports. Well, maybe for quick getaways or temporary rush jobs, but not fully fleshed out aliases with legends (spy talk for an intricate fake history) complete with backstops, supporting documents, and a false presence in searchable databases. Our team of expert identity professionals actually find those scenes kind of insulting to the complexity of what they do. It takes a lot of work and artistry to craft a complete, believable false identity that will stand up to scrutiny and research. We'll have these aliases until they're no longer useful–or until we are.

We've never had last names. Those come from your family and we don't have one of those, either. Our aliases do, though. They have all the things we don't have: full names, addresses, birth certificates, driver's licenses. Records with photographs. That was a bold move on DAAAD's part. Hard to believe Agent Zero agreed to it. I bet there are subtle watermarks in our photos that will make them digitally unsearchable. I've heard our techs can do stuff like that.

When creating a legend, you want to keep as much truth in it as possible, so it's easier for the spy to remember all the little details. Otherwise you might slip up in the field and that's bad. My new name is Simon Zachary Lenoir. My sister is now Sarah Abigail Quarterly. Not my sister anymore, apparently. I know it's fake but us having different last names feels prickly on my skin, like a rash.

I pack Simon Lenoir's driver's license, credit cards, and other pocket litter into my new wallet. Pocket litter is the stuff that makes a cover look real, like old receipts, a grocery list, a pack of gum. The things normal people have in their pockets. I pause, then pack my sister's wallet for her, too. She drools on the buttery leather of the jet's seat. One of her hands clutches her new necklace, even in her sleep. She hasn't taken it off since she got it.

The jet jiggles around and the seatbelt sign comes on. I look out the window and see the Rocky Mountains giving way to flatter ground. We're approaching our destination from the north, cruising low now. Off to the left, a faint brown cloud covers the biggest collection of buildings I've ever seen. Denver. I know it's not the largest city in the world, but it sprawls out bigger than my entire Island.

We follow along the Front Range of the Rockies, and the turbulence dies down. Houses and other buildings dot the ground below us continuously from Denver to Colorado Springs. So many houses. So many people. Each house and office building seems to have its own parking lot or driveway, with manicured lawns in the front and back. What do people even do with all that space?

It's a different beauty than I'm used to. There are hundreds of thousands of people down there, driving cars, going in and out of buildings, playing in carefully crafted parks. I've seen it all from a distance, through movies and YouTube and news programs. I've seen these people scripted and glamourized and sound-bited. Bitten? But what are they really like? What is it like to actually walk on those streets? What does it feel like to be in a shopping mall, with hordes of people just doing whatever real people do in a mall? In less than an hour, I'll know.

The mission brief is available on both my new phone and in a physical folder. It contains everything DAAAD has collected so far about this mysterious totally-not-a-government-experiment guy, and all the disturbances around town. It's pretty thin. Vandalism, almost always in a tourist area, including blurry photos and sightings of this misshapen wild-man. Online rumors are all over the place; it's a bodybuilder jacked up on steroids and having anger management issues, a linebacker who didn't make the draft and is training to be a vigilante instead, a mutant from radioactive pools hidden underneath Cheyenne Mountain. Most of these rumors are harmless but, as Agent Zero predicted, a few people theorize it might be some kind of military experiment gone wrong. Those are the ones we need to stop before they get out of hand.

It looks suspicious to me, but what do I know? This is my first mission. The scattering of subtle disinformation and inconclusive photographs seem tailor-made to start a conspiracy theory, right down to the fact that no one has reported any injuries. If people were getting hurt, local law enforcement would be all over it. And why can't anyone get a decent photo of this guy? As a photographer, I don't understand why no one in this town seems to have a decent zoom lens.

But if this chatter really is being planted on purpose, what's the point? Encouraging conspiracy theorists to break into the military bases, like Agent Zero fears? I guess that's what we're here to find out. Discover what's causing the disturbances and shut down the chatter by either exposing it or covering it up. Or at least diverting the conversation away from the government facilities to keep your average citizen from accidentally getting their hands on top-secret information while searching for some non-existent conspiracy.

We're finally starring in our own spy show, even if it's not quite the Hollywood summer blockbuster Sarah wants.

Either way, the first scene is always the same; visit the locations and look for clues. We'll use our journalist aliases to gather intel. There's a lovely irony to pretending to investigate strange happenings in order to keep anyone else from wanting to investigate strange happenings. I consider waking up Sarah to laugh about it with her, but then I realize waking up Sarah would be hazardous to my health.

The folder on the table slides as our jet adjusts its trajectory to the left.

"Y'all hang tight back there. We need to stay out of military airspace," our pilot, Agent Albert, calls from the cockpit. "And there's a lot of it around here."

He chatters with air control over his headset. Contrails criss-crossing the sky in the distance, over a thick blanket of trees. I assume the long thin lines of white clouds are from the Thunderbird fighter jets training at the Air Force Academy. None are in the air right now, but it can take hours for those trails to dissipate depending on the air conditions. We make another course correction and begin our final approach into Colorado Springs Airport.

"Wake up that little lady," Agent Albert calls again in his Texas drawl. "And then you kids just hang tight. We got ways to hustle through security where you don't have to explain those knives in your boot or nothing."

I hope Sarah didn't hear that "little lady" comment, for Albert's sake. Her eyes snap open immediately when I nudge her. I roll my suitcase out, stuff the mission briefing folder inside and my wallet into my pocket, sling my camera's strap around my neck, and prepare to land on mainland soil for the first time ever.

***

Agent Albert drives us through winding streets lined with single-family homes. House after house, complete with lawns, driveways, and people not related to DAAAD at all. People who have never even heard the name DAAAD unless it's a(n unrelated) whine coming from a kid who isn't getting what they want. I press my face against the window and stare until Sarah, with a sour expression, tells me I'm acting suspiciously.

I pull my face away from the glass.

Agent Albert parks the car in front of a yellow house with the mountains practically in its backyard. The house, a short-term rental, is adorable. A real estate ad come to life. An old maple tree spreads its branches over the pristine front yard, but I'm more interested in wonders like the paved driveway, sidewalk, and a front door without a palm scanner. Agent Albert unlocks it with a small, metal key. An ordinary, old-fashioned, absolutely fascinating actual key.

"It's just a standard two bedroom. DAAAD thought it would be less conspicuous to put you guys up in a house instead of a hotel. Smart, really. Unaccompanied kids checking into a hotel would definitely raise a few flags."

"We're not kids." Sarah leads the way inside.

Agent Albert smirks and hands me the key. "Sure, honey. Whatever you say. Still, probably best not to let people know you're staying here alone."

Alone.

There's an entire city out there. More people than I've ever seen. And yet Sarah and I have more privacy than we've ever had. No Agent Zero, no chefs, no cleaning crew, no VIPs to parade in front of, or agents bunking in the room next door.

"I reckon y'all are gonna want to skedaddle to the grocery store right quick, kids," Albert says. I can hear Sarah's teeth grind every time he says "kids." I think he's trying to enrage her on purpose.

"We'll be fine," Sarah snips. "We've been studying

how to be off-Island for years."

Agent Albert laughs. "It's a whole different ball of wax being out here in person than it is to read about it, little lady." (more teeth grinding) "Y'all might want to keep your eyes open and study what normal people do. Y'all stand out like sore thumbs."

Sarah rolls her suitcase into one room and slams the door. Agent Albert grins and elbows me like we're sharing a secret, but I don't know what the secret is. An angry Sarah isn't a game. Besides, I like her a lot more than I like this stranger who keeps calling me kid.

"This here is the kitchen," Albert leads me into a room off the main living space. I don't see a food chart anywhere. "She ever cook before?"

"Who, Sarah?" I open the refrigerator door. It's empty inside except for an alarming amount of tiny ketchup packets and one jar of pickles. "Not really, neither of us have. It's not exactly essential training. But Gus showed us a few things."

Albert shakes his head. "Well, good luck to you. But I still suggest the first thing y'all do is stock up your icebox."

That sounds like an excellent idea.

"Sarah, let's head out and grab some food for the house," I call. A grunt comes from behind her door. That means she agrees.

I drop my suitcase in the other bedroom. It's simple but pleasant; a decent bed with a poofy comforter, a dresser, and some night stands. Sarah comes out of her room carrying a purse and wearing her necklace. It's essential for a spy to keep important stuff with them. Any time you leave a safe-house, there's no guarantee you'll ever return. With regret, I set my camera on my bed. I'd hate to lose it, but it would attract attention if I brought it with me. I pat down my pockets to make sure I have my wallet and phone, then I join Sarah at the front door.

Agent Albert walks us out to the car. He hands me the keys, but Sarah grabs them instead.

"You sure you can drive on these here city streets, missy?" He raises a doubtful eyebrow.

Sarah fluffs up like an exotic bird. "Excuse me? I'll have you know I've aced every course, every obstacle DAAAD has thrown at me on both the simulator and the practical exercises. You think because I'm a girl I can't drive?"

"Now don't get your knickers in a twist," Albert says sternly, but releases the car's fob to her. "You've got a reputation is all. Just remember you're not training anymore. Life out here is serious business. These people who live here, they aren't agents, junior nor otherwise. They aren't generally evil, neither. Most of these fine people are just trying to get through the day. Don't you go all crazy on them now, you hear?"

Sarah's eyes narrow as she slides into the driver's seat. I smile at Agent Albert and open the passenger door.

"Don't worry about us, we'll be fine," I tell him.

"Where's the gearshift?" Sarah asks through the window. "This car has no clutch. You got a faulty one."

Agent Albert grins like Sarah just proved his point. "Nope, kiddo. Most people use automatic transmissions out here in the real world. It's easier to drive."

"Where's the fun in that?" Sarah mumbles, ramming the car into Drive. Then she turns back to Agent Albert. "Want me to drive you to a pickup point or safe house?"

Albert laughs again. "I'll be fine. Just gonna head back to the airport. Hate to leave you kids but I've got a mission in Wyoming and need to skedaddle. Sorry I can't stick around and babysit y'all. You kids have fun with your little—" he coughs to hide yet another chuckle "—assignment. Y'all dispense yourself some justice and keep the world safe from evil."

He reaches inside the car and ruffles Sarah's hair. Her face flushes red and I sincerely hope she won't punch him. Luckily, she just punches the directions to the nearest grocery store into the navigation system of the car, mumbling about how slow the inferior technology is.

"It's a long run back to the airport," I call from the passenger seat. "Let us drive you."

He pauses, a finger hovering over his phone. "You guys really haven't spent much time away from the Island, huh? Here in the rest of the world, we have rideshare."

"Hey, you wouldn't know where we can find a good taco truck, would you?" I ask, but Sarah pulls away from the curb, narrowly misses Albert's foot with the front tire. All I can do is watch him wave goodbye in the rear-view mirror.

Then I glance at the speedometer. "Uh, Sarah? You know streets out here usually come with speed limits attached, right?"

Her glare deepens as she eases up on the gas pedal. "It's boring to go twenty miles an hour. Oh my god, no shifting gears, driving slower than we can run, and all these stop signs. What's the point of driving like this?"

In specific environments, Sarah's driving is sensational. She can maneuver a vehicle with a blown

51

engine and three flat tires through an array of orange traffic cones, using only the car's inertia and some cleverly applied physics and geometry.

Navigating suburban streets in a rented compact car really isn't her strength.

"Turn signal. Turn signal!" I yell as a car screeches to a halt in front of us and blares its horn.

"Turn left at the next light," the car tells her in a soothing voice. "Then go straight for three blocks."

Sarah growls at both me and the car's dashboard. Then she slams down the turn signal bar.

By the time we pull into the parking lot of the grocery store, I'm curled up in the passenger seat, clinging to the little handle over the window. Sarah checks her purse as I slowly unwrap myself.

"Maybe I should drive back," I whisper.

"Why? That went perfectly. We're here aren't we?" she says to her purse. "Phone, credit card, keys... do you have the house key? Excellent. Let's go shopping."

5: SARAH VS THE GROCERY STORE

Simon pushes the grocery cart. One of its wheels wiggles as it squeaks down the aisle. We've seen the shows, and know that the one wiggly wheel is how shopping carts work. I don't understand why, but it seems to be standard. Every movie or show we've ever seen involving a shopping cart takes great pains to point that out.

Our cart's wheel is definitely wiggly, so we nailed that one.

"Where do you think the taco aisle is?" Simon asks, standing in the middle of the store to read an overhead sign. People push their carts around him aggressively.

"You're blocking the flow of traffic." I yank him over to the side. "It's conspicuous."

The grocery store is bigger and busier than we expected. We may not be sufficiently prepared. I think we were supposed to make a shopping list or something.

We've done our best to not look like teenagers. Some people look young their whole lives. It's in their genes. Those aren't the kinds of people Simon and I got our genetics from. My brother got visited by the grown-up voice fairy a few years ago, and, along with gaining access to lower octaves, he also sprouted up a foot in, like, a month, which usually means "gangly teen." Working out as much as we do, though, neither of us has ever lacked muscle. More than one guest on the Island has assumed Simon is of drinking age.

For me, it's about confidence. Don't mumble. Know what you're going to say before you open your mouth. Don't use slang. Stand up straight, don't overdo the make-up, don't over-style your hair, and don't wear three-inch heels to the grocery store. First, I don't do heels. They're impractical in a fight and for all my balance training, I just can't get the hang of them. They throw off my center of balance. And second, a lot of young people think the way to look older is to wear all the adult things, but you want to look casual, not like you're heading to a nightclub in the middle of the day. Trying too hard gets noticed. And remember not to say anything that will give you away as teenagers.

"Hey, where can we find all the junk food?" Simon asks a guy in an apron.

I sigh.

The clerk doesn't look up from the cans of pinto beans he's stacking on a shelf. "Chips and stuff are in aisle three, and soda is in aisle five."

I've never seen anything like aisle three. Bags of chips line the shelves on both sides in every flavor you could imagine. So much goodness fried, baked, or dehydrated to crispy perfection. Crackers and pretzels. Not a single person stops us as we fill our cart with dozens of bags. The soda section is similar and I can't help but stock the cart with multiple six-packs of various brands and flavors. This may be our one chance to try them before we go back to Gus's food jail.

"I did not know there were so many kinds of snacks," A doofy grin spreads across Simon's face. "Look, Sarah. Cake!"

He darts off to a section filled with bread, pies, and yes, cake. Simon kneels in front of a glass case filled with fancy baked goods. A woman with a toddler in her cart pauses, throwing him a suspicious glance.

"Hey Sarah," Simon calls, waving to me. The woman glances over as I poke my head up over the whole wheat sandwich bread. "Did you know you can just buy a birthday cake here? Nobody even checks if it's your birthday."

The woman grins, sets a baguette in her cart, and disappears down another aisle. I stomp over to Simon and whisper. "Could you try to be a little more undercover and a little less–weird? Please?"

"We're not undercover here. We're just shopping. Don't be so paranoid."

A young man balancing three bananas and a jug of milk in his arms looks at us from the corner of his eye. I tense, but he just grabs a plastic carton of croissants and moves on. Why is everything wrapped in plastic? The young man makes his way to the cart he's left in the middle of the main aisle, dumps his stuff inside, and leaves it there as he moves to sort through some boxes of doughnuts.

There are so many people I'm getting paranoid. "Come on, Simon, let's just grab some tacos and get out of here."

So here's something interesting. You can't just buy tacos at a grocery store. Who knew? You have to buy taco ingredients and then assemble them yourself. I'm perfectly good with field stripping a rocket launcher, but attempting taco assembly without proper instructions? I don't even know what ingredients to get. We stare blankly at a dizzying selection of taco shells that cover a third of an aisle labeled "ethnic foods." What makes a can of jalapenos "ethnic"? Which box do we want, and what to do with it once we get it home? I suddenly regret not watching more Teen Chef Master.

"Did Gus teach you to cook anything?" I ask Simon.

"I can make scrambled eggs," he shrugs. "I think you need eggs, milk, salt and pepper. Maybe some cheese?"

We get milk and a block of cheddar cheese. There are two people at the eggs, so I wait until they finish. One of them opens their carton and inspects every single egg.

What a waste of time, I think, grabbing the closest carton, which is big with eighteen eggs, and tossing it in the cart, on top of a bag of chips. The woman with the toddler passes by us again. She pretends to be listening to her kid, but I can tell she's watching us from the corner of her eye.

"Let's get out of here," I mumble. "All these people are making me nervous. I keep expecting one of them to attack us. Let's get back to the safehouse and debrief."

Simon nods, but the lines at checkout are long. In movies, the heroes always walk right up and check out. The real world is a lot more inconvenient.

"There's no line at the self-checkout," Simon points out and pushes our cart next to a contraption with a green light on top.

"Scan item to begin," the machine tells us. Excellent, we don't even have to talk to anyone. At least we won't have to show the entire store that we've never been through a grocery checkout before.

I grab a can of Pringles and wave them over the laser

pad. It may not be a palm reader, but at least I know how to use a laser scanner. The machine beeps and a price comes up on the screen. Success!

"Please place the item in the bagging area," it continues.

Off to the side, some bags hang on a bar. But the machine didn't tell us to put the item in the bag, just in the bagging area. Okay, I set the can near the bags.

"Please place the item in the bagging area," the machine says again in its pleasant female voice.

"I placed the item in the…" I begin, but Simon moves it right in front of the actual bags.

The machine doesn't complain so I scan another bag of chips and place them next to the Pringles before she can yell at me again.

"Unexpected item in the bagging area," it scolds. "Please remove the item from the bagging area."

"What? I thought I was supposed to put it in the bagging area," I huff.

"Unexpected item in the bagging area," it repeats as the green light on top turns red. "Please remove the item from the bagging area."

A man in line behind us groans. I feel my face getting hot. I just want to leave. Simon looks around and waves to a middle-aged woman in a black apron. She saunters over and patiently scans a card attached to her belt. Without a word, she scans another bag of chips and pulls a bag open, placing them inside. She nods at me and walks away.

I mimic what she's done with the rest of the groceries and use my credit card to pay. The machine spits out an absurdly long receipt like it's sticking its tongue out at me. I yank on the paper, stuff it in the bag, and toss them all into the cart.

Simon loads everything in the trunk while I fume in the driver's seat. Why does everything have to be so complicated? I just want to get this stupid mission over with.

I dodge a few cars on the way home, skirting around the really slow ones by swerving into the oncoming lane. Simon keeps gasping and grabbing for the handle over the car door. He's so dramatic. I'm perfectly capable of navigating these streets with a very low probability of imminent death for anyone.

We soon pull into the driveway. "Look Mr. Dramatic, we've arrived home perfectly safe."

Simon ignores me as he unlocks the front door.

It's not fair to call the house a dump, but the sightlines are horrible. It would be impossible to see an enemy coming in the front door if you were in the kitchen, or coming in the back door if you were in the front room. And you can't see the door from the garage no matter where you are. Definitely too many doors. The couch is soft and squishy, with a high back. Comfortable, granted, but difficult to vault over and, frankly, absolutely useless as cover in a firefight.

The dinner plates, on the other hand, I like. They're heavy and solid, unlike the delicate china we use on the Island. You could knock someone cold with one of these bad boys if you frisbee it just right.

"That table isn't good for anything but eating in here, Simon. It should be in the front room where the light is better so we can work on it."

Table legs squeal against the wood floor as I yank it into the front room. Much better. Maybe my alias should have been an interior decorator. We move a few other pieces of furniture around until we've set up a functional, defensible workspace.

I flop down on the soft cushions of the tactically impractical sofa. Simon collapses next to me. I'm surprised we're a little out of breath.

"I didn't expect being a mile above sea level to make this much difference," he confides. "Moving that furniture should not have wiped me out like this."

We've lived our lives literally at sea level, and now we're in some serious altitude. And it's arid compared to the tropical environment we're used to.

"Let's just stay hydrated and we'll acclimate in a day or two." I pant. "We'll have to get used to different environments if we're going to head out on assignments."

"So, you're feeling better about this mission then?" Simon asks cautiously.

I've been wondering the same thing myself. The answer is that I don't know how I feel about the mission, but I do know that we're here, and my only option right now is to do a good job.

"Let's just finish it and get home to Agent Zero. Once we show her what we're capable of, we'll be running black bag operations in no time."

6: SIMON GETS THE LAY OF THE LAND

"Let's expose this totally-not-a-supersoldier and get out of here." Sarah sets up our command center in the front room while I look for a frying pan in the kitchen. "I figure if we can get some footage of him that proves he's not an escaped military experiment and upload it to the internet, we can go home."

"Right." I toss the frying pan on the counter with a clatter. "Or we can just fake one with AI," she suggests.

"No, too risky." I reply. "If it gets outed as a fake, it will only stoke the conspiracy. We need genuine footage, preferably with corroborating witnesses. More importantly, we need a hook that's going to get people to reshare it. You can't just toss up an image and expect it to gain traction."

I can almost hear her shrug. Video editing and influencer-style marketing aren't her thing. "I'll leave that stuff to you. I'm hungry. Where's our food?"

It and the spatula next to it taunt me with high expectations. Making scrambled eggs is suddenly more intimidating than I ever imagined. The one time I made them, I really just wanted to hang out with Gus. I didn't actually pay attention. They trained me to excel at knife throwing, not egg cracking.

Delicate balance
The egg gets scrambled
Every choice matters

I grab my phone. There are hundreds of scrambled egg recipes online. I click one at random and pull out the carton of eggs. Clear, sticky slime tinged with yellow seeps into the container. Five of the eighteen are already cracked.

Better use those first.

"It's coming!" I start the egg video, muted so I can hear Sarah. On the screen, a woman cracks some eggs into a bowl, but I've already dumped mine into the pan. I pour some milk into the pan, copying the woman. "Where do we look for this guy? We'll have to anticipate his next move if we want to catch him in the act."

Gus had shredded his cheese before our lesson. There must be some sort of machine or kitchen gadget for that, but I don't know what it is. Knife skills it is, then. I don't want to brag, but knives are kind of my thing. I whip the knife from my boot and flakes of cheese fall from the cheddar block with a few quick surgical swipes of the blade.

"Let's see. El Paso County has five military commands." Sarah continues. "Fort Carson, Peterson Air Force Base, the United States Air Force Academy, Schriever Air Force Base, and Cheyenne Mountain. Also NORAD, the North American Aerospace Defense Command, and the US Space Force."

"Yeah, I remember from the briefing with Agent Zero. What do those bases do, exactly?"

"Taking them in order," Sarah calls, "Let's start with Fort Carson."

"Wait, why are we starting with these military bases at all?" I add in the cheese to my pan of pre-cracked eggs and milk. "Shouldn't we be reviewing the locations where the incidents occurred? Find some sort of pattern?"

"We'll get to that," she replies. "But I figure if we're here to stop conspiracy theorists from targeting the bases, we should learn more about them."

That makes sense, so I turn back to my video. The woman turns on her burner and sets her pan on top. I'm one step ahead since my eggs are already in my pan. Feeling accomplished, I turn on the burner. Then the woman melts some butter in her pan. I look around for some, but can't find any. Does butter come from the fridge or pantry? Or the freezer? I have no idea. My butter comes from Gus.

"So Fort Carson then," I prompt, moving to the open doorway between the kitchen and front room. "That's an army base right?"

"Yeah." Sarah has spread documents all over the table. "They built Fort Carson after the attack on Pearl Harbor in 1941 and named it for Brigadier General Christopher 'Kit' Carson. It's an army base, with combat-ready expeditionary forces used in complex environments as part of joint force teams. About 26,000 soldiers are stationed there, and 6400 civilians. It's on the southwest side of Colorado Springs. Hang on, let me mark that on the map."

A big paper map of the area crinkles as Sarah unfolds it. She pulls a few picture frames off the wall and tapes the map in their place. The smell of cooking eggs tickles my nostrils so I return to the stove. The substance bubbling in the pan doesn't look like the eggs I'm used to. I mix it around with the spatula like I've seen Gus do. On my phone, the cooking tutorial has already finished. It's auto-playing the next video.

A fluffy, multi-colored feline hangs its bottom over a toilet while upbeat music plays in the background. It's that stupid pooping cat! I growl and hit the back button. The eggs video starts up again from the beginning, as the woman cracks eggs into her bowl.

"Peterson Air Force Base and Schriever look like they're both part of the US Space Force." Sarah says while I scrape some crusty eggs onto some plates and bring one to her. "Peterson is Space Force's headquarters. Let's see, blah blah execution of eight functional space deltas, eighty mission partners across twenty-two worldwide locations. There seems to be a lot of overlap there, with the primary mission of—Oh, thanks."

Sarah takes a plate of eggs and sticks the fork in without really looking. Then stops dead as she lifts some to her mouth. Gus's scrambles are light and fluffy, and a soft yellow like little clouds of sun-drenched protein on a summer's day. Gus's eggs are packed full of nutritious meat and veggies. Mine aren't.

Sarah looks at me, then shrugs. She forces a smile and starts chewing again. Suddenly, she stands with her finger up in a "hang on a minute" gesture. She disappears into the kitchen and comes out with two cherry sodas. She hands me one and cracks open the other, taking a big swig.

"So what does the US Space Force do?" I ask as my lips close around my first homemade meal.

"Apparently," she reads, "it organizes, trains, equips, and deploys space forces to support operational plans and missions for U.S. combatants, whatever that means. And Peterson is the home of Space Command, which handles military operations in outer space, meaning everything over 62 miles above sea level. Interesting. I wonder what a space battle would be like?"

My eggs are disgusting. I try not to care, but my heart sinks. I didn't expect to do great the first time, but these are barely edible.

"I don't think we're talking Star Wars here," I answer.

"It looks like NORAD shifted operations from Cheyenne Mountain to Peterson. It sounds like a lot of important stuff is going on at Peterson. We should look into their security protocol," she continues.

"You said NORAD stands for the North American Aerospace Defense Command, right?"

"Yup," Sarah bravely takes another bite. "That's America and Canada watching the airspace over North America together. I mean, it's the government, so it's more complicated than that, but that seems to be the basics."

On the wall map, Sarah pins up strips of bright pink paper with the names of all the bases on them. She writes "Cheyenne Mountain Complex" on another strip and traces her finger down the map, moving south past the Cheyenne Mountain Zoo and west of Fort Carson to pin the tag in a green forested area, pushing it straight into the drywall underneath.

"I wish we had the big touch display in Agent Zero's office," she sighs. "But a good spy adapts to whatever they have in the field."

I point to the tag with my fork. "Tell me more about the Cheyenne Mountain Complex."

"It's a big bunker inside Cheyenne Mountain. NORAD used to be there, but when they moved the primary command to Peterson, the Cheyenne complex became the backup."

"It can't be that important if it's just a backup location." I look at the images of a big tunnel sticking out of the side of a mountain. "There aren't many pictures."

"Yeah, it doesn't seem like much goes on there these days," Sarah agrees. "It's still super top security, though. In 2021 they started calling it Cheyenne Mountain Space Force Station, so I guess it's a double backup for NORAD and the Space Force. There may not be a lot going on, but it's still one of the most secure places in the world during a nuclear attack. It's a complex of buildings two thousand feet underground with two massive twenty-five-ton blast doors that can shut in forty-five seconds with its own power generators, water sources, heating and cooling, and is self-sufficient. They made it in the 1960s during the cold war as the ultimate nuclear bunker."

"Huh, that's cool. I can see why we need to keep conspiracy nuts from infiltrating it. It probably holds all kinds of secrets." I make a spooky face at her and wiggle my eyebrows.

Sarah laughs. "Like I said, it's super secure. And it has zero strategic value since operations moved to Peterson."

"Okay then, what about the Air Force Academy? That's pretty active."

"Oh yeah," Sarah looks through the documents again. "I skipped that one, didn't I?"

I choke down some more eggs. At least they're good

protein. Still, I should have done a better job. I can hit a target at fifty paces dead-on with a thrown knife and yet I can't make a meal.

Sarah finds another page with photos of a chapel made of tall white peaks pointing to the sky, and others showing state-of-the-art fighter jets in glistening rows. Fields of cadets by the hundreds stand in measured rows.

I take another sip of my soda. It's sweet and fruity and tickles my throat on the way down. Gus only lets us have super-fancy sodas a few times a year. This plain, trashy, carbonated elixir is absolute heaven.

"The Air Force Academy is in northern Colorado Springs, and it's open to visitors." Sarah pins a tag inside a massive green area well away from the other pins. "It's where they train future fighter pilots and Air Force officers. And it's where the Thunderbirds are stationed. Graduating from the Air Force Academy is one of the few ways you have any chance of being a Thunderbird pilot. There's also a high school on the base, Air Academy High School. The whole place would be super hard to secure, it's on a huge nature preserve, so I don't know that they'd have a lot of state secrets there."

"Should we go visit it?" I ask. "Since it's a tourist destination, it sounds like a prime place for another vandalism attack by our not-a-supersoldier."

"Maybe? Let's make a list of the actual places where these incidents happened and go visit those. Then we can cross-reference—Hey Simon, are eggs supposed to be crunchy? I don't remember Gus's eggs ever being crunchy."

As she says it, my teeth grind something hard. I swallow a big swig of soda.

"Shells. I guess there were some shells in there. Sorry."

Sarah sets her plate down, but she's eaten more than half. She's braver than I am.

"Consider it field training," she smirks, patting me on the shoulder. "I'm sure we'll have to eat a lot worse than this in the future. You can't expect to do something perfectly the first time."

A weight lifts off my shoulders. Sarah always seems to know when I need a reassuring word and when I need a good, swift kick in the rear.

"Cheers," I hold up my can of cherry cola. Sarah taps it with her own. "To all our future missions. May you always be there to back me up."

"Cheers," she replies.

7: SARAH DRIVES THE INVESTIGATION

"The first sighting was in Cheyenne Canyon," I read from our notes on my phone. "Some hikers saw what looked like a super big guy, our supersoldier, hiding in the bushes. He disappeared as soon as they got close."

"SARAH!" Simon screams, grabbing at the handle above the passenger side door. "EYES ON THE ROAD!"

I turn back to the road I'm speeding down just in time to see the stop sign. Where the heck did that come from? I slam on the brakes, throwing us forward against our seatbelts. I don't see the problem, but Simon breathes heavily, clinging to that stupid roof handle.

"It's a residential area," he scolds, grabbing my phone from my hand. "You're not supposed to be looking at your phone while you drive."

I roll my eyes. "Yeah, I'm sure nobody ever does that. We're fine. I'm the Island's best driver, three years running."

"So you've said. Repeatedly. This isn't a crisis situation, Sarah. Just drive the speed limit and obey the rules." Simon continues to glare at me while I press on the gas, popping the car forward before turning left. "Including using your turn signal. Turn signal!"

Another car screeches to a stop. It honks at me as I

turn but honestly, they shouldn't have been so close to me, anyway. A good driver is always prepared to make a sudden stop when something unexpected pops up, like I did at that sign back there. What do these people learn in their driving lessons?

"Speed limit is an oxymoron, Simon." But I ease up on the gas pedal. "Speed isn't supposed to have limits. That's why it's called speed."

"No, it's not," he pouts.

We're on our way to the Cave of the Winds. It's one place that caught footage of the guy. A blurry, grainy image. Conspiracy nuts swarm to grainy cameras like ants on a sticky lollipop. They always think something's being covered up. They never seem to consider that maybe the owner of the blurry camera just hasn't cleaned the lens in a while.

My grappling hook necklace sits light and cool around my neck, as it has since ever I took it out of the box. Simon's got his camera slung over his shoulder, looking like a genuine photojournalist. We're both dressed to look like adults, and we're pulling it off well. Simon and I have business cards in our pocket litter. The cards list our fake names and our real phone numbers. It's the little details that sell a false identity. In fact, to give my alias some flavor, I think I'll go by her middle name, Abigail.

We're on the road to Manitou Springs, even further up in the Rocky Mountains. Manitou Springs, Colorado Springs, apparently there are a lot of springs around here. We pull onto Highway 24 and I push the gas pedal down a bit more. The purr of the accelerating engine relaxes me as the highway saunters through a canyon of red-tinted rock and pine trees. The road feels a lot like the training runs on HQ Mountain. I feel comfortable here. I even seem to have acclimated to the altitude. So far today, I've only run two stop signs, one red light, and swerved a little too hard to avoid a squirrel that darted in front of us. I admire that squirrel. A real risk-taker.

Not too far after we leave the last suburban house behind, we pass a sign that reads "Manitou Cliff Dwellings." People have lived in these mountains for thousands of years. It's weird to think about. As far as we know, the agents of DAAAD are the first human inhabitants of our Island, and we're the only ones ever born there.

"Wait! That's my exit!"

I yank the wheel to the right, cutting off some poor, terrified minivan driver who's too polite to honk. His eyes widen with terror as he pumps his brakes. He should take bravery lessons from that squirrel.

We follow the twisting two-lane road with my foot heavy on the gas and Simon whimpering something about speed limits again. The new road crawls up the canyon, the rock walls slanting down in a cliff on one side and rising in a wall on the other. The road curves and winds back on itself seemingly at random, but the view from up here is spectacular. You can see for miles, past buildings and streets to forests and grasslands.

I'm surprised at how full the parking lot we pull into is. Back home, parking isn't exactly a problem. There's an assigned spot for every jeep, van, helicopter, and training car. Out here it's like some kind of hero's quest to find a space. I finally skid into one at the end of a long row.

"So let's review what happened at this Cave of the Winds place." I turn the car off.

We get out and follow some arrow-shaped signs that say "Cave this way." Simon checks my phone, which he still hasn't given back to me. I grab for it but he holds it over my head, reading the screen from below.

"Someone—or something—" he wiggles his eyebrows, "got caught on security cameras here at night. They got some crappy video of the guy. He matches the description of our not-a-supersoldier; unusually muscular and kind of short. A few structures were damaged, and they left the door to the caves open. The authorities chalked it up to vandalism, but conspiracy sites linked the Canyon and the Cave sightings. And, to be fair, so did DAAAD."

"Maybe this whole thing is just kids playing around. It sounds like some kind of prank." I step on Simon's foot and he drops the phone. I grab it mid-air. "Oh! Maybe it's a gang of teenage hooligans. We could hunt them down and infiltrate their lair. Take down their organization from the inside."

"You're not infiltrating any gang of teens if you keep using words like 'hooligan.'" Simon points out.

I look back along the road leading to the parking lot, with its twists, turns, and steep sides. Then I notice something else. Or, more accurately, the lack of something else. There aren't any streetlights. Not even in the parking lot. Without streetlights, it would be tricky to navigate that road at night.

"How well do teenagers drive? I don't know much about kids who aren't spies, but I don't think they get a lot of training in survival driving skills," I click on the security photo of the not-a-supersoldier on my phone. "Besides, this is only one person. And he doesn't look like a teenager to me. You're right, we're probably not looking for hooligans. Too bad. There'd be some real potential for a story like that to circulate."

As we continue along the path, Simon takes some photos of his own. He walks backward, snapping shots of the road and surrounding landscape. The biggest arrow yet tells us we've reached the historic Cave of the Winds. We walk around some bushes and I stop dead in my tracks. Simon, still walking backward, slams into me. He spins around.

"Now *this* is my kind of place," I gasp.

A giant house hangs off a cliff, built on an outcropping at one of the steepest areas we've seen so far. Two enormous decks cantilever over the side, stacked on top of each other. They're suspended six hundred feet above the ground with a view of forever. People swarm over them, carrying trays of food that looks absolutely, deliciously unhealthy. Overly processed burgers on fluffy white buns, thick fries slathered in ketchup, soft serve ice cream dipped in a hard chocolate shell. Chicken nuggets that probably have nothing to do with chickens at all. Tourist food. Gus would lose his marbles.

Hordes of brightly clad young children chase each around, screaming. Teenage couples with hands in each other's pockets cling together. A few white-haired older people shoot disapproving looks at the parents of the young kids. Everyone mulls around on the decks looking for open tables to set their trays on and leaning against the railings, pretending to push each other over. But I'm not paying attention to any of that.

I only have eyes for the world's most incredible ropes course.

A wooden structure sits at the edge of the cliff,

between the parking lot and the house, near two glass climbing walls and a tall, fully enclosed, corkscrew slide. Climbers access the slide through level after level of round rope nets, stacked on top of each other and swarming with kids. In the distance, a chair-like contraption hurdles pairs of terrified, screaming tourists down the canyon on some kind of crazy zipline. It looks amazing.

The ropes course is shaped like a three-story cube. Tall wooden poles stand at each corner, with a few planks spanning the space between them. Stair planks suspended by ropes, rope bridges suspended over hundreds of feet of nothing, and sparse rope nets all hang within the solid-looking wood framework.

I walk towards it in awe, and am shattered when I see a giant orange sign across the front that says "closed for repairs." Something has ripped the ropes from their anchors. Stairs and nets dangle precariously. My eyes follow the trail of destruction to the top corner which is suspended over the cliff. A post topped with a crushed security camera stands about ten feet away. The post and camera would be nearly invisible at night. I don't care how unnaturally long this guy's arms are, no one could reach the top of that pole in the darkness. Not without falling to his death. It really would take an enhanced human to make that jump. Or something not human at all. So what broke the camera?

DAAAD set up a meeting for us. Simon leads us past the broken ropes course and towards the enormous house, which is labeled "tourist center," to meet our contact. People mill around outside. Discarded food and packaging overwhelm the trash cans, baking in the blistering sun. It stinks.

Our contact is an employee named Ivan. He's not an agent and doesn't know who we really are. He's just a regular employee who thinks we're doing a story for an online news site; The Stratagem Online, Real News for a Fake World. It calls itself news, but it's a hotbed of conspiracy theories. DAAAD keeps a close eye on it and got our fake identities hired remotely. Someone has written a few articles by Sarah Abigail Quarterly and turned in some photos from Simon Zachary Lenoir. It's the perfect cover for us to gain the trust of conspiracy theorists anywhere we go.

Ivan Douterton is more than a little eager to talk to reporters from the Stratagem because he's one of the people spreading rumors. I recognize him immediately from the picture DAAAD sent us and confirm with a glance at his nametag. A nondescript Caucasian of medium height and weight, with short, dark-blonde hair, Ivan wears wire-rimmed glasses. He's got on comfortable-looking walking shoes with thick black soles. He's so painfully ordinary I kind of understand why he's looking for weird stuff to happen, just to create some interest in his life.

Ivan watches us approach with a mixture of suspicion and excitement. I get into character for my first undercover interaction.

It's showtime.

"Hello, you must be Mr. Douterton. Abigail Quarterly from The Stratagem." I hand him a business card. "It's a pleasure to meet you. This is my photographer, Simon Lenoir."

"Ivan, please. I'm glad your paper understands the importance of my story. It's about time someone listened to me." Suddenly Ivan freezes, reading my card.

"You said your name is Abigail? Then why does it say Sarah on your business card?"

His voice is triumphant as if he's caught me red-handed. Just like I predicted.

"Yes, Sarah Abigail Quarterly," I point to the full name on the card and lean a little closer, sharing a confidence with him. "But I go by Abigail in person. It makes it harder to trace me. I shouldn't tell you that, but you seem like someone I can trust." I pause. "I can trust you, can't I?"

One way to divert suspicion is to be even more suspicious than someone suspicious of you. Ivan nods knowingly, a confidant in our little secret.

"Ah, I understand." He winks at me. "Don't worry, you can trust me."

He leads us into the building, but I don't follow him. Instead, I point to the "closed" sign in front of the ropes course.

"What happened here?"

Ivan sighs at the dangling ropes. "You know, in the twelve years I've worked here, nothing has ever taken out the Wind Walker course. Hail, we get a lot of hail, blizzards, and ridiculous heat in the dead of summer. High winds. We even had a bear up here once. It's a shame. I hate to see all the sad faces of people who come to do it. But we're getting it repaired as soon as we can."

Ivan looks at me expectantly. I pull out my phone and jot down some notes, though probably not the ones he thinks I'm jotting down. "Any idea what happened to it?"

He glances around, as if afraid of being overheard. Then, even though there are lots of people within listening range, he says, "I heard it was some crazy guy who escaped from a mental hospital."

Wait, an escaped mental patient? That type of rumor would work perfectly. If I can amplify it and get one measly picture, we're done here.

"Wow! That makes total sense!" I envision a photo of a guy in a hospital gown, untied with the back flopping open, waving around the broken shackles on his wrists. So perfect. Nothing military about–

Then Ivan leans closer. "Yeah, it was a *military* hospital. And the guy was an escaped—" he catches himself. "Well, you wouldn't believe it."

Sigh. Of course it wouldn't be that easy. These types of rumors always wrap every over-the-top theory back to the government and/or the military, like private citizens can't plot anything evil on their own. Still, I wonder who really could have caused that kind of damage to the ropes course. And why? Ivan might have some useful insight, hidden inside his ridiculous theories, and when you're a spy, you can't leave any angle unsearched.

"You'd be surprised what I'd believe," I prod. "Try me."

Ivan doesn't reply. We travel towards the tourist center along a wide road edged by short rock walls. A kid walks along the top of the wall, holding her father's hand. The dad smiles as his daughter fearlessly skips along as if she has nothing to fear as long as her dad is with her.

I wonder what that would feel like.

Ivan takes us to his office inside the main building. He's obviously worked here a long time. Personal photos, paperback books, plants, and a few comfortable guest chairs cram into the small space.

"Can you tell us more about this mysterious visitor?" I ask as Simon takes a few photos. "Where did he go, what did he do? Do you think there was more than one person?"

"Well, we know he climbed around on the Wind Walker—"

"That's the ropes course outside, right?" Simon asks, turning the camera on Ivan. Ivan freezes in a thoughtful pose and Simon's camera clicks a few times. Ivan's image zips straight to DAAAD's database through the camera's data-link.

"Yup, that's the one. I'm pretty sure he went into the caves, too, though I can't prove it."

"Why do you think that?" I ask.

"For one thing, the door was wide open. Also, look at this," Ivan pulls open a laptop and turns it face to us. I think we're looking at the Wind Walker course, but it's dark and I can hardly see anything. Seriously, these cameras have to be from the Stone Age. It looks like a bunch of static. A vaguely human-shaped lump comes from what might be the direction of the cave entrance. Or the gift shop. Or heck, just further down the road. "See? Where else besides the cave could he have come from? There's nothing else in that direction."

He's not telling us anything we don't already know, and I'm growing impatient. "Do you have any other clues about what he might have been doing?"

Ivan grabs a flashlight. "I have proof he went deep inside the caves. It's easier to show you. I hope you're not afraid of the dark or small confined spaces! It can take some practice getting used to being in a cave. But don't worry, I won't let anything happen to you."

He chuckles, probably thinking he's scaring us. He

doesn't know we live inside a volcano. Traversing caves is as natural as walking to Simon and I. I've never thought about how it might feel to someone who didn't grow up underground.

I follow Ivan out the door, but Simon stares at the screen. The security video is still running, as the blob of static rampages over the ropes course with what looks like unnatural strength and agility. Simon squints at it, rewinds it, and watches it again. He holds out his arms a little and moves his body back and forth.

"What is it?" I ask.

"I don't know, there's something about the guy's movement. Something I can't quite put my finger on," he answers quietly. He takes a last look at the screen over his shoulder before following us out the door.

Ivan brings us into the caves. Even for people who live inside a mountain, it's impressive. Giant caverns, drippy stalactites on distant ceilings, endless sparkling tunnels, forests of stalagmites. Several tour groups pass us as we go deeper and deeper into the earth. One guide asks his tour if they're afraid of the dark. Ivan's eyes light up. He pulls me to a stop.

"You're gonna love this," he says. "And don't worry. Remember, I'm here. Try not to be too scared."

I try not to laugh.

Then the lights go out. All of them. It's pitch black in the cavern. Like, really black. It's the type of darkness Simon and I train in, but I doubt any of these regular people have ever seen black as dark as what they're suddenly standing in. I remember I'm supposed to be one of the regular people and pretend to gasp. Ivan chuckles. Then I hear someone cry.

There's a certain feeling to being deep underground.

A preternatural quiet, a stillness, and a deep black you don't get anywhere else. All that rock above you, the lack of flowing air. Maybe if you've been in a submarine with tons of water pressing invisibly down on you, then you might have felt something like it. I wonder if it feels the same in space.

"I want to go back," a voice says, sounding small and scared in the darkness.

The lights switch back on and I see the skipping girl, still clinging to her father's hand. The father's eyes are enormous. In that same small voice, he says again, "Let's go back."

But the little girl looks excited. She tugs her father along as the tour guide moves deeper into the cave, oblivious to her father's whimpering.

Ivan motions for us to follow him down a different tunnel. This one isn't part of the main tour. There aren't any lights installed this far down, so he turns on his flashlight. The floor continues to descend until a yellow plastic ribbon stretches across yet another tunnel in our path. Someone has torn the plastic in half, but now it's tied back together to restore the barrier.

"I found this off-limits tape broken. I fixed it the best I could, but nobody but me comes down here, anyway. And no one on staff has been here since we put the tape up." He shines his flashlight into the tunnel. "I just know he came down here. I bet he laid some mutant alien eggs deep in that tunnel but, um, I haven't had a chance to look closer."

Oh boy. This guy is crazier than we thought. But I might as well check it out. Simon and I share a look and Simon, understanding what I'm thinking, nods in agreement.

"Hand me the flashlight," I say. "I'm going to check it out."

Ivan hesitates. "Nobody's supposed to go in there. It's unstable."

"I'll be fine." I grab the flashlight and scoot under the security tape.

The tunnel doesn't go very far. There's one little turn and then it stops in a small cavern barely large enough to stand in. There are no alien eggs here, but I see what looks like a scrap of paper on the ground. I stuff it in my pocket and make my way back to Simon and a nervous-looking Ivan. He gratefully takes the flashlight back and immediately starts walking us back to the surface.

"What did you see in there?" Ivan asks me.

"Nothing. No eggs, no escaped mental patients, nothing. Are you sure he came down here?"

"I didn't think he'd still be there! But I thought he would've left something behind. Some kind of spore, maybe." Ivan's eyebrows knit together. "First, he visits the caves, then he destroys the Wind Walker. I even found some fresh tread marks in the parking lot. From a big truck, like a van or a jeep. It must have been the military. They must have hacked into our camera feed and saw him wrecking the ropes, so they came to take him out. They do that when an experiment goes haywire, you know. Blamo! Erase all the evidence. I bet that's how the camera got destroyed."

It's getting out of hand, I need to take control of the situation. "I don't think you should tell that theory to anyone else."

"You're not going to report it?" He narrows his eyes. "What kind of reporter are you? Are you really from the Stratagem?"

Simon, who had been lost in thought, puts a hand on Ivan's arm. "Not yet. Ivan, we need to create plausible deniability for your safety. You know how it works, man. You don't want that truck to show up looking for you, do you?"

Fear passes across Ivan's face, then a look of gratitude. "Of course, of course. Thanks, guys."

"We have to protect our sources," Simon continues, throwing his arm around Ivan's shoulders. "You call us if you see anything else, okay? Thanks for your time, you're a real patriot."

Ivan walks back to his office with his head held high.

"Nice work," I pat Simon on the back. As soon as Ivan disappears, I pull the paper from my pocket and show it to Simon. "Almost as good as mine. Look what I found."

It's a photograph. An aerial view of the mountains. A single road twists and turns towards the mountain then disappears, probably into a tunnel. From the camera's angle, we can't see the entrance but there are several buildings along the lonely road and two large parking lots. I'm not impressed.

"Oh look," I snort. "A photo of a mountain inside a mountain."

"What's a photo doing down inside a cave in an off-limits tunnel?" Simon looks closer. "That's not this mountain. Look, it's got a different shape, and it's not in a canyon. I wonder where it is?"

"Maybe some tourist dropped it," I suggest. "Though that doesn't explain how it got down so deep."

"What tourist carries photo printouts around while sightseeing? If they were going to print them out, they'd wait until they got home."

"That's true. I'm going to hang on to it. It might be

from our not-a-supersoldier after all, even if it's not a mutant egg," I chuckle.

We walk past the wreckage of the Wind Walker on the way to our car. Simon slows down to look at the damage.

He takes a few photos of it, and mumbles, "It sure looks like someone was furious."

"How can you tell?" I watch a broken stair tread swing on its rope in the breeze.

"I don't know. This destruction, it just says angry to me. It looks like whoever was here left the caves in a terrible mood and took it out on the poor ropes." He points to the broken security camera. "And didn't like being watched while having his little temper tantrum."

"That seems a little far to jump, don't you think? Maybe the military did shoot it out. With a space laser." We both laugh while I pull out the car keys. "Where to next?"

"I don't know." Simon grabs the keys from me. "But I'm driving."

8: SIMON'S TURN TO DRIVE

Sarah and I decide to visit the locations of the sightings in backward order. Interestingly, they've all been at night so far. The most recent one was at Cave of the Winds. Check. Three nights before that, a tourist posted a ten-second video from a scenic spot called Seven Falls, which was three nights before the first sighting in Cheyenne Canyon, where hikers saw a muscular, weird-looking guy lurking in the shadows. He looked confused or scared or something, but when they approached, he ran away.

So our next stop is Seven Falls. It's a series of seven sequential waterfalls cascading down one long box canyon. It's owned by this ritzy hotel complex called the Broadmoor. We have to park at the hotel and take a shuttle to the waterfall. Sarah punches the hotel's address into our navigation system as I pull out of the driveway. She's annoyed that I insisted on driving, but I value both of our lives. I stick to the speed limit (even though we could make better time jogging.)

"Turn right on West Cheyenne Road," says the car.

Grainy videos of the not-a-supersoldier wrecking the Wind Walker course keep playing in my head. There's something off about the way he's moving. I can't put my finger on it. It's almost—

"Turn right, Simon," Sarah's voice snaps me back to the road. "Right! OMG, you drive like a twelve-year-old."

"Is this West Cheyenne Road already?" I crane my neck around to surveil my surroundings. "How do you know what street you're on?"

"By looking at the street signs." Sarah rolls her eyes. "We just passed West Cheyenne. Turn around."

I press gently on the brakes and push down my turn signal in the middle of the street. A car blares its horn at me and swerves around us as I start to pull a U-turn.

"You can't flip around in the middle of the block!" Sarah yells. Another car swerves around me, and the driver yells something nasty out the window. "You have to turn at the next street! And then turn again."

"Yeah, I get it. It's just, all these other cars are stressing me out. Traffic isn't exactly a thing on the Island, you know," I snip. I follow Sarah's instructions and glance over at her for approval, but she's playing with her phone. Probably reviewing the files again.

"We should check out the Broadmoor since we're going to be there anyway," she says.

"Why? I don't think it's relevant."

We've been going back and forth all morning because there's been a little chatter about the hotel. Sarah thinks it's connected but I'm not sure it fits the pattern. Multiple sightings, no footage, just vague comments on social media from a frustrated janitor who hears noises and can't get anyone to take him seriously. Plus the Broadmoor is a populated hotel. Our escaped supersoldier has avoided people at all the other sightings. I don't want to waste our time or get sidetracked, but Sarah thinks we should check it out, and we both know she's going to win eventually.

"Wait. Which street is this?" I get to the next intersection and wait for a car to pass before I turn. Someone behind me honks long and loud. The noise is more annoying than motivating. "Why are there so many streets? Who needs this many places to go?"

"Recalculating." The car's soothing voice irritates me.

"Go, go!" Sarah yells. I wait for another car to pass while the car behind us keeps honking. I start to turn but Sarah yells at me again. "No! Stop. Not now. You waited too long."

"Turn left," the car says. "Then turn left again at the next intersection."

"There are too many streets!" I yell at the car. I try to think of a haiku to settle my brain, but can't. "What's the name of the street I'm supposed to turn on?"

"Seriously, Simon? Just turn here. In fact, pull over. I'm driving again."

"No." I finally turn left. Tires screech as the driver behind us pops forward, released like a racehorse from a starting gate. "At least I won't kill anybody with a car on our first assignment."

"I might have to kill you with a car on our first assignment if you don't speed up." Sarah drums her fingers on the dashboard.

The digital map on our GPS spins around, and the red arrow I'm supposed to follow keeps changing. I slow down and ignore the cars swerving around me.

"Recalculating," the car informs me pleasantly.

I turn where the arrow says to turn. That makes the car happy. "In forty-five feet, turn left onto Cresta Road."

I take a few deep breaths, slowing down at the next intersection to read the signs. "I don't like the car telling me how to drive. I don't like her attitude."

"It's software, Simon. It doesn't have an attitude. Will you speed up already? Is there a speed minimum?" Sarah looks around for a street sign.

"Of course, it has an attitude." I turn left onto Cresta Road and the car seems to approve. "An attitude, a color, it's got everything anybody else has. Everything has a personality, Sarah, you just have to be open to it."

Sarah frowns at me.

The Broadmoor looms up in front of us, a majestic complex of pink buildings fronted by a long, stately, circular driveway. We cruise around the buildings towards the parking structure in the back. A walkway bisects a lake behind the main building with a cute, curved bridge. Tranquil walking paths lead to other buildings. Some families splash around at one end of the lake, which appears to be a pool. Others paddle boats on the non-pool side, chasing swans they'll never catch. The place is enormous. We circle the parking garage until I ease us into the spot.

"You missed like fifteen perfectly good parking places. Could we be any farther away? I'm driving next." Sarah grabs for the keys, but I tuck them into my pocket. She scrunches her mouth to the side but lets me hold on to them.

"Thank you for your feedback. I'll file it in the appropriate trash can." I reply. We head out of the parking garage into the simmering afternoon heat. "Do you think there's a taco truck around here? If I have to eat another chip, I think I'm going to vomit. I have this constant stomach ache."

Sarah laughs. She thumbs around on her phone, then shakes her head. "All I see are a few restaurants, but they look pretty fancy. I don't think we have time for that kind of meal."

I sigh at the thought of endless future meals made entirely out of snacks. I never thought I'd get tired of eating chips, but I miss Gus and his salmon risotto. There, I said it.

A few people wait with us at the shuttle stop to Seven Falls, fanning themselves with brochures as heat drifts off the pavement in waves. I pull a brochure from a little plastic box attached to the side of the shuttle stop's shelter. It tells us that Seven Falls is "the grandest mile of scenery in Colorado." It also says there's a food truck (not specifically taco, but maybe it's got one on the menu) in the area between the shuttle and the falls, along with a bunch of gold-mining-themed attractions like gold panning and stuff like that. I stop reading at "food truck." Eventually the shuttle swings by and we all climb aboard.

Public transportation is fascinating. The rules seem to consist mostly of pretending no one else is on the bus, yet sitting as far away from them as possible. It's an elaborate sort of geometry, so I let Sarah choose our seats. The shuttle is hot and stinks of sweaty armpits. My feet stick to something under the seat in front of me.

The bus drops us under an ornamental archway and we walk towards the falls. I keep my eyes open for the food truck, which appears from the mist like a glorious mirage.

I dash towards it. No lines, no waiting. "Second Meal is served!"

"Hey, Simon." Sarah walks leisurely, reading the

brochure. "It's closed Monday through Thursday."

I skid to a stop in front of the "closed" sign, stomach grumbling as I rejoin Sarah on the main path. Someday, street taco, you will be mine.

This deep in the canyon the air is cool and refreshing, filled with the sound of splashing water mingling with the conversations of the people around us. To our left, a stream crashes over a picturesque little stone dam and tosses cool mist into the air. Further back in the canyon, craggy cliffs speckled in moss surround us on three sides. A few pine trees dot the area, growing from the rock itself. Water tumbles down the series of falls, spilling from one to another to another, bouncing off layers of rock into deep pools then cascading to the next.

> *Streaks of timeless foam*
> *Writing stories in white ink*
> *Tales of forever*

A dizzying number of metal stairs rise up the side of the canyon. They stretch from the viewing platforms at the bottom of the falls where we stand, all the way to the top. Spotlights, artfully arranged around more viewing platforms, maximize selfies. There's a tunnel with an entrance that looks like an old mine and a sign that says "Mountain Elevator."

So much here is paved. I'm not used to smooth streets and walkways of wood or asphalt. Back home, we have to use our bare hands and feet to climb to the top of a canyon.

From the bottom of the falls, we call up the video. It's dark, taken by some trespassing kids after the gates had been closed for the night. The man in the video is wide and short, with enormous shoulders, fitting the description of our not-a-supersoldier. Every once in a while, some poor bear wanders around up here at night, and some of the video's comments insist that's what the shadowy figure is. But this is no bear.

The distant figure bounds up the stairs, vaulting and crawling and leaping from one railing to another all the way to the top. He's in constant motion as if he's doing Parkour. I can't imagine a regular person, even one in fantastic shape, moving with the strength of this guy. I don't think I could pull it off.

"This video is better quality than the one from Cave of the Winds," I point out. "At least it's in color, but it's too far away and too dark to see anything clearly. Looks like they tried to zoom in, but that just made it super shaky." I take a few shots and a video with my camera, even though the only people going up the stairs today are tourists.

Sarah compares the online video to the actual landscape in front of her. "That's about two hundred and twenty, maybe two hundred twenty-three steps. Probably a one-hundred-eighty-foot drop. Maybe there is something to this escaped experimental supersoldier thing after all. I mean, what sort of person has the strength to move like that?"

"What if he's wearing some kind of gear or tactical suit or exoskeleton? Maybe that's what's bulking him out and making him look like he has long arms and short legs." I replay the video again. There's that thing in the way he's moving again. I still can't put my finger on it. It taunts me just out of reach of my brain like a whisper in the wind.

"What makes you so sure it's a guy?" Sarah asks.

That gets my attention. Can we be so sure this supersoldier is a guy? "Look at those shoulders. They're so big."

"Like a gymnast?" Sarah suggests. "Wearing gear on her shoulders? I wonder if a guy that muscular would have the stamina to climb like that. You know, assuming he didn't have enhanced lungs or anything."

I close the video. "I think we've seen what we've come to see, and it's only given us more questions. Why visit all these places? Why always at night? What's the connection here? And of course, who is this guy?"

"Or girl," Sarah adds as we head back to the gate to meet the shuttle.

"Okay, sure," I agree. "We don't even know that for sure. But if we're going to catch this person in the act, we need to know why they're choosing the places they are so we can predict the next one. We need to figure out what they're doing, what's motivating them."

I don't point out that all the evidence indicates exactly what we don't want to think about. An enhanced human. And it's interesting that, with all the military bases around here, none of them have been hit by the vandal. Which implies that if the bases aren't victims, they are probably the perpetrators.

Are the conspiracy nuts right? Who would want to create a superhuman? The military bases around here, especially secretive places like Cheyenne Mountain, are the most logical points of origin. The concept of a genetically enhanced supersoldier persists because it makes sense. Who except the military has the resources and motivation to experiment with genetically enhanced humans? But Agent Zero said nothing like that is going on. And she'd never lie to us.

Would she?

Then a thought crosses my mind. One I know for sure would never occur to Sarah. What if Agent Zero put us on this assignment not to train us, not because it's a good first mission, but because we're inexperienced? If I had information I wanted covered up from my own organization, I'd probably pick Sarah and me to do the investigation, too. We can get the job done, for sure, but we really only on a surface level, like junior agents who just want to get the job done and get out of here. And I might even lie to them to make sure they stayed on their assignment, cleaning up conspiracy chatter, and nothing else.

But no. That's ridiculous. I won't even mention the idea to Sarah. She'd never even consider it. She'd never accept that Agent Zero was anything less than perfect. I keep quiet as we take the shuttle back to the Broadmoor complex.

"As long as we're here," Sarah presses. "We might as well check this place out."

I may not believe the Broadmoor incident has anything to do with our supersoldier, but going along with Sarah's hunch is better than telling her I think Agent Zero might be lying to us. So I call up a map of the hotel and review the posts about the alleged disturbance.

"Looks like it's happening at the main building over there. The janitor heard him on the roof—"

"Or her."

"Okay, the janitor heard *them* on the roof," I point to the building labeled as the main tower on our map. The roof is maybe eight or ten stories above the ground. "I think it's that one there if I'm reading the comments correctly. And it was barely evening. Earlier than the other sightings, but still after dark."

"Maybe they were trying to get inside." Sarah squints at the roof. "Let's go see if we can get on that roof."

We enter a formal lobby with a chandelier larger than our rental car. There's a gently bubbling fountain, glistening white marble floors, and the ceiling has a mural of the sky complete with wispy white clouds. They grouped the furniture at precise angles. Uniformed employees skitter around helpfully.

To my surprise, no one stops us as we head to the elevator and up to the top floor. We may not have experience in undercover work, but when you're a spy, you learn to carry yourself with confidence. And whether you're trying to appear older or breaking into a ritzy hotel, confidence is your number one tool to sell your cover.

Confidence is something Sarah does not lack.

We go all the way to the top floor, but can't figure out how to get to the roof. A woman's voice comes from the end of the hallway and we head towards it. The woman wears a maid's uniform and leans against a wheeled cart full of towels and buckets of tiny shampoo and lotion bottles. The wiry, balding, grey-haired man she's chatting with has on a jumpsuit that matches her maid's uniform. He's carrying a mop.

"I heard him," the man insists. "He was climbing around up there. I tell you, Angie, he wasn't human."

"Oh no?" the woman laughs. "It was a giant squirrel, I suppose?"

"They say they're making supersoldiers in Cheyenne Mountain," he presses. "And that one of them escaped. I bet that's who it was. I know how it sounds, but I swear

I heard him."

The woman chuckles. She grabs a load of towels and heads into an open room. The man grips his mop tighter. His face contorts with frustration as he calls after her.

"What if it's true, Angie? Stranger things have happened. I know what I heard."

Then he sees Sarah and me. He puts his head down and walks past us, but Sarah steps in front of him, handing him one of her business cards. "Hello, Abigail Quarterly from the Stratagem news site. I'm here investigating the escaped mental patient. I heard you talking and wonder if you could tell me what you saw."

She emphasizes 'mental patient', trying to steer the discussion away from the military base, but I don't think it's going to work. Nothing says "something's being covered up" like a bunch of blurry photos and some eyewitnesses, like this was all being done on purpose. And anyway, the janitor isn't buying it.

"Mental patient?" He looks at Sarah's card. "I heard it was the military."

Sarah nods. A good way to get someone to agree with you is to agree with them first. Sure enough, the man with the mop nods with Sarah as she continues.

"Yeah, I used to think that too, but the newest information says it's a mental patient. This is Simon Lenoir, my photographer. Can we borrow a moment of your time?"

The janitor shrugs. "Sure, I ain't never been interviewed before, though."

"Just tell us what you saw," Sarah smiles. "Or, is it what you heard?"

"Well, it was late, see. I was covering for Smitty. He

had to go to his daughter's graduation, see, so I was happy to help out." He turns his mop over and leans on it. "Yeah, so I don't usually work late, but there I was, up here on the top floor. I hear this scritch-scratching on the roof, see, and it ain't no GIANT SQUIRREL, ANGIE." He yells towards the open room. "Nosiree, it was something heavy. A lot bigger than some squirrel. But here's the thing. It wasn't trying to get in, I swear it was trying to get *out*."

He pauses to check our reaction. Sarah and I look at each other.

"Like a guest?" I ask. "Climbing out their window?"

"Are you sure they were trying to get out, and not just climbing around on the outside of the building?" Sarah asks.

"I'll show you. You bring that camera, boy, you ain't gonna believe this," The janitor motions for us to follow him, leading us through a series of doors, up some steps, and into a small room in the tower at the front of the main building. The old man points victoriously to a pile of leaves and twigs in the middle of the room's floor. Then he sneezes. "I was just about to clean this up tonight, see, but I wanted to show Angie first. I think he spent the night here and then took off the next evening after it got dark. Smitty don't have no reason to check up here, but these leaves ain't dead yet. Just wilty. So it's a good guess that they aren't more than a few days old. See what I'm saying here?"

I film a video. Knowing it's going straight to an operative back at HQ, I narrate for them, "So you found this pile of leaves where you heard a bunch of movement. Have you checked the hotel's security cameras? Or heard anything from the guests? If the visitor was here for a whole day, someone would have seen them, right?"

The old man shrugs. "I ain't heard anything from the guests, and the other workers think I'm nuts. There ain't no way Jackie would let me look at no security footage. She'd laugh me right to unemployment."

He sneezes again.

"Is it the dust up here?" I ask, handing him a tissue. It doesn't seem that dusty but some people are just sensitive.

"Naw, I'm a janitor, son. Dust don't bother me none. It ain't allergies. Only thing I'm allergic to is animals. Any type of animal, you name it, I'm allergic to it. My son didn't like that none growing up but what can you do?"

Sarah opens her mouth to say something, but the janitor shakes his head. "I gotta get back to work now. Can't afford no bad review."

"Okay, thank you for your time." Sarah shakes his hand. "If you think of anything else, please call the number on my card."

We make our way out of the building. As we head back to the car, we pass a group of families who look like they've just come back from a long day of touristing. Two men, four women, and seven kids between the ages of five to maybe fifteen. The three littlest ones are carrying brand-new stuffed animals that still have "Cheyenne Mountain Zoo" tags on them. A snow leopard, a giraffe, and a gorilla. I turn to watch as they pass.

Something tugs at my brain as they walk by. I can't figure it out. Something about those videos we saw back at Cave of the Winds.

9: SARAH FOLLOWS THE LEAD

We're supposed to report to Agent Zero this morning and Simon hasn't changed out of his pajama pants.

Without our morning routine, Simon has been sleeping in. I slept in this morning too, waking up at sunrise instead of before dawn. I took a casual run around our neighborhood, stopping at a Starbucks three miles away for a nice latte and some oatmeal. He was still sleeping by the time I came home, showered, and turned on the television to watch the news.

Color-coded paper strips cover the map I pinned to the wall, showing the military bases and all the sightings. Most of the military bases are in the south, except for the Air Force Academy, which is way up north, and Schriever, which is east. The sightings branch out from the general vicinity of Fort Carson and Cheyenne Mountain and seem to move northwards.

From the kitchen, I hear both the pantry and the refrigerator doors open. Then, over the din of the television that's still droning on in the background, I hear Simon set a bowl on the counter with a clatter.

"Hey, Sarah," he calls. "We need cereal. I'm sick of chips."

"We're not going back to the grocery store. We have

plenty of food. Let's stay focused."

"But—" he whines.

"I said we're not going back. It's a waste of time. If you want a better First Meal–or, I suppose they call it breakfast out here, wake up at a reasonable time tomorrow and come for a run. Now get in here and help me figure out what we're going to tell Agent Zero."

Simon grunts. I hear something bang against the counter a few times. He joins me in the living room a minute later, carrying a bowl and spoon.

"So, what have we got?" he asks.

"Not much." I eye his bowl suspiciously. It's full of milk and what looks like cereal. "We haven't learned anything that DAAAD doesn't already know. Argh! My head hurts. Figuring out mysteries isn't our job! We're just supposed to act on what other people figure out. If this assignment is as important as Agent Zero says, why didn't they assign someone smarter than us?"

Simon dips his spoon into the milk and crunches whatever's floating around in there. He pauses thoughtfully. At first, I think he's considering our upcoming report. Then he raises his eyebrows at the stuff in his bowl with a nod of approval.

"What are you even eating?" I sniff at his bowl. It smells soggy.

"Dorito cereal." He offers me a laden spoon. I can see broken bits of corn chips floating in the milk. "Want some?"

"Are you kidding me?" I gag. "No, I don't want some. How can you want some? What possessed you to put corn chips in milk?"

He looks at his bowl. "It's not so bad. Cool Ranch was the right choice. I don't think the flaming ones would have worked. And the Pringles definitely would have dissolved completely by now—"

"You're so gross." I shake my head and turn back to the map.

He turns to it as well, his eyes running over the colored paper trail again and again. Then he takes a deep breath.

"It does seem like, I mean," he looks from the map to me, and back to the map, then turns away. "Nevermind."

Neither one of us says anything immediately. A television commercial quietly offers us ten percent off at Andy's Furniture Emporium in the background. I know what Simon is thinking because I've been thinking it too. All the evidence does point to some kind of supersoldier experiment. But it can't be. Agent Zero said it wasn't. Unless something is going on that even she doesn't know about, and she knows everything. Facts, we have to stick to the facts.

"Let's go through it again," I finally say, but Simon points his spoon at me.

"Why?" He asks. "Look, do we even care what's really going on? I mean, what's our assignment in the end? We don't need to solve this thing, right? We're just supposed to divert attention away from the military bases."

"I don't think we can take down this conspiracy until we know the truth, Simon. No matter what that truth is." I leave the possibility that we're being lied to out of it. I have to believe in Agent Zero. If she's lying to us, then everything is a lie. Our entire world is a lie. Nothing we've worked so hard for the last seventeen years would mean what we thought. I can't believe that. We may not be the smartest agents at HQ, but we're not stupid. No, I'm going to choose to believe in DAAAD. I believe in Agent Zero. We'll figure out what's going on and I'll prove it to Simon.

But Simon isn't looking at me anymore. He sets his bowl of Dorito cereal on the table, his eyes riveted to the television. He scrambles for the remote and turns up the volume. It's the news. The anchorwoman smiles a toothy grin at the camera. It must be a feel-good piece.

Sure enough, the scene cuts to an aerial view of a zoo nestled in the mountains. It fades to stock footage of giraffes eating lettuce right from the hands of visitors. Then the camera pans to another enclosure. The anchorwoman's perky voiceover gets louder as Simon cranks the volume.

"And thanks to a generous donation, these new gorillas will find a home at the Cheyenne Mountain Zoo. Once the two groups are mixed, the zoo will host one of the largest troops of great apes in the country. In fact," the reporter continues with a good-natured chuckle, "they've had to hire a few more zookeepers just for the new additions."

Simon brings the remote to the map, using it as a pointer as he searches. "Zoo, zoo, zoo, where's the zoo?"

Ignoring the loud weather report that starts up on the news and scan the map with my brother for the location of the zoo, though I don't understand why.

"That's it!" Simon slams the tip of the remote against the map. The zoo is right between Cheyenne Mountain and Cheyenne Canyon, the location of the first sighting. He turns to me with sparkling eyes. "I know why the supersoldier moves so strangely."

I raise my eyebrows in a question.

"Gorillas!" He points to the television screen, even

though the news report is over. "He's not a supersoldier at all. He isn't even human. Don't you see? That weird way he moves? It's the way an *ape* moves. And given its size, it's got to be a gorilla. The zoo just got in a bunch of new ones. It's an escapee alright, but not from any military base. It's an escaped ape, Sarah. That's why his arms are so long and his legs are so short. That's why he's so strong. Gorillas are, like, six to ten times stronger than a human."

He grabs my shoulders, smiling at me. "Don't you see? Agent Zero wasn't lying about there not being any military experiments. We need to report in and see if they can get us an appointment with a zookeeper!"

It's improbable. Why would a gorilla hang out at a bunch of tourist locations after dark? But it's the best lead we have. And if it *is* true, then Simon is right. Agent Zero told us the truth. And now we at least have something to report at our check-in. I just have to figure out how to phrase it so we don't sound crazier than the conspiracy nuts.

***

Cheyenne Mountain Zoo sits up on the side of a mountain with Colorado Springs spreading out below. The sprawling acres of homes, businesses, and buildings blend into the faraway plains and forest beyond. The zoo itself is an oasis of concrete and carefully constructed habitats deep inside an endless forest of evergreen and aspen trees.

DAAAD set up an interview for us with the new zookeeper. The zoo brought him in specifically to handle the extra gorillas, so he's in the best position to provide us with information about them. They sent along some bonus intel on the zoo's ape population, too.

There are two sets of gorillas here; the ones they've had for a long time, and the ones that were recently acquired. A traveling circus closed down and donated all its gorillas and an old elephant. Why they chose Colorado Springs as the recipient, I don't know. Maybe they're mountain gorillas. If so, this is a good place for them.

Simon pulls our car into the expansive parking lot. He won't give me the keys back. I could pick his pocket, and I will if it comes to it, but we haven't reached that point yet.

- *Situation assessment:*
  - *Parking lot*
    - *Large. One side is the zoo, three sides are pine trees*
    - *Tree branches hang over the edges of the lot*
      - *Shade for the cars*
      - *Good cover for a vehicle*
      - *Far away from the entrance*
    - *Simon parked all the way across the lot under the trees*
      - *It's taking forever to walk across this parking lot to the entrance*
      - *Total waste of time*
      - *I'm not only a superior driver, I'm also better at parking*
    - ***Note To Self***: *Pick Simon's pocket to get the car keys back at first opportunity*
  - *Zoo wall*
    - *Twelve and a half feet tall*
    - *Smooth, no handholds, difficult to*

climb
- ▪ *Doors in wall near the back of the lot*
  - ● *Two employee entrances*
  - ● *Service gate for large delivery vehicles*
- ▪ *Fake thatched roof along the entire length of the wall*
  - ● *Impossible to grab the top edge*
  - ● *Super effective at keeping anything from crawling over the wall*
  - ● *Cheeeeeeesy looking*
- ● **Conclusion:**
  - ○ *Wall designed to keep animals in, not to keep them out, though sufficiently functional for either situation*

"If our supersoldier really is a gorilla, I'm not sure he's coming from inside there." I point to the wall as we continue our long trek across the lot to the zoo's main entrance. "How would it get past that?"

We finally reach the ticket booth and head around it to the door marked "office." I push inside.

"Hello? I'm here to do a story on your new gorillas." I tell the woman standing behind the counter.

She doesn't look up. She's untangling a large handful of lanyards. They're the kind you wear around your neck as you walk through the zoo on an audio tour, with plastic speaker boxes dangling from the end. As the woman wrestles each one free, she hangs it on a hook behind her.

I clear my throat, but she lifts a tangled-up finger to silence me. Her lips move as she counts to herself. Simon and I stand awkwardly just inside the door. She completes the untangling and hangs the last lanyard on the hook, then finally turns to us.

"Twelve! Got them all." She seems to see us for the first time. "How can I help you? Audio tour?"

"Ummm. I'm Abigail Quarterly from Stratagem News. This is my photographer, Simon Lenoir." I hand her a business card but she doesn't even look at it. She just watches me expectantly. After a few seconds of holding the card out awkwardly, I set it on the counter in front of her. "We've got an appointment with one of your zookeepers to do a story on your new gorillas. Where should we go?"

"I have no idea." She cranes her neck to look through a doorway off to the side. "Beckman? Hey Beckman, do you know anything about some reporters?"

A man in his fifties comes out of the office, wiping sauce off his face with a napkin. He's tall and muscular, with short salt and pepper hair, a long oval face, and bright blue eyes. Thick stubble covers his prominent jaw. He's wearing khaki pants and a short-sleeved blue polo shirt, like the woman with the lanyards. The shirts say Cheyenne Mountain Zoo on the breast pocket.

"What do you want?" He looks me up and down with a sour expression and picks up the card. "This you? Stratagem? Never heard of it."

Probably for the best, really. This guy doesn't look like a conspiracy nut. He looks like he beats up conspiracy nuts for fun.

"Don't be a jerk, Beckman, they say they're reporters or something," the woman says.

"That's DOCTOR Beckman, Tori. How many times do I have to remind you?"

"Apparently at least once more, *Beckman*," she drops

a lanyard around his neck and disappears into the side room. The door closes behind her with enthusiasm.

I stare at Beckman, unsure what to say. Behind me, Simon consults his phone. He reads out loud as the man sizes us both up.

"Dr. Beckman. You're the man we're supposed to meet. Our office set up an appointment to talk with you about the new gorillas today."

"Look," Beckman yanks the lanyard off his neck and tosses it on the counter along with his napkin. "I have work to do. You reporters keep coming by for your fluff pieces, taking up all my time. These animals have to be monitored constantly."

I decide on the direct angle with this guy. He doesn't seem like he'd respond well to sweet-talking. The only thing I want to know is if a gorilla has escaped. "And you've accounted for all the animals the circus sent you?"

"What kind of question is that?" He narrows his eyes. I straighten my shoulders and hold his gaze. "Let me tell you something, reporter girl. If the zoo wasn't forcing me to talk with you people, I would have you and all your questions kicked out of here faster than iced lightning. But they want their precious free advertising, so they'll accept every stupid request that comes along. Let's get this over with. Come with me."

Beckman stalks out from behind the counter and storms through the door into the zoo. He doesn't look back to see if we follow him. He travels fast down the path on long legs.

We race after him. Simon snaps pictures of the front gate and the path through the zoo to Primate World. We pass lots of open-air pens, all created to resemble the natural habitats of each animal. Except, of course, for the swarms of people crowding around glass walls and fences to stare at them and take selfies. A series of huts and walkways extend over a sunken area filled with giraffes. Excited kids offer lettuce leaves to the tall creatures. The giraffes stick out enormously long tongues to wrap around the lettuce like snakes. The kids squeal with delight as the giraffes slobber all over their hands.

"Can you tell us about the gorilla enclosure?" I catch up with Beckman.

"What do you want to know? There are some indoor spaces, some outdoor spaces, some spaces closed to the public. Everything's connected with big metal doors. We need to keep the old group and the new group separate for now so they don't kill each other. One of the new ones is having trouble adjusting. Named Bobo. Put that in your feel-good story. Gorillas are like people, they don't always want to hang out with each other. They can be real jerks."

Beckman brings us into a small building. A thick transparent wall divides the interior. Visitors stare through the glass. On the other side, four gorillas of different sizes and ages lounge on ledges, ropes, and a tire swing. On the gorillas' side of the glass wall, one open metal door leads to the outside enclosure, and another metal door, identical but closed, seems to lead to another room inside the building. One gorilla sits next to the closed door, leaning its head against the metal.

"That's Moki." Beckman points to the one by the door. "Terrible name if you ask me, but nobody asked me. These circus monkeys all came with their own names."

Simon's brows knit together. "Monkeys? There are monkeys too?"

Beckman glares at him. "It's just a figure of speech. I mean apes of course. I'm a scientist, what do you think I mean?"

"Just clarifying," Simon steps back.

"Aren't you the photographer? Shouldn't this one ask the questions?" He jerks a thumb at me. "And by the way, no pictures of me. I don't like it."

"Sure, no problem." Simon lowers his camera. It's still pointed at Beckman, though, and I see Simon's finger hit the button. I cough to hide a smile. Simon winks at me.

"Anyway, Moki is always trying to get through the door to Bobo's isolation room. But Bobo can get violent, so we have to keep him away from the others. Most of the gorillas are integrating well, but it's a slow process. They've been here for about a month. That's Suzette, the little one's Boingo, and the big silverback there is Gargantua."

The silverback hangs from a hammock near the ceiling, one arm and leg dangling over the edge. His shoulder and biceps are enormous. He absolutely could have vaulted up those stairs at Seven Falls. But could he have gotten out of the zoo?

"Can we see Bobo?" Simon asks. He takes pictures of the apes, the doors, and the rest of the enclosure.

At first, Beckman grits his teeth, but suddenly his face lights up. "He should be with Daisy right now. That's the summer intern, Daisy Damsel. Started about the same time I did. She doesn't have any experience, but she has an almost magical way with the monk...

apes. She can babysit you and answer all your questions, and I can get back to work."

He leads us through a door marked "employees only." The white room behind the door is smaller than the one in the public area but it has a glass wall, too. The cabinets, blankets, and a steel table remind me of a veterinary office, except for the security cameras in the corners. A gorilla sits on the other side of the glass wall. He's gigantic, but not as large as the silverback. This must be Bobo. He's agitated, pacing around and around the small space. One of his ears has a large nick in it like someone clipped it.

Beckman closes the door behind us. He signals for us to stay quiet as a girl, not much older than we are, stands close to the glass. She's wearing the same khaki and blue uniform all the other zookeepers wear, with her long red hair pulled into a loose braid. She stares at Bobo through the glass with her hands clasped behind her back.

The gorilla's grunts and snuffs fill the room despite the thick barrier. Suddenly, he hurls himself against the glass, the powerful thud echoing off the walls. The whole glass barrier vibrates under his power. I take an involuntary step back and drop into a defensive stance. Beckman recoils as well, and Simon almost drops his camera.

The girl doesn't even flinch. She stands still as Bobo puts his face in front of hers and roars. Giant teeth drip saliva as the sound rings in my ears. But the girl still doesn't react. She reaches out, palm up, and holds her hand in front of Bobo. The gorilla snorts and tilts his head, eyes focused on the hand.

Then, still holding her pose, the girl begins to sing.

She sings loudly, without fear or self-consciousness, projecting from the diaphragm like a trained singer. Her voice isn't amazing, but even though it cracks a bit on some of the higher notes, it's lovely to listen to. I imagine she's singing loudly so that Bobo can hear her through the thick glass and over the sound of his whoofing noises.

It's a lullaby. Not one I've ever heard, but then, it's not like anyone sang me to sleep at night when I was a kid. Bobo thumps his chest with one hand and then punches the glass, right where the girl stands.

She remains still, her hand out, palm up, and continues to sing.

Bobo tilts his head again and stops grunting. Then, slowly, he sits down and listens. The girl sets her hand against the glass and the gorilla lifts its own, making soft *ook-ook* noises. Then, he places his palm against the girl's. He stretches his curled fingers flat against the glass as if trying to wrap them around hers.

From the corner of my eye, I see Simon snap a few silent photos. Maybe he took a video, but it's hard to tell. He's staring at the girl with wide eyes. I turn to get a better view of my brother. We've spent pretty much every moment of our lives together, yet I've never seen the expression that is currently on his face. It's relaxed, dreamy. I don't understand it.

"That's Daisy." Beckman nods with approval. "And that's why she got the job."

The girl stares into Bobo's eyes for a moment longer, then softly turns, keeping her hand against the glass and Bobo's hand. A bit of sunlight through the window shines across her face, lighting up a few renegade strands of hair that escaped from her braid like fiery filigree.

Her heart-shaped face is delicate and pale, ending in a pointy chin. It's spattered with freckles beneath brilliant blue eyes. Her ears, a bit too large to be proportional, stick out to the sides. She looks like I could break her like a twig, but there is an inner strength to her I just can't place. She lifts her delicate hand from the window glass and extends it to us.

"Hello," she says in a tinkling, musical voice. "I'm Daisy. Who are you?"

Simon stares, completely frozen.

10: SIMON MAKES A NEW FRIEND

I can't move.

I can't even breathe. In front of me, the girl made of magic says something, but I don't know what it is. She's holding something out to me. After a moment, I realize it's her hand, and that I'm supposed to do something with it.

Sarah shoots me a confused look, reaches over me, and shakes the girl's hand. She says something too. The man who brought us here nods once, says something, and leaves. Everyone is saying something. I guess I should too.

"My name is Simon," I manage. The girl, Daisy, is already talking to Sarah. She smiles at me and goes back to her conversation. I take her picture.

On the other side of the glass, Bobo the gorilla picks his nose. Daisy gazes at him fondly. Maybe I should pick my nose.

No, that's ridiculous. What's wrong with me? I have to concentrate on the conversation in front of me or I'm going to sound like an idiot. I shake my head to clear it as Daisy continues to talk to my sister, what's-her-name.

"They say this little guy has to be isolated for the

safety of the others, but I don't know," Daisy says. I glance at Bobo. He's almost four hundred pounds of hairy fury. Nothing about him seems little, but Daisy looks at him like he's a soft, warm kitten. "Sometimes I think he's just lonely. He hasn't been allowed to see any of the others since he came here. That kind of isolation would drive anyone crazy."

Sarah talks but I don't register what she says. Daisy pauses and looks at the door that Beckman exited through before she replies.

"Yeah, you know, I think if he were just able to rejoin the others, maybe he'd stop hurting so much. That's the only reason he gets violent sometimes. Because he's hurting, you know?" She lifts her hands. "Don't quote me on that. I mean, I'm not the expert here. I'm just an intern and it's not my call. But—"

She walks over to Bobo again. He's hunched down on the floor, leaning against the glass. He watches Daisy approach with a sad expression. She absentmindedly runs her hand over her fiery auburn braid. It's the color of a garnet gemstone, melted soft. Like lava on its unstoppable crawl across the earth. A deep, undeniable red.

She stares into Bobo's sad brown eyes. "Sometimes I think no one understands him. I mean, we all just need a little connection, you know? Some actual contact with someone kind."

Her eyes drift off like she's not even talking about Bobo anymore. I think for one ridiculous second that she's talking about me, then I realize that of course she's not. She doesn't even know me. Yet, her words bring up something inside me. A feeling hidden so deeply I haven't even talked to Sarah about it. I haven't even talked to myself about it. Like the tickle of a coming sneeze, I feel those few words, words from a complete stranger, itching at me.

DAAAD gave us so much growing up. We've had enchanted lives. I love who I'm becoming. But despite their best efforts, the Department couldn't give us everything. They weren't able to give us the simple comfort of belonging. Being loved not for how hard I can kick, or how accurately I can throw a knife, but just for existing. They couldn't give us a hug we didn't somehow earn.

They couldn't give us the touch of connection.

"I know what you mean," I say before I can stop myself.

Daisy turns to me. She stares into my eyes for a full moment before squinting at me. "Did you know Moki is Bobo's sister? You guys are siblings, right? Maybe you understand what they must be going through, being separated like this after they've spent their whole lives together in that circus."

Moki. That's the gorilla who keeps trying to get through the door to Bobo. At least Sarah and I have each other, even if neither one of us has any answers. Even if we can't be a parent to each other, we can at least understand. Bobo doesn't even have that right now.

"No, no, we're not related." Sarah coughs nervously. I know she's trying to maintain our cover, but the words sting as she says them. "Simon is just my photographer. We have entirely different last names!"

"Who says siblings have to have the same last name?" Daisy snorts. "And anyway, are you guys even reporters? You can't be any older than I am. I find it hard to believe any newspaper would send teenagers out on assignment."

Sarah and I look at each other. Daisy is the only person we've met so far who has seen through our cover. I'm not sure what to say, and my brain is in no condition to think fast.

Any cover identity has various layers of importance, like the fact that our cover's most important job is to give us a plausible reason to ask questions, and a background identity that curious people can research via the web. Some of the small, specific details are much lower priority. Sometimes you can spin yourself out of a dangerous situation by giving up some of your cover in order to satisfy the questioner and preserve the more important parts. While Daisy has guessed we're siblings and teenagers, our relationship to each other is a lot less important than the fact that we're not even old enough to legally rent a car yet.

I say the first spin that pops into my head. "Yeah, people always say we look alike. Honestly, we're cousins. On my mom's side. That's how I got the job. Nepotism isn't always bad."

I force my mouth to stop talking, even though it wants to keep going. It's almost always better to only give the other person a few choice tidbits and let them fill in the blanks with their imagination. I'm not sure if I'm successful, but Daisy lets it go. She turns back to the now-calm gorilla who watches her with soulful eyes.

"These ex-circus animals have been through some trauma." She sits down next to Bobo. He places his hand on the glass and Daisy lifts hers to match. It's like I can literally see her heart drifting through her like clouds. "That's why they closed down the circus. See that notch cut out of his ear? They did that to him on purpose, so they could identify him while he performed special tricks with the rest of the troop."

"That's terrible," I take some pictures of the ear. Sarah, behind me, types some notes on her phone. All the data will go directly to DAAAD for agents to sort, dissect, and analyze down to each item's constituent parts. I make sure Daisy isn't in my shots anymore. It seems like a betrayal of her privacy. It's not a very spy way to think about it, but it feels right.

She leans against the glass, tipping her head to touch it. With a delicate finger, she traces a heart across Bobo's palm, which is still pressed against the glass wall. When she speaks again, her voice is soft and musical, not addressing anyone in particular. Or maybe she's talking to Bobo. Either way, I'm not sure she remembers we're still in the room.

"I've never understood why people have to cage up beautiful things. Like this town, so full of natural wonder. People see nature's incredible beauty, and decide they have to own it, pave it, and put up an amusement park and a tourist shop. Why do people feel like they have to control everything? Contain everything? Why can't we just live alongside each other?" Daisy sighs, gives Bobo one last look, and pushes herself off the floor.

She brushes off her pants and leads us out of the employees-only room, through the gorilla house, and out into the zoo.

Gorilla World extends from the gorilla house into a giant sunken yard area attached to the interior shelter through the open metal door. It's a deep pit, open to the sky but surrounded by concrete walls too high and sheer for even an ape to climb. Thick windows, embedded in the walls, allow visitors to stare in at the apes while they lounge around in their habitat. Far across the expansive yard on the side opposite the gorilla house, the concrete opens into a cave, sheltered from the prying eyes of humans.

A sturdy fence bisects the yard. On the far side, a few more gorillas stretch out in the sun. Some kids bang on a window near them, pressing their faces to the glass. One gorilla heaves itself up and lumbers into the cave.

Daisy points to it. "That cave is an indoor space for the zoo's original troop. The gorillas go in there for privacy. The original troop lost their silverback about five years ago. Integration is a slow process, but once the two groups become friends, these gorillas will have a family again, complete with a silverback. Some day Bobo will be a silverback, and he'll take over when Gargantua eventually passes away, the way nature intended."

"Nature is nice," I add, not looking at the enclosure.

> *Hair, in Garnet dipped*
> *Freckles like honey, dripped*
> *Across the petals of a Daisy*

"You guys aren't really reporting on the gorillas, are you?" She smirks at me.

"Pull yourself together, Simon," Sarah whispers, elbowing me in the ribs. Then she turns to Daisy and pretends to be embarrassed. "Is it that obvious? Look, I don't know if you know anything about our news site, but we kind of—specialize."

"Oh, I know all about Stratagem." Daisy gives us a cock-eyed smile. "I've never seen your by-line though. Abigail Quarterly?"

"My by-line is Sarah Quarterly. I'm going by my middle name to make it harder for the government to track me." She flashes the same smile she gave Ivan.

But Daisy isn't as easy to mislead. She lifts a doubtful eyebrow and crosses her arms. I know it's against our best interests, but I can't help being impressed by how sharp Daisy is, seeing right to the heart of whatever lies we throw at her.

Sarah tries to gain Daisy's confidence again by leaning in with a whisper. "We're actually investigating a mental patient that's been wandering around town."

"Oh!" Daisy replies. "The escaped government supersoldier!"

I don't know if it's because I'm sensitive to the subject, or if Daisy is just excited, but her voice seems especially loud to me suddenly. Sarah winces as some tourists turn towards us. She tries to counter with her cover story. "That's what I thought at first, too, but now we've heard it's an escaped mental patient."

"Where did you hear that?" Daisy scoffs. She continues to speak with the same powerful voice that could project a lullaby through two inches of glass. "It's totally the military. Fascinating though. Do you think they're experimenting on supersoldiers inside of one of the military bases around here?"

Sarah is losing control of the conversation. She flounders.

Learning to control dialog like this is exactly why we're here. I try to project my thoughts into Sarah's brain. *Think of it like a training exercise.*

Sarah is not only failing, she's failing in public. She's good at a lot of things, but she's horrible at failing. Sarah's eyes dart around the curious crowd who look interested in what Daisy is saying, but she can't seem to think of anything clever that will convince the listeners to listen to her instead. She breathes faster. I want to help her, but don't know what I could say that won't make the supersoldier rumor worse. Anything I say will just prolong the conversation. Onlookers are already talking about it amongst themselves.

"Hey Jennifer," one of them whispers to the woman next to him. "Isn't that what you were talking about yesterday? Maybe you were right."

The woman nods. "You know the military. They've got so many secrets."

This is exactly why conspiracy is so dangerous. Once people start talking about a wild idea, it can spread like a virus, because talking about it is fun and interesting. So is escalating it.

A teenager with a sizeable group of friends says "We should break into the Air Force Academy. I bet they're the ones experimenting."

Another teen laughs. "The Air Force? Nah, its gotta be NORAD."

Sarah listens to them helplessly. We just aren't socialized enough to control conversational group dynamics.

"Which base do you think he escaped from?" Daisy giggles, looking at the group of teens. "I mean, what are they even doing with all those top-secret labs in Cheyenne Mountain now that NORAD moved to Peterson? Somebody should find out the truth."

One teen nods in agreement.

"It's not the government," Sarah chokes with a desperate voice.

Daisy pauses. "Oh, sorry. I don't mean to make you

angry. I just thought, you know, isn't that what your newspaper investigates?"

Sarah freezes. She swallows and gives it another try. "No, no you're right. We always suspect them first. It's just that our research doesn't hold up this time."

"Ah," Daisy nods. "That makes sense. But I still wonder what's going on in that mountain, don't you? When has the government ever been *not* drowning in secrets?"

Someone else who is listening nods at Daisy. Sarah sees it too. She can't control this chatter, but maybe I can divert the whole situation by diverting Daisy.

"Say. I don't suppose—Do you know of any good taco trucks around here?"

"What? Oh, yeah, sure," Daisy nods, flashing me a smile that makes me wish I'd asked about tacos sooner. The onlookers drift away, apparently not interested in delicious Mexican food. "There's a Taco Loco that sets up in the zoo's parking lot. Have you ever tried them? Delicious!"

Once Daisy's gaze shifts off her, Sarah sends me a look of gratitude.

"Nope," I reply. "Never eaten street food at all. But I want to."

"*What?*" Daisy's mouth falls open. "Never? Seriously?"

"Yeah, I'm totally serious. There aren't any food trucks where we come from." I shrug, forgetting myself. Forgetting, for a moment, who I'm supposed to be.

"No food tr—not at all? What kind of backwater burg do you even come from, anyway? Who doesn't have *any* food trucks?"

"It's, umm. It's far away. And tiny. You've probably

never heard of it. Anyway, so Taco Loco, you say?" She must think I'm an idiot. "Would you, I mean can you, or you know if you want, maybe you can show me where it is? To go. And eat a taco." *Shut up, Simon.* "We could go eat a taco together. Because I like tacos." *Shut up, Simon.* "Do you like tacos?"

"Are you—" Daisy squints at me, then turns to Sarah and back to me. "Is he—Are you flirting with me? Is he trying to flirt with me?"

"Well, I wouldn't say flirting," I reply as Sarah lifts her eyebrows at me. "Unless you want me to, you don't want me to, well, I mean, of course not, I'm just talking about—facts."

When Daisy turns away, Sarah sends me a thumbs up. She must think I'm acting like an idiot on purpose to divert the conversation. And while that part of my plan seems to work well, I had hoped to come off smooth and suave like James Bond, not blithering like some fool.

Sarah rolls her eyes, thinking she's playing along. "He's terrible at it, isn't he?"

Daisy nods slowly. "Well, anyway, Taco Loco is closed today, so, sorry."

"Oh, yeah, okay, that's fine." I try to hide my disappointment, remembering that at least I diverted the conversation. Small victories, right?

Then Daisy smiles again, and this time her smile is just for me. "You know what, though? If you come back tomorrow, I can totally show you where it is."

11: SARAH GETS MOVING

"We need to go back to the zoo," Simon declares. "We need more information."

I roll my eyes and hand Simon a bowl full of Cheetos for Third Meal. "Yeah, I know what kind of information you need. Look, I gave that girl a business card. If she wants to talk to you, she'll call. That's how they do it in the movies."

"But you believe me now about the gorillas, right?" He wipes fingers coated with orange powder on his pants, leaving toxic-looking tiger stripes across his thigh.

"I don't know, Simon," I sigh. "It's possible, I guess. I hope it is just gorillas out having a little vacation because I want to be done here. It's been interesting, and I get that keeping people from breaking into military bases or whatever is important, but I just don't feel like we're doing anything meaningful here."

Simon shrugs. "It's not so bad."

I bring my own Cheetos to the map and glance over the notes I've pinned up. I don't want to look at it anymore. Spying isn't supposed to be hard or boring. It's never boring in the movies. They figure this stuff out in a quick montage and move on to the good stuff. Yet here we are staring at the same facts over and over again. It's not fair. I just want to make a difference in the world and have fun doing it. Is that so much to ask? And all these chips are making me feel less than optimal.

Cheyenne Canyon, three days later Seven Falls, three days later Cave of the Winds. There's a pattern there. Every three days.

"The next sighting should be tonight," I mumble.

Simon, standing behind me, crunches a Cheeto in my ear. "Oh yeah, probably. Well, that's good, right? More data? Hey if it is the gorillas and we can catch them at it, my camera can get nice, clear footage. One clear look at a gorilla on a vandalism rampage and we dispel the whole supersoldier thing better than we could have hoped."

"That's true, and it'll give the nuts a new conspiracy to dream up. We just need to figure out where they'll be. What's north of Cave of the Winds?"

"Nope. We don't have to know where they're going." Simon waves a neon orange food stick at me. "Because we know where they're coming from. We can just follow them."

"Assuming you're right about the gorillas and they're coming from the zoo," I add.

"You have a better lead?"

I don't. Simon is right, it's the best lead we have.

"Okay, so tonight we'll stake out the zoo, I guess. Why not? Beats sitting around here. If they are coming from the zoo, I wonder how they're escaping."

"And why would they want to leave?" Simon adds. "The zoo seems like a great place."

"Maybe they're bored," I offer. "Maybe they want to explore the neighborhood. I really don't care. We just need that footage."

"Yeah, and then figure out how to make it go viral," Simon's voice fades, deep in thought. When it comes to video footage and how to use it, I trust Simon. His directing decisions and editing skills are the reason Crazystuntz has over three million subscribers.

"I trust you," I turn back to the map to trace out a route to the zoo.

Simon crunches a few more Cheetos, licking his fingers energetically. "What's in these things? Magic?"

I'm less enthusiastic. "Maybe. Honestly, my stomach isn't feeling very good. I kind of miss Gus's stupid-fancy meals. He'd hate you for saying these are magic after he slaved for days on some meal we can't even pronounce and probably didn't even like. You know how much pride he puts into his creations."

"That's it!" Simon sets his bowl on the edge of the table. It teeters, then falls to the floor. Orange powder and bits of Cheeto fly everywhere, but he doesn't notice. Instead, he gazes at me with sparkling eyes. "Okay, imagine you're a big tough conspiracy theorist, right? What's your biggest weakness?"

"The truth?"

"No, not at all. Nobody cares about the truth. It's fear. Fear of looking as ridiculous as you sound."

"Okay. That makes sense." I nod. "That's a known tactic for people spreading disinformation–to make it sound like the other person is an idiot. These people have thinner skins than a soap bubble."

"Right, so, think about this." Simon paces, kicking the bowl under the couch without noticing. "Why did that pooping cat video do better than our wingsuit one? Animals. Humor. That's the best way to make something go viral. So if I'm right, and our supersoldier is a gorilla, we have our animals. We just have to add humor and our video has the right elements to go viral."

"We could post it on Crazystuntz to get it started. If even half our subscribers share with just two other people, it'll spread like digital wildfire."

"Exactly. And if it's undeniably a gorilla that looks funny and harmless, anyone who tries to make it into a dark conspiracy will look stupid and the other conspiracy theorists will make fun of them. Like trying to make those pandas who slide around in the snow look like terrorists. They'll get laughed out of town!"

"That's perfect, Simon! I love this plan," I throw my arms around him and spin him around. "I'm totally on board. We could get everything we need to finish up here tonight!"

A smile of triumph spreads across Simon's face. "We get some footage of the gorilla escaping the zoo and follow it to wherever it goes. Then we get more footage of it frolicking around, then climbing back into the zoo. I can add cute music and cut it together so the gorilla looks all bumbling and lovable. I mean, it might even be good for the gorillas, right? The zoo will figure out how they're escaping and fix it, and they'll get a bunch more visitors. That gorilla will be a star."

"Sure, whatever, that's great. We have another check-in with Agent Zero in four days. By then, if it is the apes, we'll be able to report a successful mission and ask for immediate extraction. I'll get the car keys." I pause as my hand closes over the fob. "Oh, wait, can you turn off the feed on your camera, so the unedited footage doesn't go directly to DAAAD?"

Simon, already headed to his room, stops and tilts his head at me. "Why? Don't we want them to see what we're up to?"

"Well yeah, but our agents have more important

things to do. If we stream the video, they'll be required to filter, vet, and archive it. DAAAD doesn't need to waste the manpower on some random footage we're only filming so we can edit it later. Besides, it's better if we implement our plan, see how it rolls out, and then report. What if it doesn't work? We'd still be able to fix it before reporting in."

Want to know the truth? I'm nervous that DAAAD might take over if they figure out what we're doing. Agent Zero might assign some of our experts to edit and distribute the footage, make sure it's "done right." I'm scared we won't be able to finish what we started, and show her we can do it, just because there are people at DAAAD who are better at it than we are. But I don't want to admit my fears to Simon. I want him to know he can rely on me.

"Are you sure that's a good idea?" Simon fidgets. "It kind of seems like, I don't know, like lying. Like we're hiding something."

"Nobody's hiding anything. It's just common sense, conservation of resources. If Agent Zero wanted the other agents to supervise every little detail of our mission, she would have sent someone with us. We're supposed to make our own decisions. Trust me."

Simon doesn't look convinced but nods anyway. "It's not that big of a deal, I guess."

By the time the sun sets, we've changed into black outfits. I'm sweating in long sleeves and long pants, but I don't care. At last it feels like we're doing something. We pull into the parking lot long after the zoo has closed for the evening. Simon still won't let me drive, and for now, I'm still allowing it.

The sky glows with vibrant oranges and purples.

Simon would no doubt babble endlessly about in long-form poetry, gushing about the way the clouds move and how the light paints the trees and rocks in some rhapsody of similes and deeper meaning.

I just think it's pretty.

No one passed us on the twisting, climbing mountain road up to the zoo, although a few cars still litter the parking lot. Simon pulls us under the tenuous cover of some tree branches that overhang the edge. Once he cuts our headlights, the car disappears into the background. A gigantic orange moon peeks over the horizon as darkness falls.

> *"Red of twilight's moon*
> *Eclipsing the horizon*
> *A flower's bright hair,"* Simon babbles.

"OMG are you serious?" I toss him his camera. "You're still thinking about that girl? Don't forget, if all goes well tonight, we'll be out of here. Don't get comfortable, you can't go native on our first assignment."

Simon pretends to be busy fiddling with his camera. He holds the camera to his eye and adjusts the focus, refusing to look at me.

"Remember, she has our number. Anyway, I'm sure there'll be plenty of pretty girls on the next assignment, too."

He keeps adjusting things on his camera without a word. I've never seen him like this, but I'm not worried, he'll come around when it's time. Simon hasn't ever let me down.

Stars sprinkle into existence overhead. It's not as dark as back home because of light pollution from the city, but I can still see a few constellations. I identify them without even realizing what I'm doing, automatically adjusting for the thousands of miles difference from the Island. There's Leo, Virgo, and Hydra. I can see the star Regulus. One glance at the North Star and our approximate latitude pops into my head.

Suddenly, a door along the zoo's outside wall opens. I almost miss it, a shadow hidden among the shadows. I poke Simon, but he's already got his camera pointed at it. He shows me the screen, which is in night-vision mode. A symbol on the bottom shows that he's recording.

He zooms in on the door which hangs open, blocking our view. A hunched shape emerges from behind it. Definitely a gorilla, now that I know what I'm looking at. How does an ape unlock a door? Then a human steps out behind him, facing away from us. The person is tall and wears a baseball hat, pants, and a short-sleeved shirt that might be a zoo uniform. It's hard to tell with the green-hued night vision obscuring the colors. The gorilla scratches at a band around its huge, furry arm. Then the human, still facing away from us, waves around some kind of small rectangular object.

The gorilla lumbers along the edge of the parking lot, knuckle-walking away from the flailing human who jabs something on the object with a finger. The gorilla stops, looks at the band on its arm, and changes direction.

The human closes the zoo door and follows the gorilla into an empty area of the parking lot. Simon tracks them with his camera. A giant pickup rumbles into the lot and idles in front of them with its back to us.

A heavy cage, the kind divers use to protect them from sharks, sits in the pickup bed. The human opens the door to the cage and the gorilla clambers inside.

"That's an electric Hummer!" Simon breathes. "The kind we use on the Island."

The person holding the door closes it, locks it, and then slides into the passenger seat up front. With barely a whisper, the truck hops forward, throwing the gorilla back against the door of the cage. The gorilla rocks back and forth, agitated, and clings to the bars, sticking its face through them like it's trying to drink the air.

"Did we get a face shot of that human?" I whisper.

Simon shakes his head. "No joy."

"What on earth is going on?"

He shrugs. "Not what I was expecting at all, but at least we've got confirmation that our supersoldier is an ape."

The Hummer, its Pareto Corporation electric engine purring as quietly as a kitten, keeps its headlights off until it reaches the parking lot's exit.

This is exactly the sort of situation where my best-on-the-Island driving skills shine. We'll have to follow the truck down the steep and twisty mountain roads with no headlights or street lights, guided through the treacherous darkness by only the taillights of the vehicle ahead. Without a word, I slip out my door and head around to the driver's side. Simon has already scooted over to the passenger seat.

I make sure all the lights are off and pull out far behind the Hummer, accelerating smoothly. We descend the mountain road, a dark whisper in the night.

The truck's red tail lights disappear as it rounds a curve. I measure our speed and the distance between our car and the Hummer so we can turn at the same spot. The back of our rental skids out into the empty oncoming lane. I correct our course.

Sliding down a mountain road in a dark car is like any gravity-based skill. You feel what you're doing in the depths of your body and work with the rules of nature. Our biggest problem right now is controlling our descent without riding the brakes. Keeping constant pressure on the brakes will overheat them, which will produce an immediately recognizable smell. It'll also light up our tail lights like a hey-you're-being-followed flavored beacon. This stupid rental is an automatic so I only have access to P(ark), D(rive), R(everse), N(eutral), and L(ow) gears. I mean, I can make it work, but without the finesse of a manual transmission. I'll have to hack together multiple techniques to pull this off.

A few aspen trees quake along the road's shoulder as we near a switchback, where the road has to twist and double back on itself to navigate the vertical terrain. The ground drops away in a steep cliff between the two stretches of road.

Gravity pulls our dark car down the treacherous road behind the Hummer like its shadow. I pop the gearshift into neutral as I fade into the car. It becomes an extension of my body as I lean into the curves, feeling how the various forces of momentum, friction, and speed press against us from all sides. It's like surfing, like we're a leaf carried downstream.

We speed up. I'm going to have to tap the brakes, lighting up our tail lights like a beacon in the night, or we won't make the next switchback. I cross my fingers that the people in the truck won't look back at the wrong moment, and sigh with relief when they round a bend, out of sight just as my foot presses on the brake pedal.

We slow, round the curve, and drift into the last stretch of mountain road as it enters the city. The Hummer passes under a streetlight, and I hang back until we reach an intersection. I swerve a little and switch on our headlights, hoping that, if the people in the truck notice me, they'll think I just turned onto the road.

Evening traffic is sparse, and since Colorado Springs is a mountain community, big pickups are common on the road. Under the cover of dark, no one seems to think twice about a gigantic Hummer with a gigantic box in the back. It's almost impossible to tell that the box is actually a cage.

We travel through some empty residential streets and a commercial area. I'm careful to change the distance between our car and the truck, and let some other cars come between us. Driving too closely is the number one best way to get spotted when you're tailing someone.

Soon, the Hummer turns down a long stretch of road surrounded almost entirely by parkland. It's even less traveled and there are hardly any side streets. Tall shadows, barely visible against the night sky, appear in front of us. Towering rock formations, tall and flat like giant wafers dropped from the sky, embedded vertically into the earth. A spotlight shines on one of the tallest formations. It, like so many of the rocks around here, is remarkably red. A hole along the ridge and some well-placed bumps make the ridge at the top of the formation look like two camels, kissing. My brain automatically assesses how long (about 1000 feet) and how tall (almost 300 feet in some places) the rocky ridge stretches.

I've read the tourist information about Colorado Springs, and I'm pretty sure I know where we are. The Garden of the Gods is over 1360 acres of sandstone formations created during a geological upheaval millions of years ago. It's easily one of the most visited tourist sites in the area, possibly in all of Colorado. The illuminated rock is the most famous formation, called, predictably, the Kissing Camels.

We turn toward it onto a series of unlit roads, through the formations that stand at attention as the giant, full moon rises higher into the night sky. I worry for a second that Simon will compose more poetry about floral redheads, but thankfully he stays quiet, filming our route.

Further along the road, the Hummer reaches a barrier and a sign that says "closed." It swerves around it and heads towards the Kissing Camel rock formation. I flip off our headlights again and follow it, falling back enough that they won't be able to see us. There's no one else on the road, I won't lose sight of them. It turns into a parking lot surrounded by trees. I guess we have reached our destination.

A few minutes later we pull around the trees and into the lot ourselves. Simon twists his head around as I ease the car into a parking spot. Maybe half a dozen other cars have defied the "closed" sign and freckle the lot at randomly spaced intervals. Some have occupants inside and others look empty. The windows of the nearest car are steamed up. I imagine this is where kids come when they want to be alone with each other. But the Hummer is gone.

"I can't see it. Where did it go?" I ask.

"I don't know," Simon whispers. "Let's see if there's a service road or something."

"How can something that large just disappear?" I step out into the night.

Movement, at the edge of the parking lot. Simon points his camera, still in night-vision mode, in that direction. I huddle next to him to see the screen. A bulky shape lumbers along a nearby sidewalk into the park.

"It's not a coincidence that the supersoldier gets photographed so often. They brought him here on purpose," I say. "They want him to be seen. That's why he's in all these tourist areas. To increase the chances of someone seeing him."

"It's a miracle no one has gotten hurt yet." Simon bites his lip. "It's lucky he's always been so far away from people."

"Is it?" I don't take my eyes off the lumbering shape disappearing behind a towering finger of stone. "Is it really luck? I bet the ape is supposed to stay away. Whoever is behind this must not want people to identify it. The conspiracy is no accident."

"Yeah, probably. We need to get our footage. How on earth do you get funny footage of a gorilla that might suddenly turn into a four-hundred-pound killing machine?"

"First thing?" I sprint down the walkway after the deadly creature. "Don't lose sight of it."

12: SIMON GETS SOME FOOTAGE

Twenty-five feet in front of Sarah, the massive chunk of muscle and fur vaults along the path. The backs of its knuckles plant on the ground as its powerful hindquarters and thick legs swing through and it leaps again and again, propelling the creature forward, muscles rippling under its fur. Sarah and I break into a jog to keep up.

"Why is it out here alone? Where are the people who brought it here?" I ask, focusing my camera's lens.

It's a huge ape, but with the night-vision and constant movement I can't confirm that it's the silverback, Gargantua but it's definitely male. Regardless, my high-quality footage gives us undeniable proof. Even with the green tinge of the night lens, no one could mistake this creature for an escaped human supersoldier, genetically enhanced or not.

The Garden of the Gods' sandstone formations tower over us on either side, separated by a wide sidewalk between them. It's like we're in a giant taco shell of stone. The rock faces are mostly sheer, but millennia of uneven erosion have pockmarked them with pits, notches, and grooves. Each wafer of stone widens at its base, where crevices create shallow alleyways between sheets of stone. The Kissing Camels glow in their spotlight to our left.

Grabbing a branch, the ape swings effortlessly into a nearby pine tree, bending the trunk under its weight. The path echoes with snaps and cracks as broken branches and buckets of pine needles pelt us from above. The gorilla leaps an impossible distance to cling high on a spire of stone and the pine tree sways wildly showering us with more branches.

"Is that—is that regular gorilla behavior?" Sarah asks from the shelter of her raised arms. "I didn't think they climbed rocks. Do they even climb trees?"

I don't have a clue, but the ape looks like it's struggling. I know what joyful climbing looks like, what it feels like and this is not it. The gorilla seems urgent, frantic. His massive arms hug the stone where it can, feet pressing uselessly against the rough rock. I know from my own climbing how small handholds can be. Sometimes cracks are so tiny I can barely grip them. An image of Bobo's curled fingers pressing against the zoo glass flashes in my mind. Climbing with those sausage fingers would not be fun. This gorilla is not climbing because he wants to.

But he keeps climbing anyway. I can almost feel his anger and frustration through my camera's lens. Suddenly, the gorilla roars. The moon casts his angular head and massive teeth into silhouette as the primordial howl reverberates off the rock surrounding us, lingering in my ears long after it's done. A car alarm goes off in the parking lot behind us, blending in with some shouts. Icy fear numbs my arms and the camera shakes. I do my best to hold it steady, while my stomach tries to empty my latest meal's-worth of chips onto my shoes. I have footage, but how can I make this creature look silly or bumbling? He's terrifying.

A red light flashes on his wrist, accompanied by a faint, high-pitched buzz. The gorilla throws his head back and screams again. My feet freeze to the sidewalk as I continue to record the scene in front of me. At least four times stronger than a bodybuilder and less than twenty feet away, the ape crushes actual stone in his angry fist. Stone that's stood against millennia of erosion. It just crumbles beneath his power.

Sarah pulls me off the path as the gorilla clambers onto the top of the stone spire. Without a pause, he swings his massive arms for extra momentum and hurls himself into the air once more, reaching for the stone at the base of the Kissing Camels.

Straight toward us.

I drag Sarah into a nearby crevice where we're out of the gorilla's sightline. The bad news? Now we're trapped, and though the gorilla can't see us, we can't see him either.

Sarah's muscles tense against me with each panting breath. She's poised, ready to act, but there's nothing we can do. It must be driving her nuts. We're trapped, blind, and vulnerable.

The gorilla doesn't quite make it to the cliff. He lands on the sidewalk with a meaty thump, right on the other side of our hiding place. I don't catch any of it this time because my camera is trapped between me and Sarah's back. Neither of us move. Even time stands still.

A pungent, musky scent drifts in on the evening breeze.

A snuffle comes from the other side of the rock. Protruding, leathery lips and wide nostrils snort, blowing sand off the top of the wall. It rains onto our heads, lit up like faerie dust in the moonlight.

Sarah and I become statues, not even breathing. The round nostrils flare out a few more times before they disappear. I scan the edge of the crevice with my eyes, unwilling to turn my head. It doesn't matter how well trained I am, if that animal gets those giant hands around my arms, it will tear them off without a second thought. Some things you just can't skill your way out of. At these close quarters, the knife in my boot wouldn't even slow the gorilla down before he ripped off both of our heads.

Leathery black fingers slam against the edge of the crevice wall right in front of Sarah's head. She presses against me as the entire hand, as large as my thigh, grips the rock, sending a shower of crumbled stone into her face. Another hand appears next to the first. With a grunt, the mass of angry muscle surges over our heads, blotting out the moonlight. Long, finger-like toes grab the ledge less than an inch from my hair as he surges forward, but he doesn't show any sign that he knows we're beneath him, easily within reach.

Don't look down, I think at him. *Don't look down.*

The red light flashes again. What *is* that light? The creature howls and shakes its wrist like the light burns him. His scream rips through the air echoing off the formations, and my ears go numb. Saliva drips from the massive jaws above us and onto my cheek. I don't dare wipe it off.

The spit slides down my face.

As the echoes fade and my ears start to work again, I think I hear human voices. Maybe the people in the cars came to investigate. Idiots. All I can see from my location is a sliver of the night sky, the red rock walls around me, and a bit of the ever-rising moon. Where did the gorilla go?

I squeeze Sarah's arm to let her know I'm going to move and lean forward to get a better view. I don't see anything. There's nothing out there. The hulking beast is gone.

Then I look up.

All four hundred pounds of him dangle over my head, swinging clumsily off some climbing hooks embedded into the rock.

That certainly isn't normal gorilla behavior, I think.

The beast sways above us like a piano in a cartoon. I don't know how it's holding on. We can't stay here.

The trick to moving silently is to engage all your muscles, distribute the amount of force evenly, and go slow. Sarah is good at it. I'm better. We creep out from under the precariously swaying animal. For an instant, the gorilla's head is outlined against the moon. Its left ear has a nick cut out of it.

It's not Gargantua, the silverback. It's Bobo, the unstable one. Fantastic. As Sarah and I back silently towards the parking lot, I squeeze her hand in a small celebration of not dying.

Bobo continues his perilous, ropeless climb up the sheer face of the cliff. He scales up hundreds of feet. My stomach feels like ice. How is he even getting handholds up that high? But Bobo presses on, somehow cresting the ridge.

I know he can crush us both into oatmeal, but part of me is frightened for him. He's so high. One poorly placed waddle, and he's a pancake. Which would not only be suboptimal for him but also would be bad for our plan. You can't film a pancake returning to the zoo.

I hear a gasp behind me and spin around. Two teenagers stand at the edge of the parking lot. The girl points her cell phone at the top of the rock. The boy stares with eyes wide, arms limp at his sides, his jaw hanging open.

As Bobo crawls over the top of the Kissing Camels, the boy lifts his arm, cell phone attached to his hand. Both teenagers record a video of the gorilla silhouetted by the full moon.

I've never seen anything like it. I've made enough YouTube videos to know that this—this is true internet gold. Once in a lifetime footage. The scene is so amazing, it'll be beyond viral. And it's too far away to see Bobo clearly at cell phone resolution. From this distance, he'll once again be mistaken for a human with large, scientifically enhanced muscles. Within moments of these guys uploading their shots, the conspiracy nuts will be all over it, sculpting the scene into exactly what the viewer wants to see; a brave supersoldier, escaped from government experimentation and running amok in Colorado Springs.

Sarah looks at my camera's screen to make sure I'm filming. My footage is much clearer than their phones, but these teens will get theirs uploaded first since I'm not streaming straight to DAAAD.

I consider confiscating the kid's phones, but doubt they'll give them up to two other teenagers without a fight. So unless I steal the phones, which will bring unwanted police attention, or I kill them, which, you know, is also problematic, the story is going to get out. Besides, two mysterious black-clad strangers trying to keep videos like this from being posted? That just screams cover-up. It would be like a gift to the conspiracy nuts, wrapped up in a big red bow.

Bobo howls again, balanced on one of the Kissing Camels' heads with the moon behind him. The teens scream and scramble for their car. Bobo clings to the stone and tilts his face toward the ground far below, wavering like a cat caught in a tree. I understand his fear. If you're not roped in, climbing down a cliff face can be even harder than climbing up.

Behind us, the teens' car starts up. The tires spray gravel as it screeches onto the road and disappears. Most of the other cars are gone, too. In front of us, Bobo vanishes over the rock's edge.

"Where's he going?" Sarah whispers urgently. "We can't let him out of our sight."

"What?" I spin her around to face me. "What do you want to do? Catch that violent animal? He'll tear us apart. And even if he doesn't, what would we do with him? Strap him into the backseat of our compact car?"

"I don't know, Simon. But we can't lose him. We have to find out where he's going. Maybe we can still get footage of him going back to the zoo." Sarah wrestles her arm out of my grip. "Simon, he might hurt somebody."

Sarah tosses me something small and I catch it by instinct. By the time I realize it's the car fob, she's already sprinting towards the other side of the cliff.

"You take the car, I'll try to catch him on foot," She calls back. "Go!"

I run to the car and wrench the door open. The car roars to life. Is that truck here somewhere? Those two guys? A small group of people scuttles towards the last empty car in the lot, showing their glowing cell phone screens to each other. More fodder for the internet algorithm, but no sign of the Hummer.

I prop my camera on the dash, pointing it out the windshield, and hit record. Next to it, I set my cell phone, cued to Sarah's GPS. Her location is a blip on a street map of the area. I flip on the headlights, hoping they won't wash out the camera's night vision, then throw the car into reverse and peel onto the dark, quiet roads of the Garden of the Gods.

Somewhere out there is a killing machine. And my sister is out there with it.

13: SARAH, IN HOT PURSUIT

Simon fires up the car while I'm still close enough to hear the engine growl. Gravel grinds beneath its tires. Headlights sweep across my path as he yanks the car onto the road. Then, he's gone. Everything is quiet except for my even breath and feet pounding the ground as I run.

Thump, thump. Thump, thump.

I veer off the smooth concrete sidewalk and head around to the back side of the Kissing Camels. There aren't any sidewalks here. Just clumps of tall grasses and a few pointy yucca plants and cacti. Desert plants. Not what I'm used to running through in the dark.

Without Simon, the air feels colder. Clouds pass over the moon and everything around me sinks into inky shadows. Dark. Layers over more shades of dark. My ears search for signs of the gorilla, filtering out the sounds of cars rushing along the nearby road. I may not be used to traffic noise, but I'm very used to listening for wild animals.

The crisp scent of broken sagebrush comes from the bushes ahead, accompanied by a rustling. I slow, eyes scanning the shadows. A raccoon the size of a dog bursts through the brush, right into my path, too close for me to stop at the speed I'm running. It hisses and snaps at my feet as I leap over its head. Racoons look adorable, but they're ornery enough to rip your calf muscle apart if you piss them off.

Where did it come from? Raccoons don't block someone's path without a reason. Something big must have scared it. Something a lot scarier than me. I skid to a stop and scan the direction the raccoon came from. There! Trees at the bottom of the Kissing Camels, swaying too much for the evening breeze.

Whump!

With a noise like a hefty kick to a punching bag, Bobo lands under the tree he'd been climbing down. He shoves some saplings aside, snapping one in half, as he violently bursts into the open. Without a pause, he hammers his fists into the ground and uses them to vault forward, then his high-speed quadruped run takes him away from the Garden of the Gods park.

I scamper after him. If Bobo hears me, he doesn't seem to care. Why would he? He could probably lift eleven hundred pounds, while I'm thrilled when I bench one-forty. Also, he's got really long arms. With that reach, Bobo could break me in two before I could get close enough to even touch him. Then he'd poke at the lifeless pile of Sarah and wonder why I hadn't put up a better fight.

Not to mention the fact that he's faster than me.

I lean forward, taking shorter strides off the balls of my feet. My breath comes faster while my feet pummel the ground. The moonlight glints off Bobo's hide as he catapults himself along the uneven ground. The average person runs approximately eight miles an hour. I'm probably clocking twelve, but can't gain on Bobo.

Since he's obviously not running away from me, he seems to have a destination in mind.

Staring for days at the map of this area finally pays off. I can visualize where we are by triangulating our starting point, the mountains, and our approximate speed. We're running toward the zoo. It's a good eight or nine miles away from here.

The gorilla's four-footed run devours the ground, but why? Why is he running so fast? He could probably make it by sunrise at a brisk trot if he didn't get lost, and the Broadmoor is on the way to the zoo. Actually, the hotel is between the zoo and most of the locations of the ape sightings. Maybe he uses it as a stopover point when he can't make it back home in time. But if he doesn't get back to the zoo, how do the zookeepers not know he's gone? Unless, of course, they're the ones letting him out.

And why isn't the Hummer extracting him? If these excursions are supposed to start a conspiracy and get some intrepid idiots to invade top-secret bases, why make him find his way back to the zoo on his own, and risk getting caught? When we were kids, Simon and I were blindfolded and dropped in the middle of the Island or on one of the little outlying islands a few times. With no resources, our goal was to find our way home and survive the trip. Survival training. Is Bobo being trained for something?

Even if he is, that's not our mission. If we keep track of Bobo and make sure no one gets hurt, maybe Simon can get the footage of him sneaking back into the zoo, and we finish our mission. Speaking of my little brother, I hope Simon locked into my GPS. I'll want my own extraction if this op goes south.

In front of me, Bobo slows down. He snorts, looking around. Is he lost? We're at the edge of the park, where one wide, empty street stands between us and a small cluster of residential houses. They're arranged in a series of cul-de-sacs along the edge of the park.

I use his moment of confusion to gain on him. What am I going to do if I catch him? Improvise, I guess.

His head twists to look at me, as if he's just realizing I'm following him. With a grunt, he leaps into motion again. This time he really is running away from me. I can't imagine why, but his movement is suddenly erratic, like he wants to get away but doesn't know where to go. Fleeing like a startled deer. A four hundred pound startled deer.

Streetlights line the wide road around the residential area. Ahead, someone, their face buried in the glow of a cell phone, walks a scruffy little dog. The dog stares at the oncoming gorilla and barks furiously.

"Speckles! Shut up!" The dog's owner doesn't look up. He's oblivious to the world around him, completely absorbed in whatever is on his screen.

The dog keeps barking, but the man keeps scrolling even as Bobo bears down on him. The floppy little mutt hops around ferociously at the end of its leash, yapping and straining towards Bobo. I respect the brave little guy. But the man continues to be held captive by whatever is on his screen.

The gorilla pounds past the dog in the blink of an eye. I don't even have time to scream a warning. The dog cowers behind the man's legs, still barking. The man finally lifts his head.

"What the?"

Bobo flashes under a streetlight, already past him.

The dog-walker lifts his phone to film the gorilla as I thunder past, giving the plucky little dog a wide berth.

"Hey!" The man yells, followed by some creative profanity.

Suddenly Bobo and I emerge in the middle of one of the cul-de-sac, the phone zombie far behind us. Large houses with tiny yards surround us on all sides, fences wedged in the few feet between them.

Bobo is trapped. The only way out of the cul-de-sac is the way he came in, and since I'm following him, I'm blocking his exit. But he doesn't even try to turn around. Instead, he crashes into a fence in front of him like a freight train. The fence sways, but doesn't break. Lights click on in the upstairs windows, casting Bobo into shadows.

The red light on his wrist flashes wildly. He throws both arms over his head and paces in front of the fence on his short, waddling legs. Then he roars, two inch long canines glistening.

Alarmed voices sound from the surrounding houses. Lights flare in the windows. A man's voice yells something about a mountain lion. Dogs bark, but not little yaps like Speckles. Big, gruff barks from the throats of big, rough dogs.

People are going to come out to investigate any minute now. If Bobo gets his hands on some resident, or gets caught on camera doing some major damage, there will be no way to contain it. Our mission will go down in flames. The only thing worse than a supersoldier escaping a secret base is one released into a residential area. The conspiracy will explode, and somebody could get killed.

I have to get Bobo out of here.

"Hey!" I wave my arms. Bobo's head twists towards me. I take a hint from the voice from the house and yell at the top of my lungs. "Mountain lion on the loose!"

Hopefully that'll keep the residents inside their houses at least. Bobo snorts, eyes fixed on me and shakes his blinking arm. I walk backwards, continuing to wave my hands around. Bobo knuckle-walks away from the fence.

Great!

He saunters down the middle of the empty street on all fours, looking almost casual. But I can see the tension in the set of his shoulders, how his head locks onto me no matter how his body moves. He's not sauntering, he's stalking. Me.

Not great.

Predators can see the slightest movement. Agent Albert once described it as seeing the world in black and white, but everything that moves is in color. That's why fluttering birds drive cats bonkers. They're lit up like a flare. There is simply no better way to get a predator to chase you than by running away from it. Instinct takes over, and you become the prey. Running signals to a beast that they are stronger and you are the weaker species. They can't help but chase you.

That's what training is for, to teach your body what to do, despite what your instincts want you to do. So I fight the urge to turn and run. I stop waving my arms, and keep walking backwards out of the cul-de-sac. We're almost there.

Sudden light to my left as a door creaks open. Through the open door comes the unmistakable *chung chung* of a double-action shotgun being cocked.

Here? I think. *A shotgun in the middle of the suburbs?*

Seriously?

Some damn cowboy is going to shoot a firearm randomly into the dark. The dark where I am. He's got no real chance of killing Bobo with one shot. He probably just wants to scare off the supposed mountain lion. But even if he doesn't hit me and doesn't prompt Bobo to attack him, that would still leave me on the street with a berserk gorilla. One I have zero chance of outrunning.

Tires squeal behind me. I spin around to see a familiar little car. The passenger door's latch clicks and Simon pushes the door open from the driver's side.

"Come with me if you want to live!" He says with a serious face. Then he breaks out laughing. "I've always wanted to say that."

Did I ever tell you I love my little brother?

I dive inside and slam the door shut just as the explosive crack of a shotgun blast pummels the air. Bobo leaps into action. Straight towards our car.

"Go, go, go!" I yell.

Simon slams down on the gas pedal. Through the rear window, I can see the gorilla closing fast.

"Turn left at the next intersection," the car's GPS chirps.

Simon glances at his phone and swerves right instead.

"Recalculating," the GPS replies.

"Where are we going?" I yell, punching the off button on the GPS.

"Away from people," Simon tosses me his phone. The screen displays a map app showing a large black rectangle straight ahead. It's labeled "commissary." I don't know what that means in this context, but whatever it is, it's nearby and isolated. We speed away from the shotgun cowboy's cul-de-sac into the night.

Up ahead, tall sports-field style floodlights loom at the end of a dark stretch of road. I twist around, but there's nothing behind us.

"Where's Bobo?" I ask. "Slow down."

The car jerks to the side.

I look out my window, right into deep brown eyes. Bobo shoulders the car again.

"Speed up! Speed up!" I scream.

Instead, Simon slams on the breaks. The gorilla shoots ahead towards the floodlights at the end of the street.

A tall chain-link fence with razor wire curling around the top surrounds what looks like a parking lot for trucks. And not just any trucks, food trucks. It's some kind of food truck storage depot.

Bobo reaches the fence at high speed. He catapults himself up onto the chain-link, clinging to it as it sways under his weight. At first I think he'll climb right into the razor wire, but he seems to understand he should avoid it. Instead, he hops along the fence horizontally until he reaches the gate. He gives the bars a mighty tug.

The fence groans in complaint. A thick, padlocked chain rattles, but holds the door closed. Bobo looks down at it. Most people's first reaction would be to yank on the gate, to try breaking open the lock or the chain. But those are probably the strongest part of the whole fence. I'd go under the links at the bottom, where the fence is the weakest.

Bobo drops and does exactly that. I blink in surprise. That's some good training for a circus gorilla. How did he know to do that?

With over two thousand pounds of pulling force, Bobo rips the fence's chain-link up from the ground. He slips under the torn fence into the sea of food trucks just as Simon pulls the car out of sight around the corner of a nearby building.

Simon hops out with his camera dangling around his neck. We head to the hole Bobo made in the fence and slide through after him.

A whuffling comes from the maze of trucks ahead, but it echoes off all the flat metal. It's impossible to tell where it's coming from. I check under the nearest chassis, looking for legs on the other side. Nothing. Simon signals for us to split up. He lifts his camera and melts into the shadows. I crouch low and scoot down the row, examining the underside of each vehicle.

I'm not a fan of guns. I'm an excellent shot and can field strip anything you throw at me. But we aren't killers. And guns can be problematic in the field between the noise and keeping them supplied with bullets, not to mention how easily a gun can get turned against you.

Right now, though, I wish I had one.

I check under the next chassis and find a pair of stocky, hairy legs. He's in the next aisle. I silently creep to the corner of the truck and peek around it. Bobo hunches in the alleyway between the truck I'm hiding behind and the one across from it, like he's waiting in line for a taco. He's just sitting there, rocking back and forth. In the overhead floodlights I can see his face clearly. His huge brows drawn together, the downturn of his leathery lips. I'm no expert on ape expressions, but if he were human, I'd say he looks confused. Almost scared.

He rubs his face with one huge hand and winces. With a low whimper, he brings his fingers to his mouth, wrapping enormous lips around them delicately. I get it. Climbing rocks isn't easy on anyone's finger flesh.

Suddenly, his nostrils expand and contract. *Snuffle.* Alert brown eyes snap towards me. I pull my head back out of sight and freeze as his heavy footsteps pad closer. Excitement surges through me like fire. It's a deadly game of hide-and-seek. Just like training without the safety protocol. I press myself against the truck, feet hidden behind a tire, and watch his shadow grow closer and closer.

- **Situation Assessment**
  - *Gorilla coming around the corner any second*
- *Options*
  - *Run for it (99% chance of failure. He'll be on me like wet on a fish)*
  - *Roll under the truck exactly as he comes around (timing must be perfect)*
  - *Die (which we've established long ago is suboptimal)*
- *Conclusion*
  - *Prepare to dive under that truck, and pray*

But then–*Clink.*

Something tinks against the side of a truck further down the row. A rock, bouncing off the truck's blue sun logo. There's a *whuff* right near my head. Then Bobo turns and lumbers towards the sound. Across the aisle, Simon waves to get my attention. I scurry over to him.

"I'm not sure following Bobo in here was your best idea, Simon."

He rolls his eyes. "Then maybe you shouldn't have suggested it."

"There doesn't seem to be any immediate threat," I reply. "Maybe we should fall back and regroup."

Simon frowns. He fiddles with some knobs on the top of his camera. "I still need some footage. I bet we can get some cute shots of him standing in front of that blue-sun truck and make it look like he just nipped out for a late-night snack." He lifts the camera and pushes away from the shadow of the truck. "We can still do this. Just a quick shot."

He steps into the middle of the aisle under a spotlight.

A massive shape slams into him from behind. Simon thuds face first into the asphalt with a gooey crunch. The hairy projectile slams into the ground a few feet from his still form.

"SIMON!"

The ape pushes himself upright, just steps from my brother's unmoving body. I gasp once and then stop breathing entirely as icy fear devours my body. Something wet oozes out from under Simon. Bobo snuffles and tilts his head, looking at my brother curiously.

My mind is blank. In the movies, this kind of scenario rarely ends well for the guy on the ground. But Simon is no random redshirt. He's my little brother, and he's under my protection. I dart out and step over his prone form, placing a foot on either side of him. Then, even though I know it probably looks ludicrous, I lift my hands in a ready position, prepared to fight.

"Get back," I snarl.

The ape grunts in reply. His beady brown eyes lock

on my own, and I don't look away. I know staring into a predator's eyes is threatening to them, but I want him to know I'm strong. I'm not prey. And neither is Simon, even if he looks an awful lot like it at the moment.

Bobo and I square off. Simon continues to not move, the dark puddle beneath him slowly growing. I don't care. I'm not leaving him. Bobo stands still, breathing as heavily as I am. Like it's trained to do, my body shifts into fight mode. Breathe in, breathe out. Focus on your opponent's center of mass, stay just out of reach. Get Simon to safety at my first chance. I review through the protocol in my head, waiting for Bobo to attack, or run away, or do *something*. I want him to make the first move. A light breeze drifts across the steamy parking lot, sharp and cool against my skin.

His arm suddenly emits an electric buzz. The red light flashes again.

Bobo cringes and squeezes his eyes closed. When they open again, there's a fire behind them. He draws himself up to his full height, staring me in the eye. I rise onto the balls of my feet, readying to strike. Suddenly, Bobo hammers his fists against his chest in a meaty staccato. He's posturing, trying to scare me away.

I stand firm, staring him down as best I can. The smartest thing I can do is get under a truck, where my smaller size would be an asset. But I will not leave Simon.

Bobo jerks his body side to side. Threatening grunts and growls come from his throat as he pounds his fists into the ground and jumps, crashing down again and again. I can feel the warmth of his breath, smell his musky odor as cold fear washes through me. Dust puffs up with every one of his jumps.

I can't take him, this is suicide. But I stand firm, waiting.

Why isn't he attacking? His wrist glows red against the blue sun on the truck behind him. Then Bobo turns and hammers the truck with one mighty fist, right on the painted sun like it's a target.

The metal screams and twists. Flecks of paint spray out from beneath his hand as the whole truck rocks on its wheels. He's hit one of the roll-up window coverings. He stares at the mangled dent for a second, then takes a step towards Simon and I.

CRASH!

It comes from the direction of the gate.

The gorilla is gone in an instant, running away with wild eyes. The bright red dot on his wrist buzzes like swarming hornets.

I drag Simon into the shadow of the dented truck and flip him over for an injury assessment. Even unconscious, Simon grips his camera. The lens is shattered. Bits of glass trail across the ground. I lower Simon's head gently and feel for a pulse.

It's there.

I release the breath I didn't know I was holding and search for the source of the blood that's spreading all over his clothes. Glass from the lens embedded itself into his hand. I pull out a few large pieces but he only resists when I try to pull the camera from his grip.

I leave the camera alone and look for Bobo from the relative safety of our hiding place. At the entrance, a massive force tore the gate from its hinges. Simon groans again and blinks his eyes open. I motion for him to be quiet and drag him into deeper cover underneath one of the food trucks.

A giant pickup has slammed into the gate backwards. The truck bed, and heavy cage inside it, face the interior of the commissary. The truck idles, looking like it's crouching over the bent remains of the gate.

"That's the Hummer!" Simon breathes.

Bobo moves towards it like a doll pulled by a string. His steps falter, he leans away, but still he walks on, each footstep bringing him closer to the cage.

"Who's driving?" Simon asks. He lifts his mangled camera, but it may never capture footage again. A small choking sob escapes him.

The door of the pickup opens, and an enormous foot steps out, followed by an enormous man. The Hummer springs up as the man's weight releases it. It's not the same human from the zoo. This guy is tall, yes, but he's also dripping with muscles. He looks like he could even match Bobo in a fair fight. His back is toward us as he moves to the pickup bed and opens the cage. Then he lifts a control box and smashes down on the screen. Bobo lurches forward again, climbing into the cage, and the man slams it shut behind him.

As he turns to get back in the driver's seat, the man's face is lit up by the floodlights. Simon gasps at the same time that I recognize the man.

It's Dr. Dinkelmeyer, DAAAD's number one most wanted criminal. He's brilliant, incredibly dangerous, and has absolutely no reason to be here unless he's plotting something that could destroy the entire state of Colorado, or maybe the entire country.

Things just got complicated.

14: SIMON HATES COMPLICATIONS

"Why would one of the world's most dangerous criminals be here in Colorado Springs, hanging out with a gorilla?" I limp into the rental house behind my sister. She closes the door behind us and twists the lock into place.

I think it's a fair question, but Sarah ignores me.

"Dr. Dinkelmeyer," She growls. "You know what this means, right?"

"Yeah," I set the remnants of my camera on top of the files that litter the living room's kitchen table and pull out my phone. "Time to contact Agent Zero."

"No!" She puts a hand on my phone, and eases it away from my face. "No, Simon, hang on. Let's think this through."

"Think what through? This is big news, we have to report it." I raise my phone again, but she grabs it and sets it on the table next to my camera.

The room spins and I wobble, grabbing her shoulder for support. She wraps an arm around my waist and starts to help me to the couch. Then she looks at my hand. Blood still oozes from my palm, soaking my make-shift sock bandage.

Her expression softens. "Let's at least get you

cleaned up first, okay? That's not exactly sanitary. And I want to check you for a concussion."

My blood drips a dotted line all the way into the bathroom. Even though my head throbs, my chest aches with every breath, and my legs aren't working the way they're supposed to, the thing that hurts most is my hand. The cuts are pretty deep but the pain comes from the fact that glass from my beautiful camera made them. My only birthday present, destroyed.

"Maybe the techs can fix it when we get back to the Island," I mumble.

Sarah doesn't reply. She sits me down on the closed toilet, drops the blood-soaked sock into the sink, and runs water from the faucet over my hand. Then she presses a clean washcloth firmly against the cuts.

"Hold that tight." She pulls some cream and butterfly-strip bandaids from the first aid kit as I apply pressure to the washcloth. "You know if we report in, Agent Zero is going to replace us, right? Are you really ready to get sent back to the Island when we're this close to figuring out what's going on?"

"I thought you were the one who was so eager to be done with this assignment."

"And I thought you weren't." She lifts my hand to reduce the blood flow. "Look, it's obvious there's more going on here than we thought."

I don't reply, but it's true. This mission isn't a joke anymore. It's no longer about controlling low-level chatter, or a theoretical incursion into some military base. Anything involving Dr. Dinkelmeyer is serious business. Just last year he and his cronies destabilized at least three governments, plunging those countries into chaos and civil war, and those are only the ones we know about. Thanks to DAAAD, he didn't maintain control of them, but the casualties were huge.

How many people will die if he pulls off some caper here among all these important military bases? Agent Zero needs to know. If she already had this intel, she'd never have assigned this op to us. This mission is over our heads.

Sarah lowers my hand and cradles it in her own. She takes the washcloth off tenderly and dabs a bit of blood from the edges of the cuts before squishing some antibiotic cream along the angry red lines. Sealing them closed with the butterfly strips, she sits on the edge of the bathtub and looks at me, her eyes pleading. She suddenly looks so young. She's only seventeen. We're both only seventeen.

"This is too big for us, Sarah," I whisper.

"I think we have a real chance of bringing down Dr. Dinkelmeyer here," she chews on her bottom lip. "We could be the ones to bring him down. We can be heroes. Legends!"

"We need to tell Agent Zero what's going on, Sarah. This is too big for us. We can't risk letting Dr D get away just because we want to play the hero. For all our training and skills, we're just junior agents. Beginners. This is our first mission. We aren't supposed to come up against people like Dinkelmeyer yet."

"No, hear me out." She leans forward. "It's more than just about playing heroes. How long do you think it'll take a new agent to get up to speed? For them to be chosen, fly in, and make new contacts? What if we don't have time to wait?"

That's a good point. It'll take time for another agent to acquire a new asset at the zoo, and it looks like

Bobo is the key to what's going on here. We've already established contact with Daisy and Beckman and no one knows Bobo better than they do. And what about Bobo? What will a new agent think of him?

I remember Bobo leaning against the zoo glass with his hand almost touching Daisy's. Her soft, strong voice singing to him. The way he stared up at her, the only kind face in that entire room. Watching her was like watching magic. She saw something wondrous in that screaming gorilla's soul, not just the beast that everyone else sees.

Sarah thinks Daisy fascinates me because she's pretty. But Daisy isn't the first pretty girl I've ever seen. She stood strong and compassionate against Bobo's anger, calming him down with love instead of discipline and force. She sees a living soul inside that ape. I look down at my bleeding hand and wonder what I'd think about him if I hadn't witnessed her calm him down. Hadn't seen him sucking on his hurt fingers.

What will happen to Bobo in the pursuit to take down Dinkelmeyer?

Sarah would give anything to be a hero, to do what she considers right. She's willing to work hard, make sacrifices, and take risks for the greater good. So is Bobo a sacrifice for the greater good? A wild, slathering, violent beast? Or is he what Daisy sees; a wondrous soul trapped by the violence thrust upon him? Someone who just needs some kindness to break through.

I follow Sarah into the living room, and my gaze falls on the remains of my camera. I remember Bobo's giant teeth, his ferocious roar, and feel the weight of hundreds of pounds crashing into me. Hitting the pavement and crisp, bright pain shooting through my body. Helplessly laying there, blacking out. He could easily have killed me.

But he didn't.

If a new, more seasoned agent had been in that situation instead of me and Sarah, what would have happened to Bobo? They'd fill him with lead so fast he wouldn't even take a last gasp. He'd get taken down without a second thought, and they would praise the agent. Because Bobo isn't human, he's a beast.

What would that do to Daisy? What about that other gorilla, Moki, waiting for her brother to return? And how would I feel if I let that happen, if I set the stage for it? But this is our first mission.

"Look, Sarah, we don't stand a chance of taking Dinkelmeyer down. Teams of senior agents have been trying for decades." I say it with conviction, but doubt creeps in around the edges of my resolve. "We can't keep this news from DAAAD. Agent Zero needs to know now so she can act on it. We can't let Dinkelmeyer get away."

"And if Agent Zero mobilizes a team?" Sarah asks quietly, sitting at the table and tracing a finger over the map. "Dinkelmeyer has no reason to think we're a threat. He doesn't even know we exist. We can slip under his radar. But if someone like Agent Albert or Suzuki were to come in and start poking around the zoo, how long do you think Dinkelmeyer will keep his guard down? It would spook him. He'd disappear in the wind. Then we'll never know what he's planning here."

Another good point.

My earlier suspicions creep up again. What if we, specifically, got this assignment because we aren't supposed to be experienced enough to find out about this deeper plot? If that's true, then someone at DAAAD is working with Dinkelmeyer. And they might put in a replacement agent who will let Dinkelmeyer get away on purpose. And blame us.

I know Sarah's primary motive is to be a hero, but what if she's right after all, and we're the only ones who can figure out what's really going on?

"Sarah, remember that day we were in Agent Zero's office, when she gave us this op? I saw something I wasn't supposed to. A letter. Someone wanted some agents deployed but Zero didn't think they were ready. What if we are those agents? What if someone from the Head Office wanted us here, on this assignment, despite Agent Zero's concerns? What if they sent us here because they thought we were too green to find out about Dinkelmeyer's involvement? I don't want to sound like a conspiracy theorist myself, but–"

Sarah scratches the back of her neck and nods. "No, no, that makes sense. If someone at DAAAD is trying to cover for Dinkelmeyer, that's exactly what they'd do. Send in someone good enough to get the job done, but too inexperienced to discover the truth behind it. And if that inexperienced agent discovered whatever was really going on, they'd report in immediately. The report would be a big red flag, and give them time to alert Dinkelmeyer so he could get out before the cavalry came rushing in."

"I mean, I'm not saying anything like that is going on, but we have to admit it's possible," I shrug. "So, let's say we stay dark, and I'm not saying we should. What does that look like?"

Sarah sits up straighter. "We're due to report in three days, right? We can keep that appointment. All I'm saying is that we don't call in early. If we do some digging first, we'll have more intel to report. Have you noticed a pattern in these random events? I think Bobo is being trained for something big, and we're the best placed agents to find out what it is. No one has been this close to Dinkelmeyer in years. It's not exactly *wrong* to wait until we're supposed to check in."

"It's still a pretty serious breach of protocol." But I admit, it doesn't sound unreasonable. It almost doesn't even sound like lying. Almost.

TV never prepared us for this. In a good summer blockbuster, there are plenty of moral conundrums, but the right decision is always obvious. Here I am with my first actual moral conundrum and it isn't obvious at all. It's complicated. I hate complications. I flop onto the couch next to a leftover bowl of potato chips and crunch on one.

> *Crunching chips*
> *Killing time, not hunger*
> *Need to think*

"All those movies and shows, every single one." Sarah's brown eyes sear into me with a laser-like intensity. "It's always the fresh young recruit that solves the problem, who takes out the big bad guy that no one can ever get a handle on. The new kid, right? Think about it. We're seeing things with fresh eyes, approaching a situation with a new perspective. That's what's really important in every single movie. That's the moral they teach us, right? Believe in yourself, do the hard thing, trust your team. Who has better teamwork than we do? Maybe we really are exactly what's needed to finally take Dinkelmeyer down. Who would we be if we didn't even try?"

It makes sense when she says it like that. What Sarah says always makes sense when she says it. It's only afterwards that I realize we sometimes miss something.

"I don't know, Sarah. It just seems wrong. Protocols are there for a reason."

"We're strengthening our report. Isn't that a good thing?" Then Sarah's eyes light up with a new idea. "You know, if we're gathering intel, we'll need to recruit an asset on the inside. We'll need someone who has intimate knowledge of the workings of the zoo, and of Bobo in particular."

In spy lingo, an asset is a source of information, someone you use to help you get the job done. They can be an agent, but can also be people who don't even know they're aiding an intelligence operation. A good spy spends time developing an asset. They have to get close.

And there's only one asset that makes sense to recruit in this scenario. Someone I would be more than happy to spend more time with.

"You've got a genuine connection with that zookeeper girl, Simon. That could be useful," Sarah nudges. "No other agent can get inside before they unleash Bobo again. You'll need to work your connection. Spend a lot of time with her."

Daisy. And just like that, we both know she's won.

> There once was a girl in a zoo
> Whose charm was more than she knew
> She can help find the whackos
> And promised me tacos
> And now her help we must woo

15: SARAH HAS QUESTIONS

Daisy stands inside the gorilla house with a clipboard, watching the apes through the thick glass as Simon and I approach. Moki leans against the metal door that connects the main interior space with the small white room. The littlest gorilla, the infant Boingo, crawls over her. He tugs at her arms and ears trying to get her to come play with him, but she won't budge.

"Oh, hi again. You came back." Daisy shakes my hand. She flashes Simon a bright smile, and he drinks it in. I try not to roll my eyes. "It's good to see you guys but I'm not sure I have much time to talk. Bobo is having a really hard day, it's like he didn't get any sleep last night or something. Beckman had to call in an expert. I don't think he wants to see reporters today, sorry."

"Oh no! What happened?" Simon lays a hand gently on her shoulder.

"I'm not sure," Daisy shrugs. "He gets agitated every few days. Sometimes I'm not even allowed in the room to see him. Which is weird, because he seems pretty quiet on those days. On the days I'm not allowed in, it's silent like he's not even there. Not today, though."

A muffled roar comes from the other side of the "employees only" door. From behind the glass, Moki looks towards the sound with concern.

"See?" Daisy sighs. "It's terrible. I wish I knew why he was so upset, but there's not much I can do to help. That expert won't even let me in there."

"That might actually work for us," I muse, accidentally out loud. Daisy looks at me, confused.

Simon covers for my awkward wording. "She means we came to see you, not Beckman. We need your help. It's important."

Daisy glances towards the closed door again. She seems unsure, like she doesn't want to leave the ape. We can hear gruff voices arguing from inside the small room. Daisy wavers then nods and leads the way outside of the gorilla house. It's early, and the zoo is relatively empty. A vacant bench overlooks the outside enclosure. She perches on an armrest. Simon sits next to her, but I remain standing.

"I'm not sure I'll be much help. I'm just an intern," Daisy shrugs, "But what can I help you with?"

It's difficult to get close to an asset and earn their trust. Winning someone over on a deadline, without blackmailing them is even tougher. Knowing how much to reveal is an art. You need to get them invested in helping you without blowing your cover. It's a tricky line. I'm glad Simon is leading this one. He's much better with people than I am.

"How much do you know about zoo security?" he asks.

Daisy blinks. "Security? What do you mean? I have a pass to get in. And me and the other employees use the side entrance. The one that opens to the parking lot. You mean like that?"

Simon takes a deep breath. "I mean how secure the

animals are. How easy would it be for them to escape?"

Daisy laughs. "Escape? From their enclosures? You know scientists and engineers put decades of research into these enclosures to make them secure, right? It would take a serious Houdini with superb motivation to escape one of these cages."

"So someone from the outside would have to let an animal out, right?"

Daisy's eyebrows pull together in confusion. "Where are you going with this? I don't understand."

"We saw Bobo leave the zoo last night," Simon says. Daisy looks doubtful.

I pace in front of the bench, not unlike a caged animal myself. Are we telling her too much? Daisy was good leverage to keep Simon from reporting to Agent Zero, but now I'm not so sure bringing her aboard is a good idea. I guess there's no going back now, though. I have to trust Simon.

"That's impossible," Daisy scoffs. "If this is a joke, it's not funny. Bobo is vulnerable right now. You reporters are always trying to create drama. You should be ashamed of yourselves." She stands to leave.

"Wait!" Simon grabs her arm.

Daisy spins around with fiery eyes. "No, you wait! Don't you dare write an article about Bobo escaping the zoo. If anyone believed that kind of nonsense, he'd be put down in a second. That means they'd kill him. They've been looking for an excuse. I don't know what you're trying to accomplish, but you just stop it right now."

She twists out of Simon's grip, tucks her clipboard under her arm and stomps off towards the gorilla house. Simon looks at me for help.

"It's true," I call after her in a calm voice. She stops, but doesn't turn to look at us. "He didn't escape though. Someone let him out. That can't be safe for him either."

I can't read her expression when she turns back to us. It's somewhere between shocked and curious. And something else. Respect? Or is it caution? "You guys aren't actually reporters, are you?"

Simon glances at me, then says, "We're investigating the odd sightings around town, the ones people think are an escaped military experiment. But it isn't a supersoldier, Daisy. It's Bobo."

Daisy walks back to us slowly. She lowers herself onto the seat of the bench next to Simon, staring at her clipboard. Simon reaches out to put a hand on her arm and she doesn't pull away. She just sits there, still as a statue except for her eyes. They dart around wildly as she processes what Simon just told her.

"I know it's a lot to take in," he says gently. "But it's true. We need to figure out why. You're the only one at the zoo we can trust. I know how much Bobo means to you."

"Damsel!" Beckman sticks his head out the door to the gorilla house. "What are you doing out there? Get back in here, now!"

Daisy glares at him. She shakes her head and replaces the look with a generic smile, then turns to us. "Hang on, I'll be right back."

"Don't tell him anything," Simon whispers. "Bobo's life might depend on keeping our secret."

Daisy nods. She hops up and disappears inside the gorilla house behind Beckman. I can only hope she understands. Our secret is in her hands now. I start pacing again, restless and hating the feeling of not being in control. We don't have ears in the building, there's no way to listen to what she's telling Beckman or this expert. If she confronts them with the intel and Dinkelmeyer finds out, he could spook. We'll have gone against protocol for nothing. Agent Zero would never trust us again. I'm not under any kind of physical threat, yet I've never felt so helpless.

Daisy comes back out of the door, this time carrying her purse instead of the clipboard. She signals us to follow her and heads toward the entrance to the zoo. Simon rushes after her, and I trail along a few paces back.

"I took my lunch break," Daisy explains. "I only have a half hour. Let's go get some tacos and you can tell me more. Taco Loco should be here today."

Simon flips around to catch my eye. He walks backward, smiling a bigger smile than I've seen in ages as he mouths "Tacos, Sarah! Tacos!" and throws me two giant thumbs-ups. He silent-screams with enthusiasm, and literally jumps and punches the air before speeding up to walk by Daisy's side. What a dork.

His face glows as they chat about what I can only assume are the culinary delights of street food. I don't blame him, I'm sure we'll have to eat much worse out in the field once we become full-fledged agents, but right now, I'm so sick of chips. And Simon can check off number one on his bucket list.

As we step into the parking lot, though, Daisy stops short. A line of waiting people wraps around the side of the lot. Far on the other side, above the people swarming around it, I can see the roofline of a food truck.

"Weird, I've never seen the line this long before,"

Daisy stretches around, trying to find any sort of explanation, but it's impossible to see through the masses of people. "It's moving so slow!"

With a shrug, we join the back of the line.

"That's okay, I'll wait forever," Simon says with a far-away look in his eyes. "I've been dreaming about street tacos ever since we got assigned here."

"That's a ridiculous dream," Daisy smirks, elbowing him.

"No, it's not," Simon frowns. "Why do you say that?"

"Taco trucks are everywhere. I've been eating at food trucks since I was like five years old. A dream is something unusual, like running away to a deserted tropical island or something. Food trucks are so... mundane. So boring." Daisy pokes at him, still smirking.

"It may seem ridiculous to you because you've always had them around. To me, it's kind of like freedom. Just walking up to a random truck and eating something just because it's delicious without having to check in with anyone, or log it, or optimize the nutrition it provides... to get to do something everyone else gets to do."

"I don't understand," she squints at me. "Why would you have to do all that? You mean your parents kept you on some kind of really strict diet? That sounds rough."

"Something like that, yeah. But while we're here, we don't have to follow it. I've been dreaming about food freedom since I was little." Simon sighs. "Haven't you ever really wanted something, even if it didn't make sense? Wanted to do something that seems so normal to other people? Something everyone else might think is silly?"

The smirk melts away from Daisy's face. She's quiet

for a second. Then she lays a hand on Simon's arm and gazes up at him. "Yeah. Yeah, I have. I get it."

They stare into each other's eyes for a heartbeat. The line inches up another step but neither one of them moves. I clear my throat. Daisy blinks and notices the line. She takes a single step forward, letting her hand slide off Simon's arm. He stands riveted in place, watching her. I have to give him a little shove to move him forward.

"Okay, so gorillas." I remind them.

"Right," Daisy focuses on me. "So what did you see? What do you think is going on?"

Simon replies. "We were here at the zoo last night and saw someone open the door and put Bobo into a truck. They drove him to the Garden of the Gods and we followed them. Then he climbed to the top of the Kissing Camels and posed for some tourists. That's what's behind these rumors. Bobo goes to these tourist areas at night when only a few people are around, and he stays far enough away that no one can get a decent picture. He's doing all these things that are easy for a gorilla but impossible for a human, so people jump to conclusions. They'd never assume it's a gorilla, yet 'genetically enhanced supersoldier' becomes more plausible. People are weird like that."

"Wait, you said he climbed the Kissing Camels?" Daisy shakes her head. "That's not natural ape behavior. And it's certainly not easy for a gorilla to do."

"That's what I thought, too!" Simon agrees. "Their fingers are too big, like–"

"–sausages," they say in unison. Again, I roll my eyes.

Daisy warms to the subject, speaking faster and with more confidence. "They'll climb trees in the wild. Not like a monkey or anything, but if they want something like fruit, they'll climb. But I mean, I've never heard of one, you know, rock climbing. In the wild, they live in tropical forests. I don't think they interact with rocks much at all, not even for shelter. They don't like enclosed spaces."

"No? They wouldn't go inside a cave?" I wonder what Bobo was doing deep inside the Cave of the Winds, then.

Daisy looks at me as if she forgot I was there. "I'm not sure. Like I said, rocks certainly aren't their natural habitat. Our guys here don't like to be cooped up even inside the hut. They like to sleep outside. They make little nests out of leaves and sticks and things. But it would be unnatural for one to live inside a cave."

"Isn't a cave part of your outdoor enclosure at the zoo?" I point out.

"Hmmm, good point," she agrees. "But these aren't exactly wild gorillas and they aren't living in a natural setting. They go into that cave to get away from all the zoo gawkers. For a little privacy. If they live their lives in the wild, they probably wouldn't. And if they did, like to take shelter in a rainstorm or something, I doubt they'd stay there longer than they had to. They prefer to make nests and sleep out in the open. Look at poor Bobo. He spends all day and night in that tiny little room, away from fresh air, away from the ones who care about him. No wonder he has hard days."

I think about Simon's unconscious body underneath that massive wall of muscle and have difficulty summoning up any sympathy. "Except he *is* getting out. So why would he be deep inside a cave?"

The line moves forward another single step. The people around us check their watches and crane their necks to see around the people in front of them. Daisy doesn't even look at the line. She tilts her head at me.

"When was he inside a cave? You said he was climbing at the Garden of the Gods."

I close my mouth. The line moves one step forward but we don't seem any closer to food truck paradise. Daisy checks the clock on her phone.

"I don't know how much I can help you if you don't tell me what's going on. I mean, are you absolutely sure it was Bobo? Assuming you actually saw a gorilla leave the zoo, how do you know it was him?"

"Definitely Bobo," Simon nods. "He had that notch in his ear."

Daisy blinks. "You were that close to him? And, you know, he didn't hurt you?"

Simon rubs the back of his head. "I don't think he's doing any of this by choice. Like you've said, he doesn't seem like a bad guy."

"Not a bad guy?" I blurt. "Simon, he almost killed you."

"Almost killed you?" Daisy squeaks. "He wouldn't do that. Maybe you misunderstood what he was doing."

"I don't think he meant to hurt me," Simon insists, earning an appraising look from Daisy. He lifts his bandaged hand for her to see. "I think someone is controlling him. There's a lot more going on here than we thought."

Daisy frowns and crosses her arms, "What's your real deal? Who are you guys? You're not reporters."

"Look, we just need some information to help us figure out what's going on here. Bobo clearly isn't just having little excursions. It's like he's being sent out on missions," I say.

"First it was 'playing around in tourist areas pretending to be a supersoldier', now it's some kind of what? Superspy missions? That seems a little far-fetched, don't you think?" Daisy's mouth squinches to the side. "What would be the point?"

"That's what we're hoping you'll help us figure out," Simon replies.

The line moves forward a bit, but our time is running out. Daisy throws her arms up helplessly.

"What more can I tell you if you aren't honest with me?" Daisy looks at the clock on her phone again. "And what's going on with this line? I've seriously never seen it this bad. I have to get back to Beckman."

Simon's face falls. "But we need you."

"I just wasted my entire lunch break. I have to go back now. Sorry you can't trust me." Daisy huffs. "Sorry I couldn't be more help to you on your secret mission."

She steps out of line and strides back towards the zoo entrance. Simon sprints after her and I reluctantly follow him. The people behind us smile and move into our spots. Right before Daisy heads through the gate, Simon catches her arm.

"Wait, please. We can tell you more, but not here. We're not secure here. Can you come to our house after work? I'll make you dinner to make up for missing lunch. Please, for Bobo. We need your help."

Daisy places a hand over the one Simon has on her arm. She squeezes it then pulls it off, turning his hand around to lay gentle fingers on his bandage. "Let me think about it after I check in. Give me your address and phone number and I'll let you know."

Simon pulls out a business card and writes something on it. He hands it to her, and she disappears back into the zoo.

When she's out of earshot I say, "We need to figure out a neutral location to meet at when she calls."

Simon winces. "I just gave her our address."

"*What?* Are you crazy, Simon? You gave a stranger the address of our safehouse?"

"I didn't know what else to do," he shrugs.

"Oh my god, there are a million and a half other things you could have done. Where's all that training?" I cover my face with my hands. "What are you thinking?"

"I guess I wasn't thinking. I mean, *now* I can see how stupid that was, but at the time it seemed like the right thing to do." Simon turns away. "She steals my brain with her eyes sometimes."

"Can you quit being a poet long enough to remember you're a spy, Simon?" I groan. He looks at me with big, sad eyes. My voice softens. "It's okay. We'll work around it. But try to be more careful, okay?"

We head back to the car. It's parked on the other side of the lot, close to the taco truck and the giant crowd of people waiting to be served. They must be fantastic tacos. There are so many people that the way Simon drives, it might take us hours to get through them.

The orange truck with a bright blue sun painted on the side comes into view. One of the two serving windows is dented closed. A sign on it says "Closed for repair, please use other window." No wonder the line is so backed up. They're working off half capacity. With a jolt, I realize it's the truck Bobo hit instead of me. Our first attempt to reel in an asset went south because of some random consequence from last night. In movies, you never see what happens to the buildings and cars destroyed in a fight. Some supervillain falling out of the sky and landing on a house is exciting to watch. I've never thought about the collateral damage. That's someone's living room that just got crushed. Their wedding pictures, the furniture they just got after years of saving up. What happens to the henchmen or the bystanders when the heroes are out saving the world?

Simon, oblivious to my thoughts, stares at the crowd. He groans. "I'm never going to get my tacos!"

16: SIMON'S GUEST

Daisy hovers on the threshold of our house.

She's radiant. She changed out of her zoo uniform and wears khaki shorts and a breezy tank top in a light cream color that sets off her garnet hair. The last rays of the setting sun paint a golden haze over her soft skin. She's taken out her braid, and her hair shimmers like jewels in the light. The cool, gentle breeze of the coming evening tosses a few strands around playfully.

> *She turns her face to the sun*
> *Unfolding petals*
> *A damsel, but I am the one in distress*

"Thanks for coming, I'm glad you called." I lean against the doorframe, trying to look charming. Sarah watches us from the living room. She doesn't say anything or come to join us. She thinks I have the best shot at getting information from Daisy if she stays out of the way. That might be true, but I admit getting information is not my primary motivation for wanting some time alone with the girl in front of me.

"Umm, this is where you guys live?" Daisy steps inside only far enough for me to close the door. As it swings shut, the golden light from outside disappears, along with the fresh air. One delicate hand flutters up to Daisy's nose. "It's, umm, it's nice."

My suave smile fades as I watch Daisy, picking up

all the little details. She's returning my smile with too many teeth, a smile that doesn't reach her eyes. Her breath is shallow. She's not moving inside. Something's wrong. I glance around, seeing our house as she must see it.

Clothes and towels litter the hallway, creating paths from the bathroom to both bedrooms. A pair of my underwear tops one pile. Where did that come from? I look away, embarrassed, tempted to grab the underwear and fling it back into my room. But that would just draw more attention to it.

We piled the living room chairs up to make room for the table. I never noticed that they completely obscure the front window. The couch, also shoved aside, sits at an odd angle. I can't even offer Daisy a seat without asking her to climb over the coffee table. Sarah hunches over the table that now dominates the living room. It's covered with photos, file folders, scribbled notes, and empty bowls that have leftover chip crumbs powdering the bottoms. Multi-colored sticky notes riddle the map on the wall, along with pins and a few photographs connected by string. It looks like a serial killer's lair from a cheesy movie.

The kitchen, bereft of its table, feels lopsided. Dishes and cups pile up in the sink and weigh down every inch of meager counter space. Cabinets hang open. The space the table used to inhabit now looks empty, like it's waiting for something. A few glasses have somehow made their way onto the floor there, but they only make it look more forlorn. I do not know how the place got so... well... disgusting.

"Sorry, we don't usually live like this," I blush. "It's just sort of crept up. Can I take your coat?"

"I don't have a coat. It's like eighty degrees out. Where are your parents?" Then she laughs. "Oh, right, we're still pretending you guys are adults, right?"

"We are adults," Sarah calls without looking up from something she's reading at the table. "We don't live with our parents."

That second part is true, anyway, but I suddenly don't feel like an adult at all. Would I feel differently if we had parents? Would I be better about things like picking up my underwear? It's a strange thought, one I haven't considered in years. What would life be like for Sarah and I if we'd been raised by actual people? I try not to let the rush of confused emotions show on my face, but I'm caught off-guard.

Daisy watches me with kind eyes. "Oh, I'm sorry. Did I say something wrong?"

"No, no it's fine. No adults here. I mean, no parents, just us adults. We live alone. Together." I clear my throat and change the subject. "Um, I promised you dinner, but then I realized we used up all our eggs."

"Eggs?" she asks.

I lead the way into the kitchen. Daisy hesitates, then follows, breathing through her mouth. Oh no, does it stink, too? I take a deep breath and the stench of rotting food and the sweat from Sarah's workout towels assaults my nose.

Back home someone takes care of all this for us. Our rooms are just clean. I never really thought about the fact that there must be an actual person picking up my underwear. And everywhere that's not home just feels, I don't know, temporary? When your training throws you in the middle of an untouched jungle for a week with nothing but a swimsuit and a throwing knife, you become used to living in questionable situations. We've never had to clean for guests.

"Eggs are all I can make," I admit, well, besides roasting lizards over an open fire, but that skill doesn't seem particularly useful here. "Though, honestly, I guess I don't even do that very well. I'm sorry. We aren't prepared to entertain. Obviously. But I'm glad you're here anyway."

Daisy cracks her first genuine smile. "Why don't we just order something?"

Sarah peeks around the corner. "You know how to do that?"

"How to what? Order takeout? Of course. Who can't order takeout?" Then Daisy says in a hopeful voice, "Or we can go out to a restaurant."

Sarah shakes her head. "No, too many ears. We might discuss delicate information. Plus all our intel is here. We'll maintain our perimeter. But you say you know how to order food? Noone trained us in that skill."

"What are you talking about?" Daisy snorts. "You sound like some cheesy spy movie. Ordering food doesn't exactly qualify as a skill, you just call the restaurant. I mean, you can use an app, but those have all these fees, and they charge both you and the restaurant a ton of money so it costs a ton and the restaurant and driver barely make anything. Capitalism at its worst. I like to call the restaurant directly and go pick it up."

"Sure, let's do that," I agree. "I have a credit card. You pick where to order from. Anything will be better than another night of chips for dinner."

Daisy's laugh is musical and loud and ends in an adorable snort. I think she thinks I'm kidding. She pokes at her phone. "There's a Thai place close by that I love."

"Excellent." I pull out DAAAD's credit card. "See? I knew you could help us. You've just arrived and already you're saving our butts, or at least our stomachs."

We look at the online menu, and she shows Sarah how to order and pay for the food. Sarah wants to leave Daisy and me alone, so despite Daisy's offer to drive, Sarah insists on being the only one to go pick it up.

As soon as the door clicks shut behind Sarah, Daisy turns to me with pleading eyes. "Can we open some windows at least? I don't mean to be rude but, I mean, it's a little stuffy in here."

That's an understatement. I climb over some furniture and open every window I can reach. The evening breeze enters the house a lot more eagerly than Daisy did, and works on blowing all the staleness out.

"Sorry," I apologize again. "This is the first time we've been out on our own. I didn't realize how hard it would be."

Daisy tilts her head at me. "Those overly controlling parents, huh? The ones who put you on a strict diet and kept you away from food trucks all your life? So then why are you guys here? What's your story?"

"Actually, we never knew our parents," I admit before realizing I probably shouldn't have said that. Sarah wants me to get info from Daisy, but I can't stop being the one who talks. Daisy looks at me with sympathy. "We grew up kind of isolated, looked after by a bunch of different people, but with a lot of strict rules."

She snorts again. "How totalitarian. You're so fascinating. What, did you grow up in some kind of hippie commune? A cult? Alaska?"

"Something like that," I mumble, trying not to let the fact that she thinks I'm fascinating make me say anything even more stupid.

"It must have been weird coming here alone then."

"Yeah, well, I thought I would be more prepared. I thought I could handle anything. But I didn't realize how complicated something as simple as making scrambled eggs is."

"I've been there." She places a hand on my arm and her touch tingles throughout my whole body. "Don't worry, it gets easier. It's no big thing. If you don't mind me saying, though, you really should at least take care of those dishes."

I blush again. "I–yeah. The only problem is I don't even know how to run a dishwasher. Do you just stick the dishes in and turn it on? Honestly, we haven't even tried."

Daisy's musical laugh chimes again. Even in the growing dark of twilight, the room seems brighter. She leads me into the kitchen and stands before the mountain in the sink.

"I see your problem with the dishwasher," She chuckles. "There isn't one! You're going to have to do these by hand."

I step towards the sink, enveloped by the smell, staring at the dishes helplessly. Do I just splash the water on the dishes? Put soap on them, then rinse? Fill a sink full of soapy water? How can I do that if the sink is already full? Blood rushes to my cheeks. I'm glad my back is to Daisy. I'm supposed to gain her trust by being strong, impressive, and confident. But so far all I've been able to convey is that I'm an idiot. I stare helplessly at the dirty dishes, my heart sinking. Then I feel a presence next to me. Daisy grins up into my face.

I find myself talking again as I lean on the edge of the counter, feeling like I've already screwed everything up. "All my life I've been raised to conquer any challenge, you know? It's all about being the best. Reaching the next goal. Go bigger, go higher. I've always thought I was so good at everything. But here I am, not even able to have a guest over. I'm failing here, and I don't even know the parameters."

"It's no big deal, Simon. Really. I hate how society always pushes people to do more and more. We've forgotten how to just live. How to make mistakes and grow. Everybody needs a little help sometimes."

It's my turn to snort. "That's not a concept I'm familiar with. Where I come from, the only way to get anywhere in life is to stand out. I mean, follow the rules and be the best you can be, and hopefully, your achievements will get noticed."

Daisy's face hardens into a sneer. "That's the problem with people in charge. They always think they know what's best for you. They set all the rules, hold all the power, and you perform like a trained monkey for their pleasure, hoping someone notices you and gives you a treat."

I'm speechless for a moment. "That hasn't been my experience. I mean, leadership can be harsh sometimes, I guess, but usually, they're just trying to get things done. You can't make an omelet without breaking a few eggs, right? At least that's what they say. I can't even make scrambles."

Daisy looks like she might say more, but then she laughs and her face melts into softness again. "Don't mind me. I've just had a bad experience with authority figures."

"Oh?" I ask. "That sucks. What happened?"

But Daisy just shakes her head. "I don't want to talk about it. Let's just handle the job at hand. Tackle these dishes. We can do it together."

"You'll really help me? Because, I think I need your help. I don't even know how to start. Just tell me what to do."

"You're awfully quick to do what people tell you to do, Simon," Daisy looks at me with concern. "I'm happy to teach you, but I'm not your boss."

"I'm not sure anyone who isn't my superior has ever taught me anything," I say, grabbing an egg-crusted plate.

"What about your sister?"

"Sarah? She certainly thinks she's my superior!" I laugh.

Daisy grins. "HA! I knew you guys were siblings."

I shrug like it doesn't matter, but inside I curse myself for not being more careful. Again. Even with Daisy, I shouldn't let my guard down. Sarah and I are really showing our inexperience in dealing with civilians tonight, but Daisy is so easy to talk to. And it's nice to talk to someone who isn't a spy. "Okay, I admit it, smart girl. You're right. Let's get back to the dishes before I tell you my deepest, darkest secrets."

"You can tell me while we're washing," she laughs, poking me with her elbow. "First, we have to find the sink under all this mess. Then we can fill it with warm, soapy water and just start scrubbing."

There isn't anywhere to put the dishes, so I pile them on the floor. Slowly, the sink emerges. Daisy opens the cabinet door underneath.

"Bad news, you don't even have any dish soap." She shuts the door and washes her hands in the newly exposed sink.

"Figures," I laugh. "I feel really stupid. I wanted this evening to go a lot different."

"You don't seem stupid to me," Daisy looks into my eyes and her gaze is almost protective. "It's okay not to know stuff. Everyone has to start somewhere. You've got plenty of skills. You seem like you know about a lot more than just photography. I bet you can do a lot of interesting stuff."

"You wouldn't believe half of what I can do."

"Try me."

I'm saying too much yet again. I feel like I could tell her anything. In some ways, she's easier to talk to than Sarah, even. But I need to get the intel. Time to turn the tables.

"What about you? How did you end up as an intern at the zoo? Why do you have such an amazing bond with Bobo?"

"It's a long, boring story, you wouldn't be interested."

We meander to the front room as we're talking, and she perches on the arm of the couch. I lower myself into a nearby chair at the table.

"No, seriously. Tell me, I'm interested. You know lots of things about me now, but I hardly know anything about you."

She smiles at me and looks away. Maybe it's just my imagination, but she doesn't seem used to people finding her interesting, which, frankly, I don't understand at all. Inside the outgoing, vivacious beauty seems to lurk a shy, protected soul. Or at least that's my feeling, my instinct.

"Maybe I'm just a natural with animals. Or maybe I ran away to join the circus when I was a kid." She laughs that amazing contagious laugh again and I join her. "Seriously though, I didn't come here to talk about me, I came here to talk about Bobo."

"Oh no," I press. "I want to know more about you. We can start small. When did you learn to do the dishes?"

Her smile fades a bit, and her eyes drift. "I've had to take care of myself for a long time. You have to be strong to survive in this world. But that's why you have friends, right? No one should have to learn about life on their own, Simon."

"Okay, so how am I supposed to learn to do the dishes?" I tease, trying to make her smile.

Her face lights up with a giant, authentic grin. "I'll just have to come back again later and bring dish soap."

"Really? You'll come back? Despite the shambles this place is in?"

One side of her mouth lifts in a smirk. "You've said it yourself, Simon. You need me."

I lean forward, resting my elbows on my knees, my face drifting mere inches from hers. "Where did you come from, Daisy Damsel?"

She leans in. A shy smile spreads across her face and her eyes dart down, then slowly back up to stare into mine. She pauses, breathing steadily. I can feel her warm breath against my face.

Suddenly she blinks and pulls away. A curtain falls over her face. Her gaze flits to our map. "No, seriously, I'm not here to talk about me. I'm not important. You wanted to talk about Bobo. That's quite the setup you have there. Tell me about that."

She's right. We're supposed to be talking about the mission. But at this moment I don't care. I carefully set a hand over hers. She doesn't pull away, but doesn't look at me either. "Of course you're important, Daisy. I've never met anyone like you."

At that, she laughs. "You don't get out much, do you?"

Before I can answer, the door opens and the smell of delicious peanut sauce, grilled chicken, and Thai spices fills the newly aired-out house. My mouth waters. Daisy stands, her hand slipping out from under mine, and moves to help Sarah carry the bags of dinner to the table.

"So what have you discovered?" Sarah asks, handing out our meals and some wooden chopsticks. "Solved the case yet?"

Daisy looks up, "Ah HA! A case! I knew you guys weren't reporters with all your 'perimeter' talk. What, you're like amateur detectives or something?"

Sarah swallows her noodles extra hard, throwing me an apologetic look. I shrug. Nice to know I'm not the only one making mistakes.

"Something like that," Sarah answers. "Daisy, I want to know if any of Bobo's activities could just be a gorilla playing around. Have you gone over the timeline?"

"Not yet," I say, glancing at Daisy, who is suddenly incredibly interested in her Pad Thai.

"What? Not at all? What have you guys even been doing then?" Sarah narrows her eyes at me.

I ignore the question and point to the map with my chopsticks, trying not to fling peanut sauce on the table.

"So the first sighting was in Cheyenne Canyon, and he was just hanging out, right?"

Sarah frowns at the map. "Right, then Seven Falls, then Cave of the Winds, then Garden of the Gods. And sometimes he stopped over at the Broadmoor. Those are the ones we know about, anyway. So each time it's a trip further away from the zoo. The question is why? What could they be bringing him to those specific places for?"

"Interestingly, none of these places are on any military base, but all the internet chatter focuses on him being an escaped soldier," I point out. "I thought we'd be spending a lot more time focusing on Peterson Air Force Base, but nothing is happening there. Why is he going to these tourist places?"

Daisy shakes her head. "Are you sure he's being brought there for a specific reason? I mean, you sound a little like a conspiracy theorist to me, but I guess you do work for The Stratagem, after all."

Sarah ponders the map. "No, no there's definitely a pattern here. You said gorillas wouldn't go into a cave voluntarily, so what was he doing deep inside the Cave of the Winds? You say they can't scale tall rocks, so what was he doing climbing at the Garden of the Gods?"

"What about the other place?" Daisy asks.

"Seven Falls? He climbed up the stairs fast. Not sure if he did anything else," I reply.

Sarah taps her chopsticks against her carton of Pad See Eiw. "Is that something a gorilla would do, gorilla expert?"

Daisy shrugs. "Actually, yes. That sounds like something one might do, especially a circus animal like Bobo. He's an excellent climber. According to our notes, when he was in the circus he used to have an act where he climbed up a tall tower in the middle of the show tent, like a big jungle gym."

She sets aside her carton and moves closer to the map, tracing the string connecting the various points of interest. Her eyes fall on the photo Sarah found inside the Cave of the Winds. She tilts her head and squints at it.

"That doesn't prove he's not being trained for something," Sarah rattles on.

Daisy isn't listening anymore. She lifts the photo, and looks from it to the map, and back to the photo.

"What is it?" I ask, coming up behind her. "Do you know what that picture is?"

"Where did you find this?" She asks me.

"I found it at one place Bobo went," Sarah replies. "Does it look familiar?"

"Not the photo specifically, but I recognize where it is. See this road coming in, and you can see some fences and a bit of a tube here? This is an aerial view of the entrance to Cheyenne Mountain. Why would they take him here?" She traces her finger on the map, moving down from the zoo, and pins the photo to the wall.

I look at Sarah. "Cheyenne Mountain. That's the super secure, top-secret military base where NORAD used to be located, right? Now it's a backup for them and the Space Force?"

"Yeah. That's top security, not a tourist place. It doesn't fit the pattern. You can't even visit there with a press pass." Sarah stares at the photo. "Assuming Bobo is being brought to these places to stir up internet trouble, that location doesn't make any sense at all. What do they have there?"

"Guns," Daisy growls. "Government soldiers with

guns. There's no reason to bring Bobo there. That's dangerous. Seriously dangerous."

Sarah paces. The gears are turning in her head. She's putting something together, and I know the best thing to do is stay out of her way and remain quiet. Daisy starts to say something, but I shush her with a finger to my lips and pat the couch's armrest. She sits.

"What if..." Sarah says as if we weren't even there. "Let's assume I'm right and Bobo is being trained for something. Let's just go with that. What would that look like?"

She heads over to the map, running her finger up and down. Daisy chews on her nail to keep from saying anything as Sarah taps the table.

"Cheyenne Canyon, he's being trained to be around people and be out in the open, to find his way back to the zoo, maybe?" Sarah continues. "Seven Falls, what could he do there?"

"It's tall and slippery," I offer. "He was climbing up those metal railings."

"Okay, so he's testing his climbing skills against the sheer, slippery rock face of that box canyon. Then say he spends the night at the Broadmoor. He makes a nest in that tower room. He's around a ton of people there, learning how to stay out of sight."

"That was probably a day I wasn't allowed to go into the medical room," Daisy offers. "When he was supposedly too agitated, but I couldn't hear anything from behind the door. Maybe he wasn't there at all!"

"Good!" Sarah agrees. "Good, maybe he didn't make it back to the zoo in time and had to go to ground. Or maybe he was supposed to learn to stay out of sight of large groups of people. Could be either, could be both.

Then the Cave of the Winds. What's so special about that?"

"It's a cave," I suggest. "If it's not normal for him to be inside a cave, he has to practice it. To learn how to be in there, right? How to move around in the pitch dark. Get comfortable with the lack of light and air. That's difficult for anyone. Then he maybe makes it back to the zoo or maybe spends the day at the Broadmoor again. Then the next time he goes out, we see him. That's when he goes to the Garden of the Gods."

"Where he gets more practice climbing up sheer rock," Sarah finishes for me. "And at all these places, he gets seen by tourists, but far enough away that no one knows what he really is. The rumor starts, and people are so focused on the idea of an escaped military experiment they aren't looking at any other options. So now we're at Cheyenne Mountain. Which is a big, deep cave. What if he's supposed to break into the mountain? That would certainly reinforce what people think about him being a military experiment gone wrong. Maybe scare any actual soldiers he comes in contact with by his reputation alone."

"But why?" Daisy asks, scratching her head. "What could they want to accomplish sending a gorilla into a military base with all those soldiers? They're trained killers with big guns and he doesn't know they can hurt him."

Sarah glances at the calendar on her phone. "I don't know, but if it keeps to the pattern, whatever they're training him for is going to happen tomorrow night."

"So what do we do now?" I ask.

"We have to stake out the zoo again," Sarah says. "We have to stop him, I guess."

Daisy turns from the photo she's been staring at. "Well, you're not going anywhere without me. You may have some mystery to solve, but somebody has to look out for Bobo."

17: SARAH RETURNS TO THE SCENE

The Damsel girl is becoming a problem.

Obviously, we can't take her on our stakeout, but she is surprisingly stubborn for someone who looks so delicate. And she's a bad influence on Simon.

"You need me," she declares, willowy hands on her hips. "You'll never be able to control Bobo without me."

"She has a point," Simon agrees. They're sitting close together on the couch as I pace the living room.

I throw up my hands. I've already explained it could get dangerous. I've already explained that we have to keep secrets from Daisy. Each time I tell Daisy why she can't come, she gets more and more obstinate. The girl has a real problem with authority. That or Simon laid on the charm a little too thick and she's smitten. Either way, she's a liability out in the field. I need to figure out how to handle her. I keep telling myself to think of it like a training exercise; figure out how to stay in control of the situation. But this isn't training. The stakes are too high. If Simon and I don't succeed here, not only will we fail personally, but Dr. Dinkelmeyer will succeed and people will die. I can't let that happen.

- *Situation assessment:*
  - *Bobo is being trained to infiltrate Cheyenne*

Mountain (probably)
- *It's part of Dr. Dinkelmeyer's unknown plan (probably)*
- *Bobo will go out on another training mission tomorrow night (probably)*
- *Daisy wants to come on our stakeout (unfortunately)*

- *Risks:*
  - *Failure in our primary mission resulting in embarrassment and a probable lack of future assignments*
  - *Failure in our secondary, secret mission resulting in–*
  - *–Dr. Dinkelmeyer succeeding in whatever he has planned. Unknown result, but it can't be good*

- *Complications:*
  - *Daisy getting in the way*
    - *Problem with authority*
    - *A lot stronger than she looks*
  - *Simon getting influenced by Daisy (see "Daisy" above)*

- *Conclusion:*
  - *New tactic–bend like a willow instead of standing strong like an oak*

"You don't have to be part of this, Daisy," I say. She just rolls her eyes. "We know Bobo is getting out and we have to put a stop to it."

"We need more information on why," Simon adds. "Maybe learning more about Bobo's background could help."

"Okay, I guess that makes sense." Daisy taps her lips. "I'm not sure it's helpful, but Beckman has a private office I'm not allowed in. There might be some information in there about Bobo, from the vet or something. It's always locked, though."

"Locked isn't a problem," I wave my hand dismissively. "But getting into some zookeeper files isn't our goal. Our priority is to keep track of that animal."

Simon nods, but Daisy looks from him to me, and back to him. Then she frowns. "Wait, Simon has a good idea, why are you dismissing it?"

Seriously? I don't have time to discuss Simon's feelings. "I'm not dismissing anything. I'm making a judgment call."

"Why is it your job to judge?" She asks, lifting her chin. "Aren't you and he partners? Equals?"

"He's perfectly capable of speaking for himself," I hate that I'm starting to respect her. She may complicate things, but I can't help but like the way she's standing up for Simon. Though, of course, he doesn't need anyone to stand up for him.

"I think he just doesn't want to hurt your feelings. He's too sweet to stand up for himself."

"You've known him for what? A few days? I've known Simon all our lives. I know what's best for him better than you do. Stand down."

"Maybe *he* knows what's best for him," she pokes at my chest with her finger, her face close to mine. I really don't want to have to incapacitate her. I hope she gets smart and backs off.

Simon steps between us. "As much as I appreciate you two fighting over me, we have more important things to discuss. Bobo and whatever his masters are planning."

Daisy and I glare at each other. Well, she glares and

I hold her gaze with authority. Simon gently pats the arm of the couch, lifting his eyebrows invitingly. Daisy takes a deep breath and sits down. I'm proud of him. And also, he's right. We need to stay focused.

"Okay, moving on," I glance at Daisy. "Simon, I do like your idea of gathering intel. Maybe we can split up. One of us can follow Bobo and the other can sneak into the zoo. What do you think?"

Simon nods.

Daisy talks again. Because of course she does. "What about me? Where am I in this plan? I have to go after Bobo. No one else can deal with him and I am not leaving him alone to face a bunch of armed soldiers who will only see him as a threat."

I don't point out that he actually is a threat, but suddenly have a flash of insight into why my training instructors frequently lost their tempers with me.

"Besides," she continues. "What are you going to do if you catch him, strap him into that little compact car of yours?"

"Do you have a better idea?" I snap.

"Yes. As a matter of fact I do. I'll just tell Beckman what's going on, and we can subvert this whole plot thing at the source."

"NO!" Simon and I both yell at once.

Daisy flinches. Despite myself, I feel bad for her. In other circumstances, it would be the most straightforward, logical solution. I lower my tone. "Promise not to tell him. Please. We don't know if he's involved, and we can't tip off Doctor... Um. Dr. Beckman." I catch myself before I say "Dinkelmeyer."

"Please, Daisy." Simon looks into her eyes. "Trust me on this one. I wish I could tell you more, but just trust me, you can't tell anyone about any of this. It might put Bobo in danger."

At that, she blinks, conflicted, then finally nods. "I don't agree, I think not telling Beckman what's going on is what could put Bobo in danger. But I do trust you, Simon. I promise I won't tell anyone until after tomorrow night. After that, depending on what happens next, we'll see. Good enough?"

I breathe a sigh of relief. I really didn't want to have to tie her up here at the house or anything. That would have aroused suspicion at the very least, and probably pissed off Simon.

"Good enough," I agree.

"Sarah and I have been getting some video footage of Bobo. We planned to edit it together to make him look harmless, like he's getting out of the zoo by himself and playing around. If we can get that out on the internet, people will stop talking about a supersoldier and instead pay attention to Bobo. They'll want to keep him safe. The zoo will make sure he doesn't get out anymore. But my camera got broken."

Daisy looks impressed. She spies the broken camera on the table and picks it up for a closer look. "Wow, you're brilliant. I agree, that would probably keep him safe. This is a really nice camera."

I look over at Simon with a sour expression. He's too chatty around her. I pluck the camera from her hands, a broken piece dangling from the side. I smack it shut and set the camera out of reach.

"So that's the plan?" Simon asks. "Daisy and I will follow Bobo, and Sarah will break into the zoo and collect intel."

Daisy tilts her head at him. "She can do that?"

He smirks. "There's not much Sarah can't do."

I feel strange, like I'm being left out of a conversation that's about me, right in front of me. Like they forgot I'm even there. I notice his hand sits lightly on top of Daisy's. Their hands aren't clasped, but they touch as if it's the most natural thing in the world. I don't think he's acting, because he's really never done that well in deception lessons. I make a mental note to have a nice, long discussion with Simon later.

"That plan works for me," I say, trying to get control of the situation again. "But if you have to subdue the ape, we still have the problem with the compact car. So here's what we're going to–"

"I can use the zoo van," Daisy interrupts me. "It's sometimes used by zoo personnel to transport animals. We'd have to lay down the seats and put up the gate between the back and driver's seat. That takes a little time, but once it's done, we can get him in there and drive him back to the zoo. Zoo staff do it all the time. I know where they keep the keys. They have a bunch of sets, so no one will notice if a keyring goes missing. I can try to grab one at work tomorrow."

Simon grins like a Cheshire cat. "You're so crafty. What a great idea. Are you sure you can pull it off?"

"You're not the only amateur detective around. I'll be fine." She smiles back at him, all cheeks and batting eyelashes.

I sigh.

***

Daisy ends up driving. I'm still not sure how that happened, actually. I was determined to not include her, yet here she is, dressed in black like we are, sitting in the driver's seat of her little blue car while I'm sitting in the back.

Our car might be suspicious in the parking lot after closing time, she had pointed out. But hers has an employee permit on it, and it wouldn't be the first time she's left it overnight in the lot because she sometimes hangs out with coworkers after the zoo closes.

She's a skilful driver, though not as good as I am, and she definitely knows the roads up here. Once again, I have to admit she's useful. She's even pretty good company. I'm trying hard not to like her, but soon I'm laughing along with them from the back seat as she and my little brother crack jokes.

We arrive in the parking lot just as twilight falls. The waning gibbous moon might not be full, but it's bright enough to throw down a little illumination. Daisy pulls her car into a nice, secluded spot under some overhanging trees. It's perfect.

"Did you get the van keys?" Simon asks.

She pulls a ring full of clinking keys out of her purse with a wicked grin and a wink. "No problem."

"Good job," I can't help but say. She smiles back at me proudly.

"I'll go pull the van around. It's on the other side of the zoo, so it may take a while, but you guys sit tight. I'll be back before you know it." Daisy hops out of the car, closing the door behind her. I don't have time to agree or disagree. She sends a thumbs-up to Simon and saunters off into the growing darkness.

I crawl into the driver's seat while Simon watches the girl go with a look of longing.

"Simon," I whisper. "Don't forget. She's an asset."

The smile on his face fades. It breaks my heart, but

he needs the reminder. He nods, still looking out the front windshield.

Here's the thing about assets. You can't get too close. Sometimes, assets get into trouble for the information they willingly, or unwillingly, pass along. And an asset always gets left behind at the end of a mission. If you're on an op, you need to keep your head in the game and your eyes on target. You can't get involved in what happens to your asset. Collateral damage is just part of the process.

Simon knows how the game is played.

He knows spies can't have friends in the outside world, that's just asking for trouble. He's tough, he'll get used to it. The first time is always the hardest. I don't want to see anything bad happen to her either, but we have to do what they've trained us to do. We have to follow protocol.

Protocol.

"Oh no," I sit up straighter, realizing something much more important than Simon's crush. "Agent Zero!"

"What?"

"Agent Zero!" I squirm. "We should have reported in."

Simon looks confused. "But I thought we weren't checking in until our regular appointment time. Remember? We had an extensive discussion."

"But this," I wave my hands in the general direction of the night. "This could be big. You don't have your camera. They have no way of knowing what's going on."

"But you said we shouldn't report in," Simon repeats.

"I know, but... I don't know. I mean, we were just

going to get some intel. What if this becomes an actual op? I don't mean the thing about Dr. Dinkelmeyer, I mean chasing down the gorilla that's our primary mission. If we end up with a full-blown operation on our hands, if we have to actually take down Bobo, protocol says we should have reported in before planning it. We may need cleanup or, I don't know, how can we keep this part of our mission from her? We can isolate the Dr. Dinkelmeyer part, but if we're going to take care of this supersoldier thing and complete the mission, *that* we should have reported in about."

Simon sighs and puts his face in his hands. "Sarah, why do you always do this?"

"What?" I blink. "Always do what?"

"You're so focused on getting something done that you don't think through all the consequences. And then you convince me to go along with your crazy idea."

"Now wait a minute. Where did that come from? We decided our course of action together. You agreed with me."

"Yeah but–" suddenly Simon goes quiet.

The door to the zoo swings open. I look around for the Hummer, but it's not there.

The thick, lumbering shadow of the gorilla emerges, a blip of red blinking slowly at his wrist. The equally thick, but much more graceful, shadow that follows him is unmistakably Dr. Dinkelmeyer.

Simon and I simultaneously sink down out of sight.

"He's supposed to be driving the Hummer," Simon whispers. "What's going on?"

Two other shadows, dwarfed by Dinkelmeyer's bulk, come into view. One of them is tall and wiry, the other wears a grey trench coat and hat with a wide brim. *Who are they?* I wonder. *There was only one accomplice last time.*

"We have to get closer, find out what's going on," I murmur, pointing at Simon's door. It's on the far side of the car from the group, so we can sneak out without being seen.

He inches the door open and we climb out, keeping below the silhouette of the car, and blend into the shadows. Crouching low, I lead the way towards the group. We move smoothly and find cover under some branches about twenty feet away from them.

The group isn't trying to be quiet. They don't have any reason to think they're being watched. Why would they? We're up on the side of a mountain, in a dark, deserted parking lot. Who would watch them up here? I'm sure it's not a mistake that this location is so remote.

Dinkelmeyer doesn't make mistakes.

I can't get a clear look at the other two people. Their backs are to us, and at this distance I can't even tell if their voices are male or female.

"Is he ready?" rumbles Dinkelmeyer. "The Phoenix Plan depends on him."

"He better be," the tallest of the other two people replies. "We won't get another shot at this. He's prepared on my end, is everything else taken care of?"

The third person, the one in the floppy hat, nods. "As long as he times it right, the gate should be open. The timed elements are already in play. He knows where to go, doesn't he?"

"Of course he does. He should go straight to the gate," the other one replies.

"I don't doubt the gorilla. He's smart. But with

Phoenix riding on him, I hope your tech and preparation is as successful as you promise," the shadowy hat grunts.

"Don't question me," the tall one says. "You don't rank me–"

"Enough," Dinkelmeyer barks. The other two fall silent immediately like a guillotine just sliced off their tongues. They cringe away from him. "It's time. Set the Phoenix alight."

The tall one, I'm almost positive it's a man, lifts the controller and pushes a button. Bobo's wrist blinks brighter and faster, and the gorilla squirms.

Then Dinkelmeyer lifts a powerful finger, pointing at us and addressing the ape. "Go. Burn it down."

His menacing voice sends an icy shiver down my spine. I push myself further into the shadows. Can he see us? No. He's pointing to a service road that extends up onto the mountainside from the back of the parking lot. Even Bobo cringes away from Dinkelmeyer as heads towards the road.

When he gets near our hiding spot, Bobo pauses and sniffs the air. His head flips around to look right at us. We don't move or breathe, but there's no way to hide from the ape's acute sense of smell. Bobo sniffs again and takes a step towards us with a *whoof*, muscles rippling.

Dinkelmeyer grabs the man with the controller by the arm and violently tugs him close until they are face to face. "You said he was ready."

"He is, he is," the tall man whimpers, desperately shaking the controller.

"Then why is that stupid animal stopping?" Dinkelmeyer roars in the person's face. "We have a timeline to maintain. Don't disappoint me."

"No, no of course not," the man whines. "I swear he's ready."

Dwarfed by their two companions, the person in the hat steps away from the other two men. They don't seem scared, though. Their body language broadcasts a disinterested curiosity about the plight of the man Dinkelmeyer is threatening, and distaste (but not surprised) at the violence. They seem more interested in Bobo, watching the ape with folded arms, as if assessing his behavior.

Bobo paws at the light on his arm and heads toward the road again with a last look towards us over his meaty shoulder. I release my held breath.

Dinkelmeyer goes back inside the zoo, the tall man scampering after him and the one in grey glancing in our direction before following them inside the gate. I still can't see their face, though. They close the gate behind them. We're left alone in the darkness.

My mind races. The plan. My plan. I have to pivot the plan. Should I still go into the zoo when there are three people inside? And what about Bobo? He's wandering away and we don't have the keys to Daisy's car and she still isn't back with the van. I'm glad she didn't show up in the middle of the scene we just witnessed, but I don't know what's taking her so long. Can we track Bobo on foot? What do we do if we catch him and don't have a van to put him in?

I don't know what to do.

"I have to follow him," I whisper. It's the only option I can think of. My body seems to move on its own. My brain just keeps thinking *I can't fail* over and over.

Simon grabs my hand. "No, Sarah, you can't go alone. Let's wait for the van."

Blood rushes through my head, pounding in my ears. I can't lose sight of the quarry or the entire mission will go down in flames. We can still be heroes if we don't let Bobo get away. If he disappears, we'll never know what they trained him for. We'll have no way to bring down Dinkelmeyer and whatever this Phoenix Plan is. I have to make it work.

I pull my hand from Simon's grasp just as the zoo van careens into view with only its running lights on. It bears down on us, gravel spraying from its wheels. As soon as it's clear of the zoo door, the headlights blaze to life.

They light up Bobo like a spotlight. The gorilla stops with a barking grunt, turning towards the unexpected light. He pulls himself up tall on two legs and beats against his chest with both mighty fists. The red light on his wrist flares. With a roar, he twists around and tears off down the road, moving fast.

The side door of the van slides open. Daisy has one hand on the open door and the other on the doorframe, her head hunched under the roof.

"Come with me if you want to catch a gorilla!" she says. Then she laughs. "I've always wanted to say that."

"Right? It's like we think with the same brain!" Simon bursts out laughing. "Daisy Damsel, will you marry me?"

"You weirdo." She disappears into the van and climbs back into the driver's seat.

We scramble after her. I squeeze into the passenger seat as Daisy grips the wheel.

"Follow that ape!" I yell while Simon yanks the

sliding door shut. Daisy rams down the gas pedal.
The chase is on.

18: SIMON IMPRESSES THE GIRL

"Follow him!" Sarah yells at Daisy.

"I'm on it," Daisy leans over the dashboard, peering through the windshield into the night.

Bobo careens along the road with loping strides. Instead of going back down the mountain towards Colorado Springs, this road goes up, higher and higher into altitude, dense trees, and unknown territory. And, of course, there aren't any streetlights.

The van roars up the mountain as Bobo swerves erratically, racing along the road to get away from us. The road whips around suddenly in a tight hairpin turn. Daisy slows to keep the van from tipping over, but Bobo doesn't even pause. He leaps into the air where the road doubles back on itself.

Arms out, he soars through the darkness and lands in a nearby pine tree. A hail of pine needles rains down on the van. Daisy slams on the brakes and yanks the wheel to the left, navigating the turn expertly. The road continues to twist its way up the mountain. Bobo swings through the trees, emerging onto the road just ahead of us. Daisy speeds up to close the distance.

"Have we figured out what we're going to do when we catch him?" Daisy says without taking her eyes off the road.

"We have to stop him," Sarah repeats. "Do you think you can take him out if you hit him with the vehicle? Can you knock him over the side of the road where it's steep?"

Daisy flashes wide eyes at her. "I'm not killing Bobo."

"If he really is going to invade Cheyenne Mountain, this is about something a lot bigger than one ape, Daisy," Sarah growls.

"Well, I'm only in this for the one ape." Daisy's face sets into a stern mask. We slow down.

"Speed up! Speed up!" yells Sarah. "We're losing him!"

"I won't hurt him," Daisy insists. "There has to be another way."

From the back seat I can see Daisy's profile, lit up by the van's headlights. Her eyes focus firmly on the road, on Bobo's constantly moving shape, and the cliffs we're rocketing along.

> *Soft as drifting clouds*
> *Strong as the ageless mountains*
> *The flower won't wilt*

Sarah stares at Daisy. I know what she's thinking. We don't know what Bobo's mission is, but there are probably lives at stake. National security concerns. Our future with DAAAD. Not to mention those people inside the mountain. Daisy might be worried about what will happen to Bobo if he encounters the soldiers, but Sarah will be worried about the soldiers. If Bobo makes contact with them, there will be no winners.

Sarah is a leader. They've trained her all her life to

make hard choices. If it came down to it, she's one of the few people I trust to make the hard decision to sacrifice for the greater good. She'd sacrifice anyone, Bobo, Daisy, herself, even me, if it meant the safety of others. She can do the math in her head to figure out which sacrifices are worth it and which aren't. Its difficult math. Sarah, Agent Zero, these are the only people I would trust to make the right choice, no matter the cost.

I don't think I could do it.

Our best hope is to reach Bobo before he enters Cheyenne Mountain, but Daisy's right, we can't just kill him. There has to be another way. I imagine Daisy's face. Those kind eyes, the strength and softness behind that porcelain skin. The firm set of her rose-petal mouth. What would she do if she wasn't driving? What can I do that would be worthy of her?

Then, an idea hits me.

"How close can you get?" I call from the back seat.

"Pretty close as long as he stays on the road," Daisy replies, twisting the wheel as the road curves again. I'm thrown to the side as she guns the engine. "Want me to get alongside him?"

"Do it. Get as close as you can." I press the window down button.

"What are you doing?" Sarah snaps her eyes back to me. "Simon, what are you doing?"

Wind streaks inside the van from the open window, whipping around a few stray papers like angry bats. One of them hits Sarah square in the face. She thrusts it aside and digs at her seatbelt.

"Simon!" She calls, trying to turn around. "What are you doing?"

I pull myself onto the frame of the window. There's

a rack on top of the van. I can grab it if I sit on the windowsill. Wind pushes against me, but I reach the rack with little trouble. I let go of the window frame and tug myself to the top of the van. It's not that different from surfing in a monsoon, just a lot less wet.

"Simon!" I can't tell if it's Sarah or Daisy calling my name.

Bobo continues to follow the road in his headlong run. The van's headlights waver back and forth, dipping the ape into pools of light, then plunging him into darkness as we swerve. I hunch down on the top of the van, clinging to the rack with both hands. Wind tugs at me. It's strong. But I'm stronger.

The van pulls up on Bobo's flank and Daisy holds it steady. Now's my chance. I move forward on the roof. We're going about twenty miles an hour, which may not seem fast, but it feels like a hundred when you're riding on a roof along a dark, twisting mountain road.

I lift one hand to steady myself and prepare to jump. If I hit Bobo just right, I can tackle him and then...

Then what?

One thing at a time. First, we need to stop him. He might be stronger than me, but if I add in my momentum, I think I can get him off his feet. Then I'm putting my trust in Daisy's ability to calm him down. Hopefully she can do it before he pulverizes me.

The road suddenly disappears from the headlights, veering into the darkness. Bobo leaps and is gone into the trees.

Below me, someone screams "Hold on!"

The van careens around a curve, tipping sideways as two wheels drive up onto the side of the mountain. Sharp pine branches sweep the roof, smacking into me, hard. It feels like getting punched. I drop and flatten against the cold metal of the roof.

A branch snags on my shoulders, sweeping off the roof. I scramble for the bars of the rack and cling to them with a white-knuckled grip and the branch scrapes along my back and finally disappears behind me. The engine groans as it drags the van up the incline, up and up. The searching headlights suddenly find Bobo loping along on the road ahead.

My ears clog, and the air is cool on my face as we keep climbing. I stay flat against the roof rack, watching for another chance to tackle the ape, but the roads are too curvy up here for Daisy to get close again.

Without warning, Bobo dives into the trees. The van slows a bit, hesitates, then crashes into the trees after him.

"Simon!" someone yells up to me again.

"Get back in here!" That one must be Sarah.

The van hits a bump, tossing me into the air. I slam down against the side of the roof and slide over the edge, tumbling towards the rugged terrain. This might not have been my best idea ever.

Snagging the roof rack with one desperate hand, I break my fall and smack against the side of the van with a force that leaves my feet flopping just above the fast-moving ground. I swing my other hand up to grip the rack too as the van crashes through another group of pine trees. Sharp branches claw at my clothes and hair, pulling at me like the hands of some fairytale tree monster.

My kicking feet find the open window. I brace them both against the bottom of the sill and let go of the rack with one hand, grabbing blind inside the vehicle for something to anchor myself with. The van jumps and kicks like a wild horse. I can't believe we haven't blown a tire yet. Daisy is an amazing driver but I doubt the zoo ever intended this van to go off-roading quite like this.

I find the bar above the window on the inside of the van, and let go of the rack. With one good heave I'm inside, sprawling across the rear seat.

Something wet drips down my face, irritating a million stinging scrapes and cuts. I'm not surprised to see some blood on the hand I use to wipe it away. The blood might be from my face, my hand, or another part of me. I hurt everywhere, but there's no time for that now. Daisy and Sarah peer out the front window. Trees streak by in the headlights. I think I see a flash of gorilla, but maybe it's just a shadow.

"There, to the left," Sarah points.

Daisy swings us that way. A boulder rises into view, and she yanks the van to the side, avoiding it by mere inches. We don't even slow down. Sure enough, I see Bobo vaulting over rocks and through trees. He obviously knows where he's going.

Daisy stays on his tail.

Sarah is too busy monitoring Bobo to yell at me. Small favors. She calls out more directions, pointing. "There, at three o'clock."

"I see him," Daisy snips back, but she turns wherever Sarah tells her to.

Daisy abruptly slams on the brakes. The force of the sudden stop throws me into the front seats and leaves me hanging gracelessly over the gearshift. One of my legs is still in the back seat, the other is up against Daisy's arm. My head lands in Sarah's lap.

"Use your seatbelt, dummy," Sarah smacks my

forehead.

Then she unbuckles her own belt, as does Daisy, who is out of the van before I know what's happening. I roll my legs into her seat and leap out the door after her.

We're in an open space way up on the side of Cheyenne Mountain. A trail of broken tree branches marks the path from the road up to where the van now perches like a wounded bird, teetering on the dramatically tilted ground. I can see the lights of Colorado Springs, just glittering specks miles below us.

The scene might be romantic in other circumstances.

A few feet from us, the mountain falls away into a steep cliff side of sheer granite. At the bottom of the cliff, a concrete half circle big enough to drive several trucks through sticks out from the side of the mountain. A wide road disappears inside the mountain through the round tunnel, almost under our feet.

Tall chain-link fencing fans out along the top of the tunnel and continues along both sides of the road, topped with looping razor wire. Tall floodlights shine over the tunnel's entrance at regular intervals. A barrier protects each side of the road. On one side, a steep cliff rises a hundred feet or more. A large concrete wall flanks the other side. Two men in military fatigues stand outside the end of the tunnel with heavy rifles slung over their shoulders. I can't see exactly what style of rifle they are, but they're obviously military grade. The soldiers' hands lay over the stocks casually. As I watch, the soldiers wander into the tube, and back out again, eyes alert.

About half a mile along the road that leads out of the mountain, a few low buildings surround a large parking lot along with a small green-roofed fueling area, and what looks like power generators. That area isn't well lit. Then the road continues down the mountain, meandering its way towards the city with the same switchbacks and hairpin turns I'm becoming familiar with as it navigates the steep terrain.

I recognize where we are immediately from the photo. We're right above the entrance to Cheyenne Mountain, the most secure military base in the world. So we're right, this is the place they've trained Bobo to infiltrate. The gorilla has come to a stop. He knows we're here and stares at us with suspicion. We're about ten feet away from him across a small clearing. He's standing under a huge outcropping of stone with a concrete tube protruding from it, pointing straight down. The bottom of the tube sticks out a few feet over his head, maybe seven or eight feet above the ground. It looks like a vent or water overflow large enough for a person to fit inside, assuming that person isn't claustrophobic and could somehow travel straight up a smooth surface.

Rock climbers call cracks in the rock that are big enough to climb up "chimneys." The climber spans the chimney with their body and uses the counterforce and friction from pushing on both sides at once to maneuver upwards. The specific technique you use to get up a chimney will depend on its width, handholds, and your own personal strengths. If I think of this tube like a chimney, I can see you would need really long, powerful arms to travel up it.

Arms like a gorilla.

Daisy takes a step towards him, but Sarah grabs her arm. Daisy wrestles out of Sarah's grip and approaches Bobo slowly, lifting her hand. Bobo watches her, scratching his arm. He tilts his head and makes a throaty *ook* sound.

"Stay back," she whispers to us, motioning us away with her other hand.

Then Daisy sings.

At first, Bobo fidgets. Then Daisy takes another step forward. I want to stand by her side as she faces the erratic ape. She must be terrified, and I want her to know she's not alone. Instead, I have to trust that she knows what she's doing.

Sarah edges forward, but I lay a hand on her arm to stop her. She turns desperate eyes to me that say; *I want to help*.

Wait. My eyes say back. *Trust Daisy*.

She doesn't trust Daisy, but she does trust me. So she waits and watches, ready to spring into action if things go south.

Daisy stands between us and Bobo, still singing in that adorable, slightly off-key voice. She lifts her hand, palm facing the gorilla. Bobo lifts his hand in response, his shoulders relaxed. I can see a yearning in his eyes, a desperate realization that there isn't any glass between them now. He reaches out to her. I imagine he just wants to feel her touch with no barriers separating them. To feel his hand against hers.

Then the red light flashes and buzzes on his wrist.

Bobo screams. He turns from Daisy and leaps up into the tube. Sarah and I bolt forward, past a stunned Daisy. We lunge for his legs, but he pulls them up out of our reach. I scramble forward and look up into the tube after him.

"Are you crazy? What are you trying to do, yank

him back down? That's suicide." Daisy hisses behind us. "Why did he get so angry all of a sudden?"

It's pitch black but I dig out my phone and point its flashlight into the darkness. The tube extends up as far as I can see. It would take an expert climber to scale it. I'm an expert climber, but even if I could get enough counterforce with my arms and legs, which I doubt, I'd be exhausted by the time I got to the top. That's no good if it turns into a combat situation.

Bobo scampers up it like a squirrel.

Who knows what's at the top of that shaft or how high it goes, but Bobo disappears into the inky darkness beyond the reach of my phone's meager light.

An angry howl echoes down the shaft and rings in my ears. It sounds eerie, like some kind of ghost. Or, if I were a conspiracy theorist, like a wild man or anguished government experiment gone wrong. Then, it fades, and everything is silent.

"He's gone," Daisy whimpers. She falls to her knees and drops her face into her hands. "I'm so scared for him."

Sarah stands under the shaft, doing a bunch of Sarah-calculations in her head. She points her cell phone flashlight into the shaft, notching it brighter. Then she takes off her necklace.

I kneel beside Daisy, placing a gentle hand on her shoulder. She takes a sobbing breath and collapses against me. She's warm and soft, her body curving to fit beside mine.

I wrap my arms around her, whispering, "It's going to be alright. We'll do what we can to reach him. Trust me."

She turns her tear-streaked face to me. "Do you

promise?"

"I promise."

Sarah surveys the mountainside entrance below us. "Daisy, your driving skills are crazy impressive. Do you think you can get the van out of here, and around to that parking lot? I don't think we'll be able to come back out this way."

Daisy wipes her eyes with the back of her hand. Her expression turns serious. She evaluates the terrain without moving from my arms, then nods. "Yeah, yeah I think I can. I know these roads pretty well. We're not that far from the zoo."

"Great," Sarah gives her a single, curt nod. "Get down there, set up the van to receive Bobo, and wait for us for one and a half hours. If we're not out by then, get back to town and call everyone you can think of. Police, the military bases, the press. Anyone you can think of who can get through to NORAD. Tell them they're being invaded."

With that, she makes some adjustments to her necklace and turns back to the shaft.

"There's no way you guys are just amateur detectives." Daisy searches my eyes with hers. "What are you?"

I lift her to her feet and glance over at Sarah. How much can I tell her? How much does she need to know?

Sarah sends me a warning look, though I don't think she can hear our conversation. In her hand, her grappling hook pops open. She clips the end of the chain to her belt and points the other part up into the shaft. With a click of a button, the hook shoots upwards. The chain reels out in a nearly inaudible *fffffwipp*. I hear a distant clank and Sarah groans, catching the hook as it falls back down.

Daisy stares at Sarah, then at me, raising her eyebrows. "Well?"

Sarah shoots the grappling hook again. This time I hear a more solid clink and the chain goes taut. Sarah tugs on it with a satisfied nod. She looks at me again.

"Come on, loverboy. It's showtime." With that, she presses the button again and disappears up the shaft.

"I have some secrets, Daisy," I smooth her hair out of her face and gaze into her eyes. "But I can tell you this: I promise to do my best to get Bobo safely out of there."

Somewhere deep inside Daisy's eyes, something shifts. The hard curiosity softens, replaced by the same yearning I saw in Bobo's eyes. She places a warm hand on my cheek. Then, making a decision, she rises on her tiptoes and presses her mouth against mine. Her lips are soft, like petals.

She lingers for only a second, then pulls away. "I understand. We all have our secrets. Come back safe and maybe I'll tell you some of mine. Just–don't get hurt, okay?"

I don't promise anything this time. Instead, I move to the bottom of the shaft. With one last look at Daisy, I catch the end of Sarah's necklace as she drops it to me. Then, clipping it to my belt, I press the button, and rocket up into the long, dark tube.

19: SARAH GETS SOME ACTION

The vertical shaft extends twenty-six feet straight up into the mountain. My grappling hook zips me past the smooth walls effortlessly. I love it so much.

The grapple is hooked to some kind of metal grate at the top of the shaft. My ascent slows as I approach it. I keep an eye out for the gorilla, but by the time I get up there he's gone. The hinged grate opens into the horizontal passageway. It's made of heavy iron, and appears to open with some kind of automated hydraulics, probably controlled by a remote panel from within the control room of the mountain.

The metal grate itself looks like a shutter or window blinds, with a series of hinged metal slats along its length. I think the horizontal passageway I've climbed into is an air duct, so my guess is that this grate is made to keep out intruders, like me and the ape, or even just random birds and bats. It probably opens like this for maintenance. If there were some kind of chemical or nuclear attack, these slats would be closed from the control room, shutting out the toxic air. Then this place would be totally secure.

If the grate weren't already open, there's no way even Bobo could have pried it up while bracing himself in place. Someone opened this door for him, and if I'm right, and I probably am, access through this vent is a limited time offer. Which means they trained Bobo not only to come straight here, but to get here on a time schedule. No wonder he was in such a hurry. I bet that wrist device tracks his movement as well as zapping him so they could make sure he got here on time. That's probably why Dinkelmeyer and his friends went back into the zoo before Daisy showed up. It's probably where their tracking station is. They watched his progress on GPS, and that's why his wrist started buzzing when Daisy was singing to him. Some kind of time warning. Whatever this Phoenix Plan is, it's well orchestrated. Must have been in the works for a long time.

I better get Simon up here in a hurry. I unclip my hook from my belt and lower it down, hoping he won't take too long saying goodbye to the girl. To my relief, he catches it.

Simon *fffffwipps* up the shaft, swinging his long legs clear of the opening to join me in the narrow air duct. I tug the hook free of the grate just as it beeps a warning.

"Get clear," I whisper.

The grate slams shut with an echoing boom. Nowhere to go now but forward. As the sound fades, I hear something scampering further down the duct.

"Let's get moving." I crawl towards the noise. "We need to figure out what the Phoenix Plan is, and stop it."

"And get Bobo out," Simon adds.

We turn a corner and see a square of light. Another metal grate, the same style as the first one, is open up ahead. I shimmy up and peek out.

- **Location assessment:**

- o Grate (I'm peeking out from)
  - ▪ Seven feet, three inches above the floor
  - ▪ Corridor has ten-foot ceilings
- o Network of pipes and fluorescent lights
  - ▪ Attached to ceiling
  - ▪ Running the length of the corridor
  - ▪ Suspended by wide bands of iron bolted into the stone
  - ▪ Two-and-a-half feet of clearance between the pipes and the ceiling.
- o No windows
  - ▪ (Reminds me of home (HQ Mountain), except a lot less fancy)
- • Conclusion:
  - o We are definitely deep inside Cheyenne Mountain.

I drop the seven feet, three inches to the floor without a sound, followed quickly by Simon. The hallway is empty, but I smell a lingering musk that I recognize from the gorilla house.

When you're infiltrating an enemy base (or, in this case, a friendly one) cover is your number one priority. The architects of Cheyenne Mountain Complex were smart; there's nowhere for us infiltrators to hide. Doors flush to the walls, no little nooks anywhere, and, of course, no windows or curtains. The industrial overhead light fixtures even rob us of any good shadows to hide in.

And also? There are no big, blinking arrows saying *"gorilla, this way"* anywhere. I send a hand-sign to Simon, telling him to check around the corner at one end of the hall while I move towards the other. Behind us, the heavy grate lowers itself with a *whirr* and snaps into place with a solid *thunk*. I'm glad I had the foresight to tell Daisy to take the van to the parking lot, because it looks like I was right. We definitely won't be going back out the way we came in.

I flatten my back against the wall and peek around the corner. Nothing. Just an identical hallway stretching for fifty feet in a straight line. At the other end, Simon is also flat against the wall, except he's waving to get my attention. By using hand signs, he tells me the gorilla went one way, but people are coming from the other. He holds up three fingers and makes the sign for soldier and the sign for gun.

Crap.

I look around the empty hallway for somewhere to hide. Still nothing. Then, I look up. Simon sees where I'm looking, nods, and locks his fingers together for me. I rush towards him, plant one foot in his hands and vault into the ceiling pipes. It's a squeeze, but they seem strong enough to hold us. I drop a hand for Simon as he gets a running start and leaps, rebounding off the wall and slapping his hand into mine like a circus acrobat. His long legs swing up, and he shimmies into the pipes with barely a noise as the soldiers round the corner and come into view. We watch the tops of their heads pass directly underneath us.

"Hey, what about the Thirsty Grizzly?" One of them loudly interrupts another.

Rifles hang off their shoulders, their hands laying lightly across them. Everything about their posture is relaxed. They apparently didn't see us or Bobo. All that time staying out of sight at the Broadmoor seems to have trained him well.

"Their potato skins suck, Matt," another one says.

"Maybe, but they have five different lagers on tap," Matt insists. "FIVE. I'm not kidding."

"The Thirsty Grizzly is closer to my house," the first guy points out. "I can probably swing that. With the new baby, it's not like I get out much."

The sound of their discussion fades as they turn the far corner.

Simon and I drop to the floor and rush after Bobo.

Around the corner, another identical corridor extends fifty feet with a series of doors set flush to the walls. Each metal door has a numbered plaque. The floors are polished concrete. In fact, everything, the walls, the ceiling, the floors, it's all concrete. Everything except the hairy leg disappearing around the corner at the far end. A pungent, musky scent lingers in the corridor. I guess if we lose sight of him, we can always follow our noses like bloodhounds.

We round the far corner just in time to see him take yet another turn. It's like a maze in here, and all the corridors look the same. HQ Mountain is a lot less, I don't know, clinical. I never really appreciated the artistry of our gently sweeping hallways and recessed lighting before.

Somewhere in front of us, a door clicks closed. As we turn another concrete corner, our corridor dead ends into just one doorway. It's even got a little window in the door. Simon yanks it open.

It's a stairwell. Muffled scruffling drifts to us from below, so we follow it down. I'm pretty sure Bobo can hear us, but it doesn't seem to bother him. He's not making a lot of noise, but he's not exactly sneaking either.

I have no idea how we're going to find our way out. And I certainly don't know how we could possibly extract Bobo. The only thing I know for certain is that we have to stop him from doing whatever he's supposed to do down here and try to keep him from wounding any of these soldiers.

Simon doesn't want to hurt him, but I don't have that luxury. I'll do whatever it takes to stop him. We might have to make a hard decision. If it comes to a choice between Bobo and the security of the nation, or the lives of these soldiers, I'll have to be the one to make the call. Simon is an excellent agent, great at following the rules and doing whatever is asked of him. But he can't make sacrifices.

I love that about him. It may not make him a better agent, but it makes him a better person. I hope he never learns how to sacrifice something he loves. If he ever has to make a choice like that, I want to be with him. I'll be the bad guy and make that decision so he doesn't have to, even if it means he'd hate me. I'd rather he hate me than lose that part of himself. Let's hope it doesn't come to that tonight, though.

The bottom of the stairwell leads to yet another door, which leads to yet another corridor, but this one is a little different. It's about thirty feet long, stretching from the stairwell to an elevator on the far end. There are only three doors, two regular ones on one side, and a set of double doors on the other. Behind us, voices echo down the stairwell and feet tromp towards us.

"Come on." I tug Simon towards the double doors. They look important. We disappear inside and find ourselves in, surprise! A hallway.

This one is wide and doesn't extend very far. It's

about ten feet long with double doors at each end and a side door halfway down that says "maintenance". On the wall across from that side door, humongous white painted letters say "Section B8, Sublevel 6." And along the back wall, a smaller sign says "without power, it's just a cave." Nothing else. Nowhere for cover, no ceiling pipes.

No gorilla.

"Where did he go?" Simon asks. "Where's Bobo? How does something that big just disappear?"

"I don't know, but he's obviously not here. Let's backtrack."

Before we get a chance, the double doors behind us slam open.

"You there! Stop!"

I swing around. Three guards stand in the doorway, rifles at the ready. Two of them edge into the room, keeping their guns trained on me and Simon. The third locks the doors open against the walls. Then he lifts his own rifle.

"How did you get in here?" the first soldier barks again. "Who are you? Hands up."

"Hey, they're just kids," says soldier number two, surprised. "Does one of your parents work here? What are you doing all the way down here?"

I wonder if they're the ones who passed underneath us upstairs. The ones with a new baby and plans for after work. Whoever they are, they certainly don't look casual and relaxed now. A thrill runs through me. It should scare me to look down the barrel of multiple military-grade rifles, but it's just like training. Except I'm not wearing a bulletproof vest. Kind of exciting, huh?

When someone with a gun tells you to do something, it's best to do it (at least until you have another plan worked out). I lift my hands over my head, and motion for Simon to do the same.

A dark, hairy shape slams into two of the soldiers like a missile. They go down with a thud, one rifle skittering across the floor. Bobo stands, silhouetted in the open doorway. He brandishes the other rifle over his head like a club and screams.

The sound doubles and triples in volume as it echoes off the surrounding walls.

The last soldier spins, his rifle raised and ready. Before the soldier has time to comprehend the situation, Bobo swings his firearm like a club. It hits the soldier with a meaty thud. I hear something crack but can't tell if it's Bobo's rifle, the soldier's arm, or the soldier's rifle hitting the floor.

The man, still standing, looks down at the rifle at his feet, his expression blank, confused. His arm dangles uselessly above it. He looks up at Bobo just as the gorilla beats the stock of his gun into the man's face. The soldier crumples. One man behind the gorilla begins to stand and Bobo grabs him by the leg, throwing him down the hallway towards us like a rag doll.

The soldier hits the floor and spins to a stop. He doesn't get back up.

The harsh red light on Bobo's wrist flashes a pattern. *Flash, pause, flash flash flash, pause, flash, pause, flash flash flash.* He shakes his arm violently, like it's covered with biting ants, but the pattern keeps repeating.

"Through there," I call to Simon, pushing through the double doors behind us. Then I realize Simon isn't with me.

He faces Bobo. The gorilla straddles the still form of a soldier, rocking back and forth, watching my little brother. Bobo grunts in several sharp bursts. He slams his knuckles into the floor, the boom echoing in the hallway. The floor, I notice, not the man beneath him.

"I think he's trying to help us." Simon doesn't take his eyes off the menace in front of him.

"Are you insane?" I hiss, holding the door open for Simon. "Get in here. You can't help those people if you're dead."

Bobo steps over the soldier on the floor, kicking him out of the way carelessly with one back foot. From the corridor outside, I hear more footsteps running towards us. Bobo hears them too. He takes one look over his shoulder.

Then he turns and charges straight at us.

Simon hurls himself through the doors I'm holding open, and together we slam them closed and throw our bodies against them. Bobo crashes against the doors from the other side, rattling the knob and rocking both Simon and I where we stand, but we hold it. Simon locks the heavy latch before Bobo can throw himself at the door again. It should keep them closed at least until we can figure out what to do. Mighty fists hammer against the doors from the outside. They're metal and made to last, but Bobo thunders hard against them. He wants in.

Why doesn't he just run away? Why does he want to get in here so bad?

The pounding suddenly stops. Gunfire crackles outside. Then we hear a lot of screams. It's hard to tell which ones are human. An icy wave grows in the pit of my stomach. There's nothing I can do to help those soldiers. I have to focus on keeping Simon safe and making sure Bobo doesn't complete his mission. That's all I can do right now.

Where are we?

A giant, poorly lit cavern. Six large blue machines, each one the size of a taco truck, fill the space, half-sunken into the floor in a row. Teal pipes travel along the tops of each machine, connecting them to fat conduits running across the far wall. Next to the conduits, cooling pipes lead to large containers bolted to the walls. Each machine has a sign attached that says "on the line" over a box of electronic controls.

Generators. Gently humming. A long row of enormous electrical generators.

"Simon," I gasp. Bobo's fury to get in here, the importance of this room. It all fits together like a puzzle. "This is it. Why they trained Bobo to infiltrate Cheyenne Mountain. This is Bobo's destination."

"The generator room?" Simon asks. "What could he do in here? According to our brief, Cheyenne Mountain gets most of its electricity from Colorado Springs. These generators are only important if the mountain goes off-grid."

"Which it would do if it went into lockdown," I nod, puzzle pieces flying together in my head. "Maybe Dinkelmeyer is planning to take out the entire power grid, disrupting every one of the military bases around here and all their supporting services. Cheyenne Mountain goes into lockdown, relying on its generators, which would be essential for NORAD to track the airspace over North America until they can get the main grid back up."

Simon's eyes get wide as he realizes the

implications. "The blast doors would close in seconds and without the generators, there would be no way to get them open again, even once the main system was back up, because they'd already be disconnected from the grid. Everyone inside would be trapped with no generators to circulate the air, run the lights, or pump water. Eventually, everyone in the mountain, including us and Bobo, would die a slow, painful death."

"I guess that's why Dinkelmeyer and his cronies trained a gorilla to do this job instead of doing it themselves. If he doesn't make it out, Bobo is expendable, and he can't reveal any information even if someone captures him. Talk about plausible deniability! *Dude, I'm a gorilla. I just do what the blinky-light bracelet tells me to do.*" I shrug. "So all these 'harmless' vandalism events serve multiple purposes. They train Bobo, create a distraction from Dinkelmeyer's real plan, and hype the conspiracy nuts into a frenzy."

The buzz of electricity fills the room, standing my arm hairs on end. It's cold, but the machines pump out a lot of heat. Even as a backup base, there must be massive amounts of data generated from the airspace surveillance here. A lot of data takes a lot of power.

"Airspace surveillance!" I choke. "Is there an even deeper layer here? Some sort of air attack? Without NORAD, the North American airspace would be blind until they cobbled together a backup. With no one watching the airspace, Dinkelmeyer's organization does what? Burns Colorado Springs to the ground like his proverbial Phoenix bird with some kind of air attack?"

Simon considers it. "That would take an insane amount of logistics. Could they pull that off without DAAAD getting wind of it?"

An alarm squeals, coming from everywhere at once. I can't hear the fighting from outside the doors anymore. I'm not sure if it stopped, or if the alarms cover it up.

Boom. Boom.

Pounding on the door again, louder and faster now. Bobo must have won the fight. What else could he do but fight back, though? And what else could the soldiers do but start shooting? They can't exactly reason with him.

"Maybe you're right," I agree. "Maybe I'm overthinking this. Any of these steps would cause chaos by themselves. Dinkelmeyer doesn't need to attack anyone, he just needs to talk people into doing it for him. We may not know how his organization gets its funding, but we know how they operate; by planting the seeds of doubt and suspicion. With the rumors of a rogue supersoldier rampant, killing people and taking out Cheyenne Mountain, the military bases in Colorado Springs would look suspicious. Either a traitor has infiltrated them, or the government really is doing secret medical experiments. Conspiracy theorists would invade the bases, trying to expose a supersoldier program that never existed and, in the process, probably uncover dozens of state secrets. Just like Agent Zero fears. The American government, which many people already don't trust, looks even more rotten from within."

Simon grabs my arms. "Sarah, it would look like the start of a civil war. Which could even become a civil war once the ball gets rolling. We can't let Bobo destroy anything in here."

"Yeah, including ourselves." That's the power of

disinformation. There doesn't have to be an actual physical attack, just a bunch of people unwilling to talk with each other or get over their prejudice in order to fight together for a common goal. Then it just takes one trigger event for everything to explode.

If we don't stop Bobo, we could very well have front row seats to the takedown of America, maybe Canada too. If I'm even kind of right, this situation is astronomically above my paygrade. We need an army of high-level agents to save the day, but thanks to me, we don't have one. I could have stopped this entire plan, but instead may have paved the way for Phoenix to happen. I don't know what to do. Agent Zero would know what to do, she always knows, but it's too late to call for backup. And to make matters worse, we've lied to her. All because I wanted to be a hero.

Why did I think I could handle this all on my own? I may have aced every lesson back at the Island, but this is the real world. It's a lot more complicated than I thought. I have to stop Bobo somehow. How can Simon and I take out a monster that clear-cut an entire regiment of armed soldiers by ourselves?

Again and again the ape hammers against the door with his massive ape fists. Red lights flash overhead and a message blares from the loudspeakers, repeating over and over, "Alert! Alert! Code Five disturbance, section B eight, sublevel six. This is not a drill. All stations to section B eight, sublevel six."

We're no good to anyone if we're dead, but we're trapped. There's no way out except for the door Bobo continues to pummel against. One of the upper corners of the door squeals and punches inward. Muscular fingers thrust into the tiny opening of the corner, tugging until the metal of the door bends.

There's only one place to go. I plant a foot on a yellow and black railing around generator number one and vault onto the top. I can wedge myself between all the valves, pipes, and attachments up here and hide while I figure out what our next steps are. Hopefully, the grease and electricity dulls my scent. Simon sees me and springs up on top of generator two.

While I invent and discard plan after plan in my head, Bobo gets his full hands inside the bent corner and continues to destroy the door. It groans in protest. His entire arm shoves through and he rips the mutilated door from its hinges, tossing it aside. Through the newly exposed doorway, I can see the mangled metal fall on top of what looks like a pile of laundry. A closer look reveals that it's actually uniforms. Uniforms with people still inside. Soldiers. The door lands on top of one of the outstretched legs with a sickening squish loud enough to be heard over the alarms.

Bobo opens his mouth startlingly wide, pulling back lips to expose gigantic teeth as he roars. He beats his chest, then knuckle-walks slowly into the room, looking around. His shoulders roll with every step. I press myself deeper into the pipes.

The alarms suddenly cut off. The unexpected quiet is almost more disturbing than the noise was. Bobo pauses. In the silence I can hear him sniff the air with loud snuffling snorts. He takes another few steps and pauses again.

Then his eyes land on the generators. At first I think he can see me or Simon, but then I realize it's the machines he's looking at. His expression changes, going blank like a robot, and he moves deeper inside the room to the machine beyond Simon. Generator three. He tilts his head.

Almost playfully, he reaches out and grabs ahold of the yellow and black railing that surrounds the front of the generator. With a mighty yank, he just about uproots it, then shakes it violently, his face maintaining the same dead expression. Without warning, he lets go of the railing, reaches onto his back, and pulls out a small bag that's buried in his fur. It's small enough that I hadn't even seen it before now.

Then he and the bag disappear around the back of the third generator.

This is it. He's supposed to use whatever is in that bag to do something to the generators in this room. And with a name like the Phoenix Plan, it's got to be explosives. He's going to rig the generators to explode in flames like the legend of the fiery phoenix. A mythical bird. When it gets old and tired, after its feathers drop out and it's too sickly to continue, it bursts into flames. The fire devours the phoenix until it's a pile of ash. Then the phoenix is reborn from its own ashes, beautiful, new, and pure. Full of hope once more.

A grandiose and whimsical name for a complex and violent plan, but I don't pretend to understand the mind of a man who runs a secret terrorist organization. I understand that this time he's targeting the US military even though he's never moved against a first-world nation until now.

Simon waves to get my attention. He points to Generator Three and signs "destroy" and "purpose." I nod. He's figured it out, too. Then he signs "calm" and "gorilla." And "flower." *Huh?*

To my surprise, he slides down from his generator. I wave at him frantically. What is he doing? I slide down to join him but he motions for me to stay where I am.

I hesitate.

He glares at me.

With a sigh, I pull my legs back onto the generator, trying to get into position to tackle the ape from above if I need to.

Bobo appears, waddling out from behind the machine. He sees Simon and stops with a *whuff*. His face still has that dead expression, which, I suppose, is better than angry. The small bag is still in his hand, but he holds it like an afterthought. Like he doesn't even know he's got it. The red light isn't flashing anymore. It looks like we've interrupted whatever he was doing back there. If we can just get him out of here before he resumes his work, maybe we can still be heroes. Even if no one ever knows.

Suddenly I realize what Simon is trying to tell me. Not "flower."

"Daisy."

Simon lifts his hand, palm facing Bobo. The ape blinks a few times and shakes his head, but stays where he is. His nostrils flare. He sniffs the air. I wonder if he can smell Daisy's scent on Simon. Simon keeps his hand up, looking intently at the gorilla. Bobo stares at Simon's hand, then down at his own.

Then Simon sings. The same lullaby Daisy sang, gentle and loud, having apparently memorized the words and the tune. Simon has a lovely voice. I've always enjoyed listening to him sing, but now I'm frozen on top of the generator, unsure what to do. The ape is barely a foot away. I'm itching to tackle him, but I force myself to trust Simon.

Bobo shakes his head again. He closes his eyes for a moment and his giant brow ridge contracts. Then he lifts one hand to his face, looking a lot like Agent Zero when she has a headache (an expression I've seen frequently.) He covers his eyes and pinches the bridge of his nose, just like she does.

Simon continues to sing and hold up his palm. Bobo's face relaxes, and he opens his eyes. His hand and curling fingers hover a few inches away from Simon's, as if there were glass between them.

Then Simon bridges the gap. He moves his hand a bit more and touches his palm to Bobo's. The moment their hands touch, Bobo shivers. I tense, ready to throw myself onto the gorilla with full force.

But in his deep brown eyes, I see nothing but longing. Bobo makes small whimpering sounds, almost as if he were crying. His long fingers wrap around Simon's hand. His shoulders relax and he looks into Simon's eyes. The dead expression is gone. The anger is gone. He clings to Simon's hand like it's a lifeline.

Maybe it is.

We may not be armed, but apparently Simon has the only weapon we need. Love. Kindness. Understanding and forgiveness, stronger, at least in this case, than all those soldiers outside and their guns. Simon's soul may save us all. I slide off the generator, and step closer. Bobo pushes Simon behind his back, standing between me and my little brother. I narrow my eyes, but Simon places a hand on Bobo's shoulder and leans close to him.

"It's okay, big guy," Simon says in a sing-songy voice. "She's one of the good ones. Sarah is a friend.

Friend."

Bobo tilts his head at me. He lifts his hand, grunting out a rough approximation of the lullaby. It's probably better than I can do, so I don't even try to sing. In awe, I place my palm against his. It's warm and leathery, like a comfortable chair that's been basking in the sun.

What do you know? Maybe I have a little poetry in me, after all. It just took a gorilla to find it. Sometimes, maybe we do all just need a little connection.

Then I hear a ding, and the sounds of the elevator door sliding open, followed by shouting and boots thundering toward us.

20: SIMON MAKES A NARROW ESCAPE

Bobo jerks upright, looking wary, but not angry. I set a hand on his arm to soothe him. The ape looks from me to the doorway, then leans into my hand. A few low, gentle grunts come from deep inside his chest. He glances out through the gaping doorway of the generator room into the hallway beyond. The pounding boot steps come closer. In a blur, he grabs me and tosses me over his shoulder. My solar plexus slams into his back, knocking the wind out of me. My long legs dangle almost to the ground but he doesn't seem to notice.

The loudspeaker calls again: "Alert! Alert! Code Five disturbance, section B eight, sublevel six. This is not a drill. All stations to section B eight, sublevel six."

Bobo leaps onto the nearest generator. I bounce around on his shoulder, trying to cling to his fur like his giant, incompetent baby. The ceilings are taller here than in the corridors, at least fourteen feet, and there aren't any overhead fluorescents. Task light pools around the generators, but everything else is in shadow, including most of the ceiling. The generators' cooling pipes branch out and spiderweb across the walls, hanging from the ceiling at irregular angles. Bobo vaults into the pipes. He lands silently and eases me down next to him. I sprawl like a floppy stuffed toy over the pipes before I can get myself together. He looks me in the eye and *ooks*.

The noises outside continue to grow louder. I see movement below. Sarah waves to get my attention and tosses me her grappling hook. I snap it around a rod that holds the pipes to the ceiling. She clips it to her belt and shoots up, the *ffffwipp* entirely lost in all the thudding boots. Her feet disappear into the shadows just as the first rifle barrel sticks through the mangled doorway.

Beneath us, a troop of soldiers enter the room cautiously. Some of them carry rifles, and some have handguns. All of them look dangerous. I think about the man with the new baby at home. Is he one of these below us? Is he out in pile in the hall? Are any of them out there still alive?

I send Sarah the "don't engage" sign. She nods, then bites her lower lip and glares at the ape. Bobo doesn't look like he wants to engage either. He stays completely still, watching the men and women in uniform move into the room underneath us. They fan out, alert, and disappear deep into the cavernous room, methodically checking every nook and cranny around the generators.

But no one looks up.

As the last soldier vanishes behind the thrumming blue machines, Bobo traverses the pipes towards the door. We follow through the shadows without a sound, like predators in the night. At almost the same time, all three of us drop to the floor in silence. Bobo leads us out the door.

People litter the floor out in the hall, the mangled door sitting on top of some of them. Bobo skirts along the wall, as if he doesn't want to touch the bodies. He doesn't even look at them, but I can't look away. A few of them move or groan. I don't know how many, but it looks like at least some of them are still alive.

Sarah hesitates, her eyes on the downed soldiers.

The loudspeaker calls out: "All available medical personnel to section B eight, sublevel six, stat. Medical emergency, section B eight, sublevel six."

We can't help these men and women, but their fellow soldiers can. The doctors are on their way. Right now we have to make sure Bobo doesn't hurt anyone else. We seem to have interrupted whatever Bobo was supposed to do.

I promised Daisy I'd get him out.

Bobo paces in front of the elevator doors at the end of the hallway. Before I can push the call button, he plants his palms on the doors and his entire body tenses. Massive shoulders surge with muscle as he pulls the elevator doors apart. They groan and shutter as they open until the gap between them is large enough for Bobo to get first his arm, and then his whole body inside. Bracing his back against one door, he pushes against the other with both hands and a foot. The doors shiver, then slide open, exposing an empty elevator shaft that disappears into the shadows in both directions, with an elevator car down below. The elevator cable hangs taut in the middle of the shaft. Beyond it, rungs are embedded at regular intervals into the concrete of a narrow service alcove. Sarah runs straight at the shaft, diving through the open doors between Bobo's outstretched arms and the floor. She grabs the elevator cable, using it to swing her legs forward, then releases. Her feet hit the rungs, neatly followed by her arms. She sticks to the ladder like a flying squirrel on a tree trunk. Then she climbs.

I dive after her, copying her moves. Behind me, Bobo launches himself at the cable. As soon as he lets go, the elevator doors slide shut with a breathy whisper. He climbs straight up the elevator cable as I scurry along the rungs after Sarah.

The backs of another set of elevator doors come into view as we climb up to the next level. Embedded in the concrete is a giant red button.

"What's this?" I call up to Sarah, reaching for it.

She looks down and hisses. "Are you crazy? Never push a big, red button. Geeze Simon, have you never seen a single TV show in your entire life? When has pushing the big, red mystery button ever worked out for a character?"

Point taken. I pull my hand away and we keep climbing. Each set of closed doors has a number painted on the side and one of the big red buttons near the service alcove. The numbers count down as my arms tire (don't judge, it's been a long day.) FOUR, climb, THREE, keep climbing. Finally, we make it to ONE.

At least Sarah does.

The shaft continues past her another ten feet or so, where it becomes a space filled with all the elevator mechanics. She stops at the double elevator doors, which are closed of course, and runs a hand over them. The call button is on the other side, so she needs to find the latch release on this side in order to open them. I'm still half a floor below her on the metal service alcove rungs.

A rumbling vibration convulses up from the depths of the shaft.

The elevator cable springs to life as the car rises

towards us, fast. Sarah scampers into the mechanical space. Even if the elevator car comes to the first floor, it will stop before it reaches her. The cable grinds under Bobo's hands and feet, and he launches himself at the rungs just below Sarah. There's enough room for me in the safe zone as well if we all squeeze. But I won't make it.

The car thunders its way towards us, the whooshing air from its motion whining in my ears. I'm only at the bottom of the doors marked ONE. The car rockets closer, filling the entire space in the elevator shaft, skimming up smoothly on its guard rails. I lunge up the rungs as fast as I can, but it's on me before I can even think of a plan. There's only a few inches between the walls of the elevator car and the hard cement walls of the shaft. I think about a windshield wiper squishing a bug across the windshield, smearing its guts against the glass as it wipes across the surface, and I climb even faster.

The car pushes a wave of stale wind ahead of it. The wind hits me, the car only a few feet behind. I drop my feet off the rungs and press as far as I can into the service alcove. The metal rungs dig into my ribs and stomach as I squeeze the rung in my hands with all my strength. Above me, Sarah gasps loud enough for me to hear her above the whoosh of air and the sound of my clothes sliding against the side of the elevator as it overtakes me.

I'm shoved against the rungs as the car's sides slide up my back, and lifted upward. The elevator glides into place in front of door ONE. My ribs, trapped between the elevator and the rungs, won't expand. I'm glad I'm not claustrophobic, enclosed in my crowded little coffin of an alcove. I can't hear Sarah anymore.

Voices from inside the elevator reverberate through the walls against me like I'm a living stereo speaker.

Many, many booted feet tromp inside. Authoritative voices bark commands. Guns cock and gurney wheels squeak and people say medical things. The car shakes on its cables, pushing me even tighter against the metal that grinds into my chest and hips, pressing what's left of my breath from my lungs. Then a restless silence falls, and the elevator grinds back down, pulling me down while making its way to the lower level. I cling to my rung so tightly my fingers ache.

Then the elevator is gone, leaving me dangling free. I take a deep breath, just because I can. Then my feet find their rungs again.

Sarah climbs down to me. "Are you okay?"

"Yeah," I reply. "But there was a giant troop of soldiers waiting outside those doors. If we'd gotten them open before the elevator came to get them, we would have stumbled out right into their midst like a bunch of noobs."

Sarah nods. "We have to be more careful. Do you think the corridor is empty now? We can't stay in this shaft forever."

I shrug. "Sounded like it, but, without visibility it's hard to tell."

Above us, Bobo is getting restless. As soon as the cables stop moving, he leaps back over to them and kicks at the closed doors.

It's not a loud sound, but if anyone is on the other side, there's no way they could miss it. I cringe. We have to get that door open. The forbidden big red button. It

239

has to be an emergency release, right? What else could it be? Why else would it be here?

"We have to take our chances." Before Sarah can say no, I smash my hand against it.

The doors slide open.

Bobo immediately leaps out. Sarah scowls at me, but hurdles across the shaft and through the door. I follow them. As I get outside, Sarah bops me upside the head.

"That was dumb," she whispers. "No more pushing big red buttons until I say it's okay."

Behind us, the elevator doors close with a whisper. Fortunately, the lobby is clear. It's definitely a lobby. Unlike the rest of the utilitarian complex, this place is as decorative as it is functional, large enough to accommodate several dozen people, with white tiles on the floor and painted walls adorned with big paintings of the Air Force Space Command and NORAD. The American flag hangs on a pole near some fake potted plants. The main floor of Cheyenne Mountain. And somewhere around here we'll find the door that will take us out into the mountain tunnel and beyond.

The way out.

Above a pair of open double doors at the far side of the lobby, a glowing amber sign reads "exit." Nice to have something clearly labeled for a change. Between us and the exit, wide hallways branch off from the lobby, one to the right and one to the left. The fluorescent lights burn bright and harsh overhead. There's no furniture, no nooks, nowhere to hide. We need to get Bobo out of that exit. We're proverbial sitting ducks here.

In the cave's tunnel beyond the exit door, I can just

make out a guard post structure. It's about forty-five feet away. Two soldiers stationed there have their backs to us, watching the two mile long cave-like tunnel that leads outside the mountain. Out to where Daisy waits with the van. One guard is inside the small structure and the other paces outside it. She shifts and I can see she, like most of the soldiers here, carries a rifle.

"Simon."

I turn at Sarah's soft voice. She points to the number six lit up on a panel next to the elevator. It blinks out and number five lights up. The steady thrum of marching boots reaches us in stereo from both the right and left hallways, getting louder by the second. The elevator, behind us, blinks off number four.

Soldiers in front, soldiers coming from left and right, and more rising in the elevator behind us. We're surrounded. I don't want to engage with friendlies, but what choice do we have? I crouch down into a fighting stance and slide one of my throwing knives from my boot. Sarah undoes her necklace and pops out the grappling hook, but there's nowhere to grapple.

Bobo tugs me back with one shaggy arm and steps in front of me protectively. While I appreciate the instinct, it won't do much good considering the threat is coming from all sides.

The elevator light blinks on for the lobby level. It's here.

I put my back against Bobo's and prepare to fight, the throwing knife an uncomfortable weight in my hand. Sarah, with a tortured look on her face, swings her grappling hook around like a weapon. Neither of us want to hurt anyone, but we can't get caught. And I can't let them hurt Bobo. They'll be out for his blood, thinking he's a monster.

And since that's what they'll think, that's what he'll have no choice but to become.

Suddenly the lights blink out. All of them, everywhere, at one time. We're immediately plunged into deep darkness.

The marching feet pause, replaced by questions and yelling. The elevator doors don't open. Fists hammer on them from the inside, along with angry voices yelling for help.

But the elevator still doesn't open. Even the tunnel drowns in the complete darkness of the underground. Darkness like in the Cave of the Winds. Or like back home. I'm used to navigating this kind of suffocating blackness, and apparently Bobo is too now, because he's not freaking out. Our backs still press against each other and he's silent. The three of us stay calm, but the soldiers panic.

The ones in the hallways move again. Their footfalls get louder and heavier and faster, their voices shrill. Sarah lunges for the exit door. Bobo already heads that direction, so I follow. Maybe this was all part of the plan. Maybe it's supposed to be Bobo's one chance to get out and make his way back to the zoo. It's doubtful he could have made it this far without me and Sarah, but if he manages to get out before anyone finds him, then this whole attack looks even more like an inside job. Who would believe a rogue gorilla caused all this chaos if there's no gorilla there?

The amber sign, dark like the rest of the lights, no longer tells us where the exit is. We find it anyway and rattle down a few metal steps to the floor of the cave. Soldiers burst into the lobby behind us, barking commands and crashing into walls, which covers the sound of our escape. A muffled voice screams in terror, *the elevator doors are jammed.* A commanding voice tells them to focus their attention on opening those elevator doors, NOW!

Past the exit door, in the tunnel now, I reach out with my well-honed senses. Just a hint of a breeze fights against musky gorilla, human sweat, and the stale air of the cave. That's the way we need to go, towards that light whisper of fresh air. The tunnel's road is a flat, smooth surface under my feet. The sounds of chaos behind us fade and up ahead, the guards argue at their post.

"What happened to the lights?" the woman fumes. "Why aren't the emergency lights kicking on?"

"I don't know," the other voice snaps back. "It must be connected to the disturbance inside."

"What good are backups if they don't back up?" She growls.

Sarah's hand pats its way down my arm to find my hand. She grabs it with a quiet rustle of cloth and starts moving. Blind, I follow her lead and reach back towards the direction of Bobo's scent and his warm puffs of breath. He doesn't flinch at my touch as I search the massive wall of fur for his leathery hand. I drag him after us, surprised that he doesn't pull away.

He whimpers like a scared child, but I haven't forgotten those bodies inside or how brutal he can get. Am I doing the right thing bringing him out to Daisy? Can I protect her if he gets violent again? She believes in him and I hope she's right, because I can't leave him behind.

Even though the guards can't see us, I crouch low.

Sarah pulls us around the guards with a wide berth.

"Hey, my flashlight isn't working!" a guard says. "Somebody took out the batteries. What's going on here?"

"Hang on, let me get my cell phone," I hear a pocket unzipping. "I'll use that flashlight."

A dim amber string of emergency lights flickers on. They're like Christmas lights, showing location but not providing much illumination. It's just enough to make out the two massive blast doors looming in front of us. When I say massive, it's no joke. They're each about three and a half feet thick and must weigh twenty tons at least. I read they can close in forty-five seconds.

The light is just enough to see through the 2 inch thick plexiglass transparent backs of the doors. A dozen thick rods on either side stand ready to launch into the rock and seal the door once it shuts. They're made to withstand a nuclear blast. Nothing will move those doors once they're closed. And if they can't open them, anything outside stays out, and anyone trapped inside will stay in. In the terrifying, debilitating dark.

I feel a palpable relief once we're past them.

Off in the distance, more faint amber lights glow at spaced intervals, leading us along the road's curving path. By the time the soldier gets out her cell phone and snaps on the flashlight, we're around the bend. Her light sweeps the tunnel behind us, but it can't reach us now.

My eyes are getting used to the dark, but I don't see it when Sarah stops. I bump into her back, then Bobo bumps into me. He gives me a little shove.

"There," Sarah points to a tiny speck of light far off. "The entrance to the mountain is just under two miles away. Looks like more emergency lights are working out here."

I groan. "That's a long jog with a tired gorilla."

"Then let's get moving."

Bobo doesn't make a sound. He nuzzles up against me, almost knocking me over.

"Come on, big guy," I whisper. "Hope you're not too tired to go home."

We settle into a steady pace. I keep listening for sounds up ahead or pursuit from behind us, but all I hear are the quiet patter of our feet and the steady pant of our breathing. Soon we make out the stars in the night sky and lights of the city through the tunnel's entrance. It feels like freedom.

Almost there.

I remember the guards wandering around the tunnel entrance from when we looked down at it from above, but they're not here now. Did they pull back to the interior post when the chaos started? Whatever the reason, it looks like the coast is clear.

A light breeze, warm and soft, rustles into the tunnel, bringing with it a clean pine scent. Then we're out of the tunnel and jogging down the road towards the parking lot where we're going to rendezvous with Daisy.

I laugh out loud. I can't believe we made it out!

Maybe Sarah is right about plucky kids sometimes being able to do what lots of grown-ups can't. I doubt anyone expected two teenage spies and a gorilla (with a little mysterious electronic help) to invade the world's most secure military base. How could anyone possibly have prepared for that? We've stopped Bobo from doing whatever he was going to do, and I kept my promise.

Daisy waits for us. For me. I can still feel her petal-soft lips on mine. We saved the gorilla, foiled the plot, and I might even get the girl. Time to roll the credits.

Tension leaves my body as we trot into the parking lot. There are a few streetlights in the lot, bright enough that I can just make out the zoo van, tucked away behind one of the low buildings. They seem to have escaped the blackout at the base, but the winding road towards the sparkling city is just a black ribbon, lit only by the moon and stars. Daisy moves in and out of sight behind the buildings. It looks a little tall to be Daisy, but who else could it be? Exhausted beats at me like a hammer. I can't wait to get back to our house, declare victory, sleep until noon, and eat something besides chips. I'm so hungry. Maybe Daisy knows of a food truck that's still open this late.

> *Victory flies in*
> *On the wings*
> *Of a taco*

A smile creeps over my face as we cross the broad, flat asphalt of the parking lot. Daisy will bring the van around any second now.

But Daisy doesn't pull the van around.

Instead, a shadow peels away from the building. A hulking shadow, bald, broad-shouldered, and well dressed. He steps into the light. Sarah, Bobo, and I freeze simultaneously.

It's Dr. Dinkelmeyer. And standing next to him, almost lost in his muscular bulk, is the tall wiry figure of Beckman, from the zoo.

"Bobo, you've brought guests. This is a surprise," Dr. Dinkelmeyer drawls in a low, deep voice. "I don't like surprises."

And Beckman pulls out a gun.

21: SARAH IS IN OVER HER HEAD

At least it looks like a gun. It takes my tired brain a moment to realize it's actually the control device for that thing on Bobo's arm. The red light thing that we never took off his arm. I'm so stupid! I twist like lightning and grab Bobo's hairy wrist, tugging at the buckle so fast that Beckman barely has time to react.

He smashes down on the button just as I'm loosening the strap, but before I can get it off entirely. I'm still holding it when it buzzes and the red light flares. Stinging pain shoots up my arms. My hands tingle even after I've yanked them clear of the device. Bobo grunts and shakes his arm, the bracelet zapping and crackling, swaying loosely but still not coming off.

Beckman flips a screen out from the device, glaring at it intently.

"Well?" Dr. Dinkelmeyer seethes, keeping his eyes trained on us like a laser scope.

"He's been to all the right places." Beckman whimpers. "Bobo! Give bag."

Bobo growls and tosses him the little bag that I didn't even realize he was still holding. Beckman catches it and gives it a shake. Nothing comes out. Satisfied, he nods to the enormous man next to him.

"Looks like he deployed the package," Beckman says with satisfaction.

Deployed? No, he didn't have time. We interrupted him before–

"There's no way to know if he did it correctly. If these kids interfered," Beckman snarls, waving at us, "they might have thrown him off his game. It's not my fault. The technology worked flawlessly. Blame them. Obviously the subroutines opened the grates and turned off the lights, but I doubt we'll get any good video for the web now that they messed up our schedule. Our conspiracy friends will just have to work with what they have."

Dr. Dinkelmeyer frowns, an expression that looks natural on his face. A rough, sandpapery stubble covers his square jaw and upper lip, accentuating the scowl. I don't move a muscle as Dinkelmeyer replies to Beckman.

"The conspiracies have done their job distracting the authorities. If they can't use what we've already given them to rouse their army, then they are of no use to us. I'll prepare a squad to dispose of them if needed. We have more important issues here in front of us, like these children. What shall we do with them?"

A chill runs through me. I'm paralyzed, legs like jelly, breath coming in short, sharp gasps. This man is three times my mass, and he's looking at me like no sparring partner or instructor ever has. Here is a man who won't stop even after he's won, a man who won't pull any punches. There is a deep, deep anger in his eyes, like nothing I've ever experienced. And absolutely no compassion. He looks like he's used to getting what he wants. My life, my death, would be nothing more than a tiny bump in the road to him. This Phoenix Plan is real. It's not a game to him. Not a training exercise, not a show. Lethally real. We've jumped straight to expert level.

I've never been so scared in my entire life.

"I'm not pleased, Claude," he tells Beckman, locking cold eyes with me. "Not pleased at all. This step was hard to set up. There's no room for error or going back to fix it, Claude."

"Yes, I know," Beckman, or, apparently, Claude, replies. "It's these—"

"Please, call us 'meddling kids'," Simon quips. "I've always wanted someone to say 'if it weren't for you meddling kids'—"

"Shut up," Dr. Dinkelmeyer growls.

Simon falls silent.

"And if the creature has deployed the package properly," Dinkelmeyer demands of Claude. "Can we gain control of the systems and overload them? Blow the grid? This operation is pivotal to our plan. It needs to function as intended."

I'm right. The Phoenix Plan is to take out the city's power grid then blow up the generators and trigger an emergency lockdown, and do serious damage to the government.

But nothing blew up. The doors didn't close. So despite Claude's reassurances, we foiled the plan.

Right?

"Yes, if he set it up the way he was trained, it'll work. Our other agents are still in play." Claude says. "And Bobo extracted himself."

"Himself?" Simon laughs. "You think he made it out here all by himself?"

"Good," the giant man replies to Claude, ignoring Simon. "It works better without the soldiers capturing the monkey."

"Ape," Simon says.

Dr. Dinkelmeyer and Claude both glare at him.

Shut up, Simon, I try to project the words into his head. *This isn't a game.*

"I would advise you to not make me any angrier," Dr. Dinkelmeyer snarls at Simon. Before we can react, he holds up a camera and clicks our picture. "I'll have to find out just exactly who you are, or were."

Then he turns and walks away. Bobo sits in a slumped heap, pawing at his wrist and whimpering. Claude scrolls through something on the device in his hands.

Where is Daisy with the van? No, she's smart enough to stay out of sight while these bad guys are around, assuming they didn't already find her. And kill her. I shiver at the possibility. Where is the third person from the zoo? Is he lurking around the shadows? Burying Daisy's body?

Maybe I can make a break for it. Disappear into the shadows while they're talking, or use my grappling hook like a weapon. I could distract them long enough for Simon to get out his knives.

But I don't do any of that. I don't do anything at all. We could die. Die for real. Simon could die. Forever. The thoughts freeze me in place like cold ice crystallizing my spine from top to bottom. I'd always assumed with all my training and skills that once I was in the field, nothing would stop me. That I was invincible. That I really was that plucky kid who would always make it out by the skin of my teeth.

But I'm not. Suddenly I realize no one even knows we're here.

"Claude," Dinkelmeyer calls over his shoulder as he disappears into the shadows. "Take care of our guests."

Claude smiles as he raises the device.

"With pleasure. I'll catch up with you soon." He points the device at Bobo. Then, he presses the button.

Bobo screams.

22: SIMON GETS MAD

I'm mad. I do stupid things when I get mad.

Like taunt people who are trying to kill me. Just for the record, that's a stupid thing to do. Don't try this at home. But the man formerly known as Beckman points his little gadget at Bobo and hurts him. Adrenaline courses through my body. Tiredness and hunger melt away, my breath gets faster, my vision and mind get crystal clear.

"Stop it, Beckman," I snarl. "Nobody hurts my friends."

"That's DOCTOR Beckman," he yells.

"I bet that's not even your real name, *Claude*."

He ignores me. Sarah hasn't moved since she did a stare-down with Dr. Dinkelmeyer.

Beckman looks me in the eye, holds down a button, and says, "Bobo. Smash."

"That's your trigger word?" I sneer. "Super original. And that's sarcasm in case you didn't figure it out. It's not original at all."

Behind me, Bobo rises, a hulking shape in the darkness. There's danger in his eyes. He doesn't seem to know who I am, like he's a whole different animal. He saunters towards me, walking tall on his knuckles. I see Sarah in my peripheral vision, moving again. She's skirting around the ape, spreading out the targets and getting into a better position so we can attack from multiple sides. But I don't want to attack.

Claude watches eagerly from the sidelines. I think I hear someone call my name from behind the buildings, but it might be just a trick of the wind. But what if it's Daisy? What if she needs me? Why hasn't she come to get us yet?

Sarah and I circle Bobo, moving in and out of shadows, staying out of his reach. He whips around, trying to keep both of us in sight, pawing at the ground and making loud whuffling noises. I can tell he's getting scared, feeling threatened, and it's making him angrier. I stop in a pool of light and let him see me.

"Please Bobo." Half-singing the words, I hunch down and lift both hands to show I'm not a threat. "I don't want to fight you."

The streetlight shines down on my dark hair and shrouds my eyes in shadow. I tilt my head up so he can see my face, but I don't know if apes can even recognize human faces. He probably knows me by scent. Well, at least that's not a problem. After the two-mile jog and all the running around, I'm sure that smelling me is easy.

Whether or not he recognizes me, Bobo doesn't attack. He seems to be trying to stay calm. I want to keep him facing me, not Sarah, since he seems to like me better.

Then that horrible electric buzzing sounds again as Claude smashes more buttons.

"Bobo, smash," he growls through gritted teeth. "Smash!"

Bobo shakes his head like he's trying to clear out a bad dream, but his shoulders tense up. He smacks his fists against the ground and jumps up and down. Suddenly, his eyes glaze over, and he lunges.

I dodge out of the way, feeling his arm brush against me. He shoots past and before he can turn around, I've already danced out of reach. He howls and grabs at me again. I skip back several feet, trying to keep my face to him, trying to let him see me.

"Your knife, Simon," Sarah calls from the other side. "Get your knife."

But I don't. Instead, the next time he lunges, I roll under his arms and pop up behind him. We've maneuvered away from Sarah. She's eyeing the control box in Claude's hands and edges towards him.

"Take him out, Simon. You have to," she yells. "I know you don't want to, but you don't have a choice. Don't let him get a hold of you. He'll rip you to shreds. Maybe you can just knock him out, but you have to fight back!"

Claude glances at her just as she flips around in a spinning roundhouse kick, aiming for the device in his hands. She's like lightning, but he dodges with shocking agility for an old guy. Her leg skims just over the top of his hands. She lands with a bounce, flips to face him, and drops into a fighting stance, fists raised and ready in perfect, best-of-the-Island precision.

Claude towers above Sarah by over a foot, which gives him a longer reach, and more leverage behind his punches. The trick to fighting someone taller than you is to either stay inside or well outside of their reach.

I know which one Sarah will go for.

Sure enough, Sarah skips in close, too close for Claude to take advantage of his long arms and legs. She's sacrificing her ability to dodge, but she'll strike first and hard, hoping to take him out quickly. And she has another advantage. Claude wants to hang on to the thing he's controlling Bobo with, and keep it functioning. Sarah just wants to destroy it. Protecting the device is a serious liability for him, but his respectable-looking fighting stance mirrors Sarah's. He looks like he knows what he's doing. For a moment, they size each other up.

I'm only distracted for a second watching them. Bobo slams into me, sending me sprawling across the pavement. My head hits the ground, and the force of impact knocks the breath from my chest. I struggle to pull in enough air. Stars dance in front of my eyes and my mind spins. Bobo really turned on me. I thought we had a connection. My vision clears enough for me to see him loom over me, ready to pound both his raised fists into my skull. His arms hover. He pauses to stare into my eyes.

For a moment, everything is quiet. I look up into Bobo's confused face.

An ear-splitting scream comes from behind the buildings. Then, *thump*. Loud, like a huge sack of flour thrown to the ground. That scream sounded a lot like—

The van roars to life. Headlights shoot out from between the buildings, lighting up a dark form crumpled on the ground. Tires squeal and the van tears forward, swerving to avoid the dark lump as it streaks across the parking lot. It slams to a halt in front of Bobo. The door slides open.

—"DAISY!" I yell.

But it isn't Daisy who emerges from the van. It's a shadowy figure in a grey trench coat, wearing a matching hat with a wide brim. The third person standing with Claude and Dinkelmeyer back at the zoo. Shadows from the hat's brim obscure his face. From the ground where I lay, he looks upside down. My eyes dart to the lump on the ground near where the van used to be. It's not moving.

"What have you done to Daisy?" I scream at the figure.

Bobo, arms still raised to strike, turns to the shadowy man, then lumbers menacingly towards the van's open door. The shadow man doesn't flinch. He raises a calm hand at the oncoming beast.

Then he shoots Bobo.

"NO!" I flip around, my addled brain trying to reorient, and flop my arms and legs trying to scramble up. They don't respond like I want them to.

I expect the deafening crack of a pistol, but hear a tiny pop, like a cork pulling out from a bottle. Wires lead from the shadow's hand to Bobo's chest. Electricity crackles. Bobo's body goes stiff.

"Bobo!" I get an elbow under me and shove the front half of my body off the ground. I reach my other hand out towards him, but what could I possibly do to help?

The gorilla falls like a toppled statue right into the van. The shadowy figure heaves him the rest of the way inside, hops in after him, and slams the door shut. Then, the van peels away, leaving a stinking cloud of burned rubber in my face. All that's left of the van and Bobo are two long black tire marks on the road.

I watch the van's tail lights disappear down the winding road and collapse to the ground again. Everything happens in slow motion. Really it's only been a few seconds. Sarah and Claude are as still as death, eyes locked on each other, each waiting for the other to make the first move, neither can afford to be distracted by the van. Behind them, deep in the darkness between the buildings, the crumpled pile lies still as death.

I force myself upright. Pain shoots through the entire left half of my body. My muscles scream. My left arm and leg just won't work. I hope nothing broke. A single gorilla's punch can shatter a human skull. Two thousand pounds of force. It's like being smashed by a compact car. I'm lucky to be standing at all.

The sheer fact that I'm still alive proves to me that Bobo didn't hit me as hard as he could have. I stumble towards the crumpled form.

Claude slings the control device at my head. Now that Bobo is gone, he doesn't need the device anymore, but I didn't expect him to throw it. I stop and lift a sluggish arm just in time. The remote smashes into it, the impact smacking my hand into my own face. In other circumstances it would be funny.

Then he throws a punch at Sarah's head. She blocks it and counters with a wicked left jab followed by a harder blow with her right. She lands them both square on his face, snapping back his salt-and-pepper head. At home when we spar, we pause to make sure the other person is okay after landing a good punch. Instinctively, Sarah pauses.

But this isn't a sparring session.

Claude's eyes blaze. He catches Sarah's upper arm. In the split second it takes her to realize her mistake, he spins her around into a headlock.

Then he squeezes his arms together and chokes the life out of her, lifting her onto her toes. She kicks out wildly, eyes desperate, scrabbling her fingers against his muscular arms, ripping at his flesh. It doesn't do any good.

I stumble towards them, my sense of time untethered, unable to tell if I'm moving fast or slow, if I'm watching my sister die in slow motion or if my brain just can't process it. I move forward, but with each step the distance between us seems to grow. Sometimes when you have a concussion, you walk backwards. Am I doing that now?

All I know is my sister needs me. There's no one else to help her. She needs me and I can't seem to get to her. It's like one of those bad dreams where you're running down a hallway towards a door that keeps getting further and further away.

Claude holds Sarah tight, gritting his teeth as she rips at his arms. She reaches a clawed hand toward his face and he shakes her hard. Her arms flap out like a rag doll, eyes bulging as much with shock as with lack of air. She hasn't lost a sparring session since she was twelve. But this opponent won't let her go, even if he wins.

Have you ever heard the expression "you'd win in a fair fight?" When you're a spy, when you're fighting for your life, there's no such thing as a fair fight. What does fair mean when two people are trying to kill each other? No actual fight is ever fair. Winning is more important than fair. Winning is more important than dead.

In horror, I watch helplessly as Sarah gasps for breath. Her face turns red. Drool pours from the corner of her mouth. Her eyes glaze over.

She does everything right. He pins her against his body as she kicks back at him, up on her toes unable to get any leverage. She tries to slip out of his arms, reach his face, claw at his eyes. Tilts her head forward and throws it back, but Claude is so tall, she only taps against his clavicles. She does everything right, but she's still losing the fight and I won't reach her in time.

We should have called for backup. We shouldn't be here alone.

Claude gives Sarah another shake. Her lips turn purple, her feet kick slower and slower. He leans back and lifts her entirely off the ground.

She makes a strange gurgling noise.

I reach down and pull a knife from my boot. Normally, I could hit Claude with no problem. If I were thinking clearly, seeing clearly, I wouldn't even worry about accidentally hitting Sarah. But I'm not thinking clearly. My hand shakes, fingers clunky and thick, my arm still a mess of screaming nerves. I can't be sure I'll hit a moving target at all under these conditions, much less not hit my sister's head. But what else can I do? I have to do something.

I drag myself a few steps closer. I'm getting stronger, each step coming a little faster, but as I watch Sarah's eyes roll upwards and I see her body twitch, I know I can't get there in time to save her.

Claude knows it too. A wicked smile creeps across his face as she slumps forward, her head falling over his arm. He relaxes a bit in victory, his back slumping under Sarah's heavy, dead weight. It's just a fraction of an inch. He thinks she's given up.

But no. Not my Sarah. Sarah never gives up. Claude slumps just far enough for her to get her feet flat on the ground. Her legs snap straight and her head slams back, right into his face.

He howls in pain. Blood pours from his nose as the howl turns into a strangled gargle. He coughs blood all over her face and shoulder, trying to reestablish his grip on her neck. With her feet solid under her, Sarah elbows him in the gut, forcing his breath from his body. His grip loosens.

Sarah grabs the arm around her neck with both hands and ducks low, knocking him off balance with a backwards thrust of her hips. She curves her back and throws him over her head. He sprawls on the ground, dazed, then rolls on his side and coughs, spitting up more blood.

Sarah sucks in great lungfuls of air with a wheezing rasp, bracing herself with her hands on her knees. She blinks rapidly, then suddenly seems to notice Claude laying on the ground in front of her.

She opens up her mouth to say something witty, wiping away a long string of drool with the back of her hand. No words come out.

Finally she gives up and settles for a swift kick to Claude's head.

23: SARAH SHOULD HAVE CALLED IN REINFORCEMENTS

I kick Claude in the head. It feels spectacular.

My throat burns. Coughing feels like I'm rubbing sandpaper along the inside of my neck. Drool pools in my mouth and my muscles rebel when I try to swallow. So I spit, but can't suck in enough air. Instead, drool drips, uncontrolled, from my mouth. I look down at Claude, wanting to feel victory. Instead, I can't shake the feeling of dangling from his grasp, my air disappearing, my vision blacking out. Sounds muted, like plastic wrap covering my ears.

Claude moans. I lift my foot to kick him again.

But before I can, a loud, slow clap echoes from the shadows on the far side of the lot. A car fob beeps, headlights turn on, and an engine roars to life with a throaty growl. A massive muscular silhouette blots out the headlights. They flare out around him like an angry sun.

"Dr. Dinkelmeyer," I rasp. "I thought you'd gone home."

He steps forward, into the light where we can see him more clearly. He's not smiling, but he does raise an eyebrow. "Hmm. You seem to have me at a disadvantage, young lady. You know who I am. Who might you be?"

I consider saying "your worst nightmare" but decide against it. Instead, I just stare at him.

Simon still looks woozy. He's standing and walking, but swaying enough to make me wonder if he has a concussion. I hope Dinkelmeyer is just here to taunt us. I don't think we can take another fistfight.

Dr. Dinkelmeyer scowls at my silence. "Very well. I suppose it doesn't matter. My associates can find anything on the internet. They'll soon track down everything about you from your photo. Your parents, your birth certificates, even your favorite restaurant."

Joke's on you, I think. He'll run himself dizzy chasing after an internet trail for us. Agent Zero won't be pleased that he got a picture, another in a long line of things she won't be pleased about. Of course, assuming we live long enough to report in, we can't actually report in at all. Deep inside of my aching chest, part of me smiles at the fact that if Dr. Dinkelmeyer kills us tonight, he'll never solve the mystery of who we are.

"I underestimated you. Claude doesn't fail very often. But I can't have you interrupting my plans. They're too important." He pulls out a gun. A real gun, not a control device or a taser, and points it dead at me.

I cough again, ripping more sandpaper against my throat. The hand I wipe across my mouth comes back tinged with blood.

Simon scrambles over. He's dragging one foot and holding one of his arms at a funny angle. He still looks dazed. Not a surprise the way his head cracked when it hit that pavement. A cold part of me thinks that he's being sloppy and merging the target for the enemy. Another part is just happy he's here.

"Ah." A smile, no less terrifying than his frown, spreads across Dinkelmeyer's face as he realizes Simon's tactical error of joining me. "I thought you might be trained agents, but now I see you're nothing but lucky amateurs. Are you sure you won't save me some trouble and tell me who you are?"

"We're your worst nightmare," Simon says.

Oh no, Simon. No.

Dinkelmeyer lets out a sharp laugh.

"At least you have a sense of humor," he drawls. "I enjoy a good laugh now and again."

"What's your plan?" My voice is hoarse and still raspy, but I push the sound out. "If you're going to kill us anyway, you might as well tell us. Brag a little."

He narrows his eyes at me shrewdly. "You won't bargain for your life? Ask for a few minutes to say goodbye. Plead on your hands and knees?"

I glare at him. I'm bloody, a gasping, limping mess. But I hold my head up and stumble in front of Simon. "I don't plead."

"Good." He nods approvingly. "I can't stand pleading. Unfortunately, though, I won't be going into some long monologue. I'm not some rank amateur. I'll just kill you and carry on. Goodbye, it was nice chatting."

He raises the gun and points it at my head. Simon snuggles up against me as I squeeze my eyes shut. I reach out to grab his hand, but it's not there. I crack one eye open just in time to see a blur of movement and hear a *whirr* whiz past my ear.

Simon's hand is outstretched, the way it gets after

he throws his knife.

Metal flashes as the knife spins through the air and thunks square into the meaty back of Dinkelmeyer's hand. He yelps in surprise and pain. The gun falls into the darkness. I hear it skitter away across the parking lot.

Up the mountain road, the tunnel into Cheyenne Mountain lights up. The floods around the entrance come on, and some headlights and flashlight beams flare out from the inside. Jeep engines rumble, and I can hear commands being shouted in crisp, military style in the distance.

Dr. Dinkelmeyer frowns up towards the commotion. He pulls Simon's knife from his hand, glares at it, then smiles at us as he licks his own blood off the knife.

"I've wasted too much time on you. Now I'm behind schedule, and those soldiers who are heading this way. It's time for me to go, but don't worry, I'll find you and get rid of you when you least expect it." He turns without a second look and casually swings himself into the driver's seat of the Hummer.

The Hummer shoots straight at us. I grab Simon's hand and squeeze it tightly. He squeezes back. I tug him out of the way, hoping we're covering enough ground, but Dinkelmeyer doesn't even swerve. He just disappears into the night.

Simon collapses into me as soon as the truck passes. I sling his arm around my shoulders and watch the Hummer's tail lights disappear down the road below.

Suddenly I remember Claude. I turn to where I left his prone form, but it's an empty patch of asphalt. He's gone, only the dark pool of blood from his broken nose left behind.

"We need to go too," I rasp at Simon. "Those soldiers from the mountain will be out looking for someone to blame. They won't know we're the good guys and we can't tell them who we are."

A cool breeze dries some of my sweat, but my little brother and I both stink. We're spotted with blood, limping and dizzy. But we're alive. It's been a long night, and as the city sparkles below us, I realize it's far from over. It's going to be a long walk home.

As I tug Simon towards the road, he suddenly pulls away and drags his sore leg back towards the buildings at an awkward run.

"Daisy!" he calls. "We have to find her!"

24: SIMON'S SURPRISE

I drag my aching body across the parking lot, towards the back of the buildings where Daisy was supposed to be waiting. Towards the dark lump laying on the ground. As I limp nearer, the lump takes the shape of a sprawled body. I rush over, the pain in my leg disappearing under the force of my fear. Sarah follows at a distance, monitoring the military's activity above us.

I flop down beside Daisy's still form, brushing her soft garnet hair away from her face. It looks extra pale in the moonlight. With trembling hands, I feel for a pulse. She's warm and stirs at my touch.

I let out my breath in one long sigh of relief. Daisy's eyes flutter open. The breeze plays with her hair as I help her sit up. She rubs her head and looks around.

"Simon? What happened? Where's Bobo?" Then she blinks. "Wait, where's the van?"

"What's the last thing you remember?" I ask in a gentle voice.

"I was waiting in the van. Then I heard something, and got out to see if it was you guys," her face clouds over, "and there was something, well, someone I think. It scared me. And I don't remember anything else."

That shadowy figure in the grey coat. Who is he? What does he want with Bobo?

"Did you get a look at his face?" I ask.

She shakes her head. "All I saw was a shadow."

"We have to get moving," Sarah chokes out.

"Oh my gosh, Sarah," Daisy says as I help her stand. "You sound terrible. Are you okay?"

Sarah nods once, then motions for us to follow. The beams from individual flashlights pour out of Cheyenne Mountain's entrance tunnel above us. The soldiers move around up there like ants swarming out of a kicked over anthill. An ambulance shoots out of the tunnel, siren blaring, and careens down the road past us. We press against the wall of one building, hidden from the main road.

Once the ambulance passes, things settle down a bit. Some flashlight beams move back inside. A military truck emerges and parks by the front. Its headlights shine on the road, but they don't reach down here.

"What's going on?" Daisy follows us towards the dark road.

"The shadow guy took the van. It's gone and we need to get out of here," Sarah says.

"What, we're going to WALK all the way back to Colorado Springs?" Daisy groans.

"Unless you have a helicopter hidden in your pocket." Sarah heads off down the road without a backwards glance, trusting me to follow. "Let's get moving. Those soldiers will be here soon."

I try to help Daisy, but stumble against her as we walk down the long, dark road. She lifts my arm across her shoulders, and stretches her own around my waist, supporting me. She feels strong at my side. Warm and safe and soft. Like she belongs there.

"You don't look so good," she whispers. "Are you alright? Bobo didn't do this to you, did he? I mean, you'd be a splat on the tarmac if he'd gone ballistic on you. So I'm assuming it was someone else."

"I'll be fine. Just a little bruised." It's mostly bravado. I'm more than a little bruised, but I don't want her to worry.

"You're avoiding the question. Who did this to you?"

"Okay, it was Bobo," I admit. "But it wasn't his fault. Oh, Daisy, you should have seen him inside the facility. He was magnificent. We had a genuine connection. I held his hand. He helped us get out."

She stops and looks up at me with tears in her eyes. For a moment she stands still, looking at me with an expression I can't read. Then she breathes, "So you really got him out?"

I smile, and gently nudge her to keep walking. "Yeah. We got out together."

"Then," she looks around. "Where is he?"

"Remember the shadow that knocked you out and stole the van? He took Bobo. He had a taser. I don't think he wanted to hurt him, though, or he could have just rammed him with the van."

"He was gorillanapped?"

I nod.

"What? We have to find him."

"We can look for him once we get back to town." I reassure her. "Right now we have to get off this mountain,"

"I guess so. I mean, if anyone is in trouble, it's the gorillanapper, right?" Daisy chuckles and speeds up to catch up with Sarah. "Bobo isn't going to let some random guy hurt him, and if he feels threatened, he could totally break out of that van in no time.

Apparently he knows how to find his way back to the zoo, so I guess we don't have to worry about him right now."

"I wish I could get some footage of him going back into the zoo so I could make that video. Then he'd really be out of danger. The zoo would keep an extra close eye on him." And it would destroy the conspiracies, but of course I don't tell her that.

Daisy nods, deep in thought. Then she shrugs. "I'm just glad you got him out. I'm glad he didn't squash you. How did you connect with him?"

"He just needed a little reassurance that not everyone in the world is trying to hurt him." I hold her tighter than I actually need to for support. "You were right, Daisy. You laid the groundwork. You knew him, and you were right."

Daisy doesn't say anything for a while.

It's quiet as we walk. Daisy hasn't even mentioned how bad I stink. She really is amazing. Below us, the lights of the city still seem so far away, but I can't bring myself to be upset about it. The warm air and refreshing light breeze soothe my aches. These may not be ideal circumstances, but to be here in this beautiful setting with my arm around Daisy, her arm around me, it feels right in a way I've never known.

"Thank you for saying that," Daisy's voice is so quiet I barely hear it. "It's weird. I don't think anyone has ever made me feel so accepted, so seen before. I've never met anyone like you, Simon."

The road clings to the mountainside, switching back on itself again and again as it makes its way cautiously down the steep incline. The moon is bright enough that we aren't in much danger of plummeting over the road's shoulder or walking into the occasional solid cliff on the other side of the road.

Sarah coughs again and spits. The sound brings flashes in my mind. Images of her purple face, her eyes rolling back. I'm worried about her. Not because of her injury, she's had worse, she's tough. Physically she'll be fine. But she's been uncharacteristically quiet, and I don't think it's just because of her throat. There's doubt in her posture. I can't remember the last time I've seen Sarah anything but sure of herself. I guess being brought to the brink of death changes a person.

When Bobo smashed me, I didn't feel any sort of failure. He's stronger than me. If he'd chosen to squash me, there wasn't anything I could do about it. No one's life was at risk because I messed up, not even my own. It was like jumping off a cliff, or skateboarding on the side of a volcano. Just me up against a force of nature. Some days you win, some days you lose.

Throughout our training, whenever an agent held our head underwater, or swept our feet out from under us, or stuffed us into a tiny locked box we had to escape from, we'd always been prepared for it, known the exercise was teaching us something, and known that at the end, if the agents had to, they'd let us out. Sarah hated knowing she was being protected. She's always wanted to pit herself against real challenges.

I can only imagine how she's feeling now. The first time she goes head to head with someone who isn't protecting her, she almost loses. Really loses. I imagine she's confused. And furious. And when Sarah gets angry, she becomes not unlike a force of nature herself. She's got something to prove.

I wouldn't want to be Claude right now.

We continue on in silence about a mile down the road.

A shape rises from the darkness on the mountainside above us. It takes form before we can register what's happening and launches into Sarah like a missile. No noise, no warning. She tumbles to the ground underneath it, taken completely by surprise.

Daisy freezes, then slips out from under my arm, taking a few steps towards Sarah. Ahead of us, Sarah is on her stomach in the middle of the road. A tall grey-haired man sits on top of her, yanking her arms behind her back and wrestling them into a length of rope. It's too fast for any of us to react. He tugs the rope tight and stands to face me.

It's Claude.

One of his feet is on Sarah's back above her bound arms, holding her face down on the ground. A ragged scream comes from her damaged neck. She lashes back and forth on the ground like a shark in a fishing boat, unable to flip herself upright. I stare at her. It all happened in less than thirty seconds.

I lunge at him but I'm off target. He grabs me and uses my momentum to swing me into an off-balance headlock, my back to Claude and my legs sprawled over Sarah's body. I can see Daisy in front of me, frozen. She looks angry and confused.

"Beckman?"

"That's DOCTOR BECKMAN!" Claude screams.

One of my off-balanced feet is all that holds me off of Sarah's chest. As I shuffle the other foot over her to get my balance, Claude loosens his grip just enough that I crush Sarah beneath me. Claude and my combined weight bear down on her ribcage. I squirm but that makes me crush Sarah, her breath forced from her lungs by my weight. She grunts and I stop, concentrating instead on keeping my weight off her and keeping Claude from pressing his foot down. Sarah stops thrashing but her growl sounds ominous from her raspy throat.

"Daisy! Quick! Grab a rock or a stick and hit him over the head!" I yell. "I know you can do it!"

Claude jerks at my neck. It's a warning to stay quiet. I tug at his arm, but he's surprisingly strong, and even taller than I am. I prepare to flip him as soon as Daisy springs into action.

But Daisy squinches her mouth to the side and puts her hands on her hips. She narrows her eyes at me. No, not me, she's glaring at the man behind me.

Sarah manages to twist around, knocking Claude off of her. He drops me and skips a few steps away. I lunge towards him, but stop short as he raises a gun at us. It looks like the gun I knocked out of Dr. Dinkelmeyer's hand. He must have found it when he ran away.

"You again," Sarah hisses. "Where did you come from?"

"Shut up and put your hands on your head." He waggles the gun at her.

"Why didn't you just pull that gun out in the first place?" I ask. "Why did you tackle us at all?"

"I—," he pauses, and glances at the gun. "Yeah well, shut up. I've got the gun now so raise your hands."

"Idiot," Sarah rasps under her breath as I lift my hands above my head.

She's already Houdini'd out of the rope he tied around her wrists and tosses it at him as she lifts herself to a standing position. It bounces off his face and falls harmlessly to the ground at his feet. He doesn't even flinch.

We're standing on the side of the road in front of a steep drop, with nowhere to go. Sarah glances at the cliffside below us.

She has no choice and lifts her hands with a sour expression. "I hate you."

Daisy hasn't moved except to cross her arms over her chest and shift her hips to one side. I don't know why Claude hasn't just shot us. He seemed perfectly happy to kill us before. The only difference between then and now is that now Daisy is here with us.

"That's not Beckman, Daisy," I say. "He's working for a notorious criminal."

"Criminal?" Claude gasps. "How dare you! And I don't work *for* him. We work together. We're liberators. Heroes. You? You're the criminals. I'm sure the police will be very interested in the people who broke into Cheyenne Mountain. Doctor Beckman looks forward to a substantial reward and a hero's welcome when I turn you in. You're just kids, aren't you? Imagine, teenagers, able to get into the most secure military complex in the world. It's going to humiliate the military, they'll have to make an example of you. Your story will be more popular on the internet than that pooping cat! Have you seen that wacky little guy? He's hilarious."

"We're not criminals, we're the good guys," I reply. "Daisy, come on, while he's got the gun trained on us. Get him!"

Claude chuckles. "Damsel, there are some zip-ties in my pocket. Come get them and get these idiots contained. They're more dangerous than they look."

Wait. "Daisy?"

Daisy throws her hands into the air in exasperation. "Dammit Claude, I had everything under control. What are you playing at here? This is completely unnecessary. Now we'll never know who they are."

My mind goes blank. "Daisy?"

She pulls the plastic cords out of Claude's pocket. "I'm sorry Simon. I really am. I was hoping it wouldn't come to this. And it wouldn't have if Doctor Stupid over here hadn't been, well, stupid."

"Oh, so now you call me Doctor?" Claude scowls.

"Only a doctor of stupid, Claude," Daisy turns to me and her voice softens. "I really didn't want this to happen."

My head spins. "Daisy?"

"Simon please," she pleads. "Stop. I didn't–I don't–I was hoping you wouldn't have to find out. Spending time with you, it's just been so–"

"You've been lying to us? To me?"

"No!" She fiddles with the zip-ties. "I just, you know, I mean I told you I have some secrets. You haven't told me yours, and I haven't told you mine. I'm not lying to you any more than you're lying to me."

Claude nudges her in the back with his elbow. "Enough. Tie them up, let's get out of here before the soldiers widen their search."

"Why are you even here, Claude?" she asks. "And more importantly, why was Bobo here? You said he wouldn't get hurt. You said he was just a distraction to encourage people to dig into military secrets. But you sent him against soldiers with guns with no backup. That wasn't the plan."

Claude sneers. "It was always the plan, Damsel. He told *me* everything. I guess he just trusts me more. You've always had a soft spot for that dumb ape, ever since the circus. Why did you let these kids follow him? Who are they? Did you find out anything about them? Did you at least find out where they live? We'll want to look through whatever intel they've gathered."

Daisy pauses. She glances at me from the corner of her eye. "What, do you think they gave me their actual address?" She chuckles. "How stupid do you think they are? We were on our way to their place now, but I guess we'll never know the location, thanks to you. No one was supposed to get hurt, Claude."

Claude rolls his eyes. "Don't worry, he'll get all the information he needs out of them. Why do you think they're still alive? He never fails. You're soft, Daisy. You think you're such a badass warrior for justice, but if you keep getting wrapped up in each individual monkey, you'll be more trouble than you're worth."

"You're an idiot Claude. Don't you get it? This world needs change, we both know it. That's why we're doing what we're doing. But if we lose sight of the ones we're trying to help, we've already lost. Bobo is innocent in all this. We can't use and discard innocents. If we do, we're no better than they are." She motions vaguely towards the soldiers up on the mountain.

Claude just shakes his head. "You are so naïve. Just get these two contained and we can take it up with Dinkelmeyer."

"Why don't you just kill us, Beckman," Sarah rasps. "Think you'll fail like you did in the parking lot?"

Daisy glares at Claude. "You tried to kill them? Dammit Claude, is that why they look so awful? What have you done?"

"He told me to. Take it up with him, now get those zip-ties on them or so help me I'll shoot you all."

Daisy gives me one last pitiful look, throws an angry scowl back at Claude, and steps forward, raising the plastic ties towards me. I don't even resist. I just lower my hands and hold them out to her, palms up. Under my breath, I hum the lullaby. A look of sadness crosses Daisy's face. Her eyes dart to Claude for a moment and her expression hardens. She glances at Sarah, meeting her eyes.

For one moment, as she brings the ties towards my outstretched arms, Daisy steps between us and Claude blocking us from his line of fire. The second it's obscured, Sarah immediately drops to the ground, sweeping my feet out from under me.

I fall.

Training kicks in and I tuck into a ball, rolling down the hillside, arms protecting my head. Sarah throws herself after me, rolling down the slope nearby. Sagebrush and rocks beat against me as I fall farther and farther away from Claude.

Away from Daisy.

I hear a gunshot go off back up the mountainside, followed by three more in quick succession. The ground on one side of me explodes in a shower of dirt and rocks. I roll and roll, branches tearing at my clothes, until I feel myself slowing to a stop as the ground levels out.

I stay tucked into a ball, shaking. All my energy bled away. Then I hear Sarah's voice, and feel her hands tugging at my arm.

"Up. Up, we have to go."

I try to make sense of what she's saying. "Go? But

what about Daisy? What if she's hurt? What if he shot her?"

"Daisy? Seriously?" Sarah's voice sounds better, not as raspy. Which makes it worse. It makes it more real now that she's sounding like Sarah again. "It was an act, Simon. She's one of the bad guys. Come on, Claude still has that gun. Man, I hate that guy."

She looks up the hillside to where we came from. We've rolled far, far down the steep slope. There's no light up there, no way to see what's happening on the road. Sarah yanks me up to stand next to her. Then she slides a bit on the gravel as she pushes me away from the road.

"No, you're wrong," I protest. "She's not a bad guy. It's all some kind of misunderstanding."

She grabs me by the shoulders and looks deep into my eyes. "Daisy betrayed us, Simon. Don't be stupid. I know it sucks, I liked her too, but we have to deal with reality."

"No, that's not possible." I wrestle out of her grip. I won't believe it. I know Daisy's heart, she can't be evil.

Sarah groans and turns away. She makes her way through the sagebrush, getting further and further ahead. I walk, but it seems like I'm walking through a dream. My legs follow Sarah, but I look back towards the road. What were those gunshots? Did Claude shoot at us or Daisy? When she stepped between us and Claude and gave us a chance to escape, did she do it on purpose? She must have. She's secretly on our side. And if she is, did Claude shoot her for it? What if she's up there somewhere, bleeding? What if she needs me?

But no more sounds come from the road above us. No girl looks over the side to see if we're okay.

Nobody gets thrown over the edge, either. Up on a much higher section of the road, beams of light cut through the darkness. Military trucks start coming down the road. The rumble of their engines and heavy tires reverberates all the way to where we are.

I can't go back there.

Sarah slides, jumps, and picks her way down the mountain as far from the road as she can get. I take one step, then another, and follow my sister towards the cheery, sparkling lights beneath us. My legs feel heavy. My arms and shoulders are wooden.

"Where are we going?" I ask, not really caring. "Is it safe to go home?"

Sarah calls back to me in a low voice, "I don't know where else to go. We're covered in blood and dirt and obviously injured. We need to go to ground, clean up and get some rest. Anywhere else we could go is going to be filled with people asking too many questions. Sounds like that girl is covering for us, for whatever reason. That doesn't mean we can trust her, but we'll have to take a chance."

> *My heart, filled with lead*
> *My feet, filled with lead.*
> *A long walk back to the house.*

25: SARAH'S DECISION

My phone blinks on the nightstand where it's been sitting since last night. I roll away and tug the blanket over my head. I didn't close the shades before collapsing into bed, and now the sunlight streams in through the open window. It paints the room a cheery yellow color.

Everything hurts. I know the blinking light means I should check my messages, but I just lay in bed for another twenty minutes. Then, I stagger into the bathroom and let hot water pour over my head while steam fills the shower. Twenty more minutes later, wrapped in a slightly too-small towel, I make my way back into the bedroom.

The sheets smell horrible. They're stained with grass and dirt from my hair and the clothes I didn't take off last night. The clothes that are now in a stinky pile on the bathroom floor. Nobody has snuck in to bring them to the laundry. Nobody has changed the sheets since we arrived. I try to remember when the sheets back home even got changed. I never really thought about it. They've just always been clean.

I strip the bed and sit on the naked mattress, the sheets in a pile on the floor. The light on my phone still blinks evenly. It hasn't sped up or anything so I don't think I'm in trouble. Yet.

I dig out my last clean pair of underwear and find some pants and a shirt that pass the sniff test.

Then I go looking for coffee. A wave of homesickness washes over me. I miss Gus. I miss his coffee and his hash browns and his overly fancy meals. I miss the invisible housekeeping people that changed my sheets and washed my underwear.

I miss feeling invincible.

A heavenly, caffeinated smell wafts from the kitchen and I can hear water percolating in the coffee machine. I don't think I could love Simon any more than I do at this moment.

Steam drifts lazily from the mug he holds out to me. I wrap my hands around it and lean against the wall in the empty spot where the table used to be. Simon gets the milk out of the fridge and sets it on the counter, stepping lightly around the pile of dishes on the floor. Then he grabs a mug emblazoned with a yellow sun-glassed happy face on one side and the words "smile like it's Friday, baby" on the other.

Simon is not smiling like it's Friday.

"What time is it?" I mumble, reaching for the milk. Its putrid odor assaults my nostrils. I glance at the expiration date, and set it back on the counter, pouring extra sugar into my mug instead.

"Eleven thirty," he tells me with dubious accuracy, not even bothering to look.

I dig my phone out of my pocket and toss it on the counter. The light on the side continues to blink, steady and patient. "Agent Zero has something to tell us."

Simon nods. His phone sits on the counter too. He unlocks it and slides it over to me. The screen flares to life with a single message: "Congratulations on successfully completing your first assignment. Look forward to your full report. -Agent Zero."

I raise an eyebrow at my little brother. He shrugs.

"Isn't there any more?"

"Yup, take a look."

What looks like security footage shows Bobo climbing back inside the zoo over a broken part of the wall. Below it, there's a list of multiple websites where it's posted. It looks like all the conspiracy sites have gotten ahold of the footage. A video, just like the one we'd planned, is getting a ton of views along with the raw footage. A cute, harmless ape bumbles out of the zoo and messes around at some local tourist traps with text splashed across the screen saying "Gorilla Takes a Vacay," then the security video of him going back in. All to upbeat music. A lot of the footage is from Simon's camera. Most of the clips streamed to DAAAD as he shot it, so no wonder Agent Zero thinks the video is our work.

Comments fill the pages. Just as we'd hoped, it looks like almost everyone believes the gorilla was just an ape out on the town. It's clear he's sneaking back in of his own free will. Mystery solved. The "Escaped Ape" is quickly becoming a folk hero. There's no more talk of a supersoldier. And there's no mention of an incursion into the Cheyenne Mountain compound at all.

It's been executed as well as if Simon had done it himself. So who did it?

Agent Zero doesn't seem to know about last night, and she certainly hasn't found out about Dr. Dinkelmeyer or the Phoenix Plan, or that light would flash a lot faster. In fact, she seems to be proud of us. Simon listlessly watches me scroll through the conspiracy sites. Then he takes his phone from me.

"Here's one from a local station. You'll want to see

this one." He clicks play, holding the phone screen so I can see it.

I lean my head against his shoulder as we watch. A reporter stands in front of the zoo's ape enclosure. There are a lot more visitors than usual milling around behind her.

"Security at the Cheyenne Mountain Zoo is under scrutiny today as unconfirmed reports indicate that one of their gorillas has been sneaking out at night to enjoy all that Colorado Springs has to offer. Though there is no solid evidence regarding the truth behind these claims, one of the zoo's head zookeepers has resigned over the allegations. This zookeeper, Mr. Beckman, was hired recently to oversee the new gorillas. His resignation closes the books on a series of reports and rumors around town. This is Becky Chambers with KKTV News 11, at the zoo. Back to you, Ted."

I lean against the wall. "Well, that's good news."

Simon shrugs.

Then another headline catches my attention. Dozens of Cheyenne Mountain Space Force soldiers injured in a training accident. Two are in critical condition, but expected to survive. No deaths reported. I read that again.

No deaths reported.

A lump forms in my throat and things get blurry. I take a gulp of coffee and wipe at my eyes before Simon can see the tears of relief.

"Looks like Bobo is back home safely. The shadow gorillanapper may not have been on our side, but they helped us out anyway by saving Bobo. At least he's safe." Simon scrolls back to the security video and zooms in. There's a notch in the ear of the gorilla climbing back into the zoo. If there were any doubt, it's gone now.

I place a hand over his. "I'm glad."

He squeezes my hand, then tries to set his mug in the sink on top of the pile of dishes. There's no room, so he places it on the counter instead. I wave my empty cup at him and he refills it without another word.

I breathe in the sharp, nutty scent of hot coffee as steam drifts around my nose. Maybe we can't cook, but Simon has really gotten the hang of this coffee maker. The cup warms my sore hands that are covered in tiny scratches. Our injuries will be mostly healed by the time we get back to the Island, disappearing like they were never even there, leaving no trace.

"What are we going to tell Agent Zero?" I ask. I expect Simon has already written a full report, coming clean and detailing every event from the past few days. But he just shrugs and looks out the window.

"Whatever you want," he says without emotion.

I pause. "It looks like we took down the Phoenix Plan. I mean, nothing happened in that generator room. If the mountain had locked down after we left, it would have been all over the news, right? No civil war, no collapsed governments. We aren't living in the Dinkeltopia this morning. I can't believe we did it. And survived."

He shrugs again. "Bobo protected us. He was on our side all along. You just didn't believe in him."

"I know, I'm sorry. But you did. You were right about him, and your instinct saved us. Nice work, little bro." I put a hand on Simon's shoulder, but he just turns and walks into the front room, letting my hand slip off. I follow him. "Do you think we should try to get back in and verify that Bobo didn't actually plant some weird device? I know it's over but, I don't know, I feel like there should be some big sign blinking 'mission accomplished' or something."

"There's no way we could get back in there alone. The only reason we got inside in the first place is because of the subroutine Beckman planted in their systems. The one that opened the grates. Plus, I'm sure the base is on high alert now that everyone is–" He swallows hard. "Everyone's in the wind. Besides, they said timing was important. I agree that if Phoenix was, as Dinkelmeyer put it, set alight, we'd know by now. Chalk one up for the ape."

He flops on the sofa. I climb over the coffee table and sit by his side in silence. "I guess out here in the real world things don't always wrap up with a big, red bow when you win. We've saved Bobo and no one even died. Phoenix crashed and burned. Roll credits, maybe wait for the post-credits scene, right?"

Except now I have to make the hardest decision yet. I have to decide whether we tell Agent Zero what really happened here or not. Do we tell her about Dinkelmeyer, that we infiltrated Cheyenne Mountain, and about the Phoenix Plan? Or do we keep her and DAAAD in the dark, and just let them think we solved the rumor problem with a clever video?

In retrospect, that was a stupid plan. I just wanted Agent Zero to be proud of me, and now I've layered lie upon lie.

So now what do we do? If we tell Agent Zero the truth, she'll put us on perpetual desk duty and Simon and I will never see the outside world again. Or maybe she'll throw us out into the cold. That's spy lingo for getting fired. Somehow, we'd have to live normal, boring lives as accountants or something, assuming they didn't send us to rot, forgotten, in some secret prison somewhere. No matter what, she'd be disappointed in us. In me.

Not only would getting burned suck for us, it also wouldn't be fair to DAAAD. Agent Zero invested a lot in preparing us for the field. If we never go out on another mission, that's seventeen years down the drain.

But how do you keep secrets from an entire network of spies? And also, even if we foiled the Phoenix Plan, DAAAD needs to know about it. It's a pretty big deal that Dinkelmeyer is targeting first world countries. DAAAD could learn a lot from knowing the details of the plan, and what Dinkelmeyer was plotting. How can we put all that in our report without destroying our futures as spies?

In movies, heroes win, and that's the end of the show. My life should just auto-play the next episode. The hero doesn't have to make some big moral decision, they're too busy having a happy ending and walking away into the sunset with the love interest.

"Tell me she's okay," Simon rests his head against my shoulder, as if he could hear me think the words *love interest*. "It's not even what she did that bugs me, honestly. Daisy was just doing her job. And she's right, we both kept our secrets. I know she's not evil, not in her heart. She didn't want anyone to get hurt, you know. And now I'll never see her again. That's the worst part."

"I'm sure she's fine. She's strong. Believe in her." I'm surprised that the thought makes me feel better, too. I have so much to worry about, and someone who betrayed us and broke Simon's heart is pretty low on my priority list. Yet I can't help but like the girl. And I honestly hope the soldiers didn't shoot or catch her.

Simon nods and leans against me. I put an arm around him and he makes a small noise. Then, like he used to do when we were really young, he curls up and rests his head in my lap. I lay a hand on his hair as my mind drifts back to our decision.

"So the way I see it, we have two options for our report. We can either tell Agent Zero everything, or tell her nothing. Let her think we posted the videos and shut the book on the entire mission, or face the consequences of our–of my bad call."

Simon doesn't respond. He gazes out the front window watching the cars drive by on the street. A woman walks her dog and some kids chase each other down the sidewalk. He watches all the things we might never see again. All the exotic, normal things that he's been waiting his whole life to be part of, gone. Just because I didn't realize how much I still have to learn.

How will I ever become the agent I'm supposed to be if I'm not allowed to make a mistake here and there? I mean, I get it. When you're a spy, mistakes are expensive. They're expensive in very real ways, like people's lives. The right thing to do is to tell Agent Zero about Dr. Dinkelmeyer and Phoenix. Tell her everything and take our punishment.

I watch that beautiful, normal world outside with my heartbroken brother and know that I won't.

"No one can ever know, Simon. We can't tell anyone what really happened here. As far as they'll know, Bobo did just escape at night and play around. We found him, followed him, filmed him, and shut down the rumors. They can't ever know about Dinkelmeyer, or Claude, or Phoenix. Or Daisy. We can't ever tell. Understand?"

Simon closes his eyes and asks the same question that's haunting me, too. "How do you keep secrets from the head of a spy agency, or all of DAAAD?"

"I'll just have to solve that problem if it ever comes up." I try to sound confident. "As long as we have each other, everything will be okay. Are you excited to get back home?"

"Yeah, actually." He sits up and tries to smile. "I'll be sad to leave all this behind, but it's time, right?"

"One more thing before we go. Get your jacket." I stand and grab the car keys. I think I know how to bring that smile back for real. "Let's go to the zoo."

Simon beats me to the car.

***

The woman who had been sorting the audio tour lanyards the first time we came here is at the front gate today. I remember her name.

"Hi Tori, remember us?"

"Oh hey, the reporters. Back for more, huh? Seems like everybody's coming to see the Escaped Ape today. Sorry, Beckman's not here. He quit after the story broke about the gorilla getting out."

"Is Daisy here?" Simon asks with bright eyes.

"The intern?" Tori shrugs. "No idea. I haven't seen her, but then again, I've been here at the gate all day. Want to go see? Go ahead."

We thank her and head over to Gorilla World. There's a small crowd of people around the outdoor enclosure, pointing and staring in at the troop. Kids make monkey noises at them, but I doubt the gorillas can hear them through the thick viewing glass. The apes seem excited about something though. Restless.

Inside the gorilla house, people mill around in groups. Simon peers at all the faces one by one but doesn't find the face he's looking for. A woman of average height, serious looking and thin with a few grey strands in her brown hair, stands by the "employees only" door. She's checking off a few items on a clipboard. As I approach, she checks her watch.

"Hi." I smile, pulling out my fake business card. "Is Daisy Damsel in today? We're reporters with the Stratagem. She's been helping us with a story about the new gorillas."

"Oh yeah, the reporters." The woman glances at my card and checks her watch again. "Daisy told me about you. Where's the other one? The guy she said was cute?"

I point to my little brother, who presses his face against the window glass, looking at the two apes inside. Neither of them is Bobo. It looks like Moki and the baby, but Simon is making absolutely sure. I wave him over.

"Ah yes, that would be the one." The woman smiles. "No, I'm sorry. Daisy didn't show up for work today. Left us in a bit of a scramble, actually. We're releasing Bobo into the general population today and she's the best with him."

"Bobo?" I fish.

"Yes, the gorilla we've been keeping in isolation. I never agreed with Beckman about that approach. Now that Beckman is gone, I've taken over the integration. I'm the head of veterinary service here at the zoo."

"Pleased to meet you." Simon shakes her hand with a smile, but there's an edge of desperation in his voice. "Daisy introduced us to Bobo. I heard he was the one escaping. Is that true?"

The vet nods again. "We believe so. He's been in the isolation room, so we're double checking the security in there. He has a few injuries I can't explain. As you can imagine, all our security protocols and enclosures are being checked and rechecked. Honestly, part of me doubts that footage could even be real. But, that's for security to deal with. Meanwhile, you're here just in time for the release. Would you like to watch?"

She leads us into the back room. Bobo paces in front of the metal door that connects his room with the other one. He looks up when we enter. His eyes light up when he sees us, and he waddles over to the glass. Then he sits down on the floor. Simon sits on the other side and leans against the glass, putting his hand up against it. Bobo places his own hand on the other side. He's not wearing the bracelet with the red light anymore.

The vet blinks. "Oh my. I've never seen anyone except Daisy do that. I understand now why she liked you. It's Simon, right? She talked about you a lot. I'm going to miss her."

"You don't think she'll be back?" Simon asks.

The vet shakes her head. "No. She was only here on a summer internship. It was almost over anyway. And with Beckman gone—It's a shame. She was a good person. Sweet. And she sure cared for Bobo."

"Really?" I scoff. "You don't think it was an act? Just doing her job?"

The vet looks at me with a half-smile, like she's amused by my innocence. "No, trust me. I've been around. I know when someone is for real. You just can't fake that kind of affection. Speaking of affection, I'm surprised she didn't say goodbye to you, Simon. Want to give me your card in case she comes back? She wouldn't stop talking about you."

Simon turns his head towards Bobo so we can't see his face. He doesn't answer, so I hand the vet a card.

"Thanks. We're leaving town tomorrow, but that number will still work."

"You know, I think it was Daisy who really turned Bobo around. I was afraid he'd have to be euthanized. He was really aggressive. I don't know why or how or even if he was the one getting out, but honestly? He seems to have found whatever he was looking for out there. He's been almost affectionate all morning. This will just be a test, reuniting him with a few familiar apes from his circus days, but I bet it goes well. He'll be ready for general release in no time."

The vet babbles on but I'm not paying attention anymore. She fiddles with some paperwork as I move over next to Simon. Bobo looks up at me. He looks relaxed. I start to hum the lullaby. Simon joins in and by the third line, we're both singing out loud. Bobo sets his other hand on the glass near me and I match it with mine. He grunts along with our song.

A thunk and a mechanical whirr come from the metal door. Slowly it lifts, opening to the other side. Bobo hops up and in a second he's at the door. He stands there, scratching his arm nervously. He looks back at Simon, then cautiously peeks out the doorway.

A furry little hand reaches in and pokes him in the nostril. He snorts and shakes his head. I tense.

But instead of getting mad, Bobo plunges eagerly through the door. Simon scrambles up and into the main room. The vet and I follow close behind.

Another gorilla stands in front of Bobo, holding Boingo, the baby. The little one sticks its full hand into

Bobo's nose. Bobo *ooks* and gently plucks it out, letting the baby climb onto his head. One of its little feet slips, landing against Bobo's mouth. He sticks his lips out to help little Boingo climb up over his head and onto one of his massive shoulders. The baby sits there, happily flicking at the ear with the notch in it.

Moki moves in closer to Bobo, picking through his fur. She plucks something out and sticks it in her mouth.

"Excellent! Grooming already," the vet mumbles approvingly. "Moki, his sister, has been trying to break into the medical room since we put Bobo in there. If anything is going to complete Bobo's healing, it's her and her baby Boingo there. She's been so protective of him."

I throw an arm around Simon and squeeze. "That makes perfect sense."

26: SIMON GOES HOME

The bowl from my Dorito cereal is the final straw. The stack of dishes slides with clinks and scrapes into the sink. Luckily, nothing breaks. There are so many dishes in there the stack doesn't have room to fall very far. All the cabinets are empty. Everything smells horrible. I carefully balance my coffee cup on top of the others as my stomach rumbles. I wish we had time to hit Taco Loco before we leave. They must have fixed their window by now.

I regret many things about this mission, but not being able to eat a street taco is pretty high on the list. Next mission, I'll make it a top priority. I will have my street taco some day, just not today.

"Ready?" I call towards the back of the house.

Sarah comes out of her room. Sheets mound in a sloppy pile next to her bed, covered in a few damp towels. The wheels of her suitcase clack along the floorboards. She slept in my room last night because we couldn't find any new sheets to put on her bed, and she refused to put the dirty ones back on. My sheets are stained and stinky too, but at least they're on the mattress.

"We have one hour and twenty-three minutes to get to the jet. Where is Agent Albert?" She grabs her coat and the keys, adjusting her necklace.

I make my way through the front room, past the

piles of crumpled paper and the furniture we've moved around. My suitcase is already in the hallway, shattered camera on top. Thoughts of Gus-cooked meals float around in my head and linger on my taste-buds. Long chats with him. Clean sheets. Well-swept floors. I've never had such a strong appreciation for them before. I'm looking forward to being home.

A knock sounds at the door. Scratches come from the lock and the deadbolt twists open by itself. Agent Albert walks in, wearing his cowboy hat, jeans, and a plaid flannel over his white t-shirt.

"You need to work on your lock-picking, Agent Albert. Your style is sloppy." Sarah's voice is crisp and formal. She doesn't smile, but Albert graces her with a wide, toothy grin.

Then his eyes drift around the wreckage of the cute little house. He lets out a low whistle. "Sheeooot, girlie, you sure do know sloppy. What kind of hurricane came through here?"

He starts to close the door, then he sniffs the air inside the house and thinks better of it.

"I'll wait outside. You got the keys?"

Sarah tosses him the fob, and he disappears back outside. I take a last look around our first home away from the Island. I won't miss the mess. But despite the dirty sheets, Dorito cereal, and Sarah's crazy driving, there's a lot I'll miss about Colorado Springs.

A lot.

But it's time to leave behind the things I don't want to take with me, things I don't need anymore. If I leave my heart here, maybe it will find its way to where it belongs.

"Do you think he'll be okay?" I ask. "Bobo?"

Sarah gives me a tight hug. "He'll be fine, Simon, he's stronger than he looks, and he has his sister to look out for him. Bobo is a survivor. And he doesn't have to worry about Claude or Doctor Dinkelmeyer any more."

"What do you think they're planning next?"

"I don't know." Sarah shrugs. "Trying to take over another country's government I guess, now that we've ruined their scheme here. It's not our problem anymore. DAAAD will continue to track him when they can, chase him, and thwart him. But that will be a problem for more experienced agents. We succeeded at our first mission. Flying colors, Agent Zero said. I'm sure our next assignment will be a lot bigger."

Our next assignment. A few weeks ago, all I could think about was going off on another assignment. Now all I can think about is the empty ache in my chest. After this operation, I've learned an important lesson about who I can trust. All I need is Sarah. She'd never betray me. And I'd never betray her. I don't need anyone else, ever.

Tell lies long enough
Even the mists of your soul
Will start to listen

As I lock the door behind us, a blue car pulls away from the curb and disappears around a corner. I only notice it because they've trained us to notice everything, but my attention is focused on Agent Albert standing by our rental car, waiting to take us home.

"The hosts ain't going to be none too happy about the state that house is in. DAAAD's gonna have a hefty cleaning fee, I tell you what. Also, this car has quite a few more dings than when I passed off the keys to you."

He watches us load our bags into the car, eyeing my broken camera as I carry it to the back seat.

Sarah shrugs. "It's a rental."

Agent Albert rolls his eyes. He walks around to the driver's side, then pauses.

"Oh, this here's for you." He hands me a white bag.

I take it from him. It's warm. A bright blue sun with an orange background is printed on the front. Underneath it says "Taco Loco."

Three warm, fresh, beautiful tacos nestle inside. A heavenly scent wafts from the bag and embraces my nostrils. I breathe deeply. Agent Albert climbs into the driver's side and starts the car. "A pretty little gal just left those for me to give you."

I look around for the blue car that just left, but it's gone. I climb into the back and place the camera next to me, setting the warm bag on my lap. There's a note inside.

It says "For your trip home, wherever that is. Love and kisses until we meet again, Daisy."

Taped to the note is a memory stick, the one from my camera. Sure enough, the flap to the memory stick slot is one of the many parts hanging loose. Daisy must have taken the stick when she was over that night. I put it in the camera and turn it on. Through a spiderweb of cracks in the screen, a video plays. There isn't any sound but between the skipping playback and cracks I can tell it's the one of Bobo's vacay. I smile. Apparently Daisy is almost as good at editing video as I am.

As we pull away from the curb, I bite into the most delicious street taco I'd ever imagined. Juices warm the back of my throat. I pull out another one and pass the bag up to Sarah, delirious with a deep sense of content.

For a brief moment I forget about everything else.

EPILOGUE: INTO THE LIGHT

He sits in the sunlight, a fresh breeze rippling across his fur.

The little one has brought him a stick. He wraps his fingers around it and lifts it to his searching lips, nibbling on the end. The little one, content, tumbles off to find more treasures. The air smells like pine and junk food out here, far away from the little white room. He only goes back there once in a while now.

The girl hasn't returned, and he misses her. Maybe she'll be back. She sang to him when he needed it. She wasn't like the others, but those other people, the cruel ones, are gone now too. The new people who sometimes bring him into the small white room are gentle. They give him apples sometimes. He likes apples.

Before now, he'd done everything they trained him to do. Whether they hurt him or gave him treats, he obeyed. Now no one wants anything from him except some grooming and to appreciate the gift of a stick.

He could climb out of here, the way he climbed the tower back in the circus, or climbed the slippery waterfalls, but he doesn't want to. He wants to be with his family. To protect them. He has everything he needs right here. No more crawling through dark caves, no more fighting angry people.

His sister leans against him, and he grooms her. He likes it here. No one makes him do tricks or perform in front of people. No one makes him go into dark caves anymore. They just look at him and make funny faces and noises from the other side of the invisible wall. That bothers some others in his family, but he doesn't care. He's finally free.

He's finished everything. Every trick, every job. The very last task had been to stick the thing from the bag onto the big humming machine inside the mountain. He did that exactly like they trained him to do. Now he can rest.

PREVIEW: SARAH & SIMON, THE SEVEN-CARAT CONUNDRUM

Prologue: Testing 1, 2, 3

The sky should feel like fire, a blazing sun scorching the sand and anything else dumb enough to try to grow here. But it doesn't. Instead, a dappled shade cast by tall trees shelters the man as he carries his special package towards the inconspicuous door. It's hot enough, for sure. But the deadly desert sands gave way to life years ago, and now joyfully colored buildings line pleasant streets filled with plant life and the sounds of insects buzz around him.

The tall man can't wait to get out of here. Back to the cool grey mists and subdued colors of home. This place is too hot, too sticky, too bright. He misses the cozy feeling of curling up in a thick, warm sweater and watching wild waves crash against the dark rocks. But he has a job to do.

No bells tinkle as he pushes open the door. This isn't a shop, not the kind of place decorated to invite you in. You only come here if you have a reason.

The room beyond the door is perfectly comfortable. Nothing dingy or dark. Just inauspicious, comfortable-looking couches and chairs, arranged in a conversational layout. A few tables scattered around. Everything is a comfortable shade of brown. The only nod to the colors out on the street are some orange and yellow curtains. They're currently drawn closed, and glow in the sunlight like a stained-glass window.

A woman sitting in an armchair looks up as he enters. She doesn't smile.

"I'm here," he says, feeling uncomfortable. What if she suspects something?

But she just nods and gestures to a chair across from her. He sits down and places a black leather pouch on the coffee table between them. It looks like an old-fashioned doctor's bag, stiff without being formal, and a comfortable size to carry. Not unlike a purse. He pulls it open and reaches inside.

The woman leans forward, her relaxed veneer cracking a bit to show excitement. Slowly, the man pulls a piece of fine-quality, soft cloth from the bag. He lays it on the table and sets the rest of the bag next to him on the chair.

The woman's eyes dart up to him, then focus on the cloth bundle. She reaches out and pulls the corners of the cloth aside, unwrapping a glittering jewel. The sapphire's deep blue color almost seems to glow, even in the low light of the room. Sparkling dots, reflected by the jewel from the overhead lights, splash over the walls of the room like bubbles.

If the man was prone to fancy, he might have thought it looked like hundreds of light fairies had burst from the sapphire as soon as it was unwrapped. But instead he just scratches at his short salt-and-pepper hair and leans forward. His eyes meet hers as he looks up. He raises an eyebrow quizzically and she smiles.

"He really did it, then?" the woman whispers. "The bastard really sold it?"

The man shrugs. "That's what I'm here to find out. Is this really the Sapphire of the Panda King?"

The woman lifts the jewel from the table, bringing it closer to her face. The glistening gem perches in a setting of rose gold. The prongs cleverly hold it so light can touch every expertly carved facet. The setting splays out like leaves, creating a delicate backdrop and connecting the jewel to a chain. She squints at it.

"It's definitely seven carats. The setting looks authentic, see this scratch here? That's from an attempted robbery back in 1923. Hang on while I get my loupe."

The man fidgets nervously with something inside the bag while the woman pulls a gadget from the table's drawer. She flips out one of its magnifying lenses and peers at the jewel through it, holding the sapphire to the light and twisting it around and around.

The man fidgets some more, waiting.

The woman grunts, talking to herself, and finally nods, setting the sapphire back onto the cloth. She looks up at him with a sideways grin.

"It's wonderful workmanship." She runs a finger across it, playing with the chain, poking it into the shape of an S, then a C. "But it's not real."

The man's tense shoulders sag. "How can you tell?"

The woman lifts the jewel by the chain and slides it over her neck, then holds up the sapphire. "The clarity is slightly off. Even if I hadn't been trained so well to recognize the Sacred Seven crown jewels, I probably would have caught it, but it's still an excellent copy. There's something unusual about the crystalline structure though. And the setting is a little heavier, a little larger than it should be."

The man nods slowly. "Right. It wasn't easy to get the crystal to form that way, but I hope it will be worth it."

The woman tilts her head at him. "What do you mean? Is this your counterfeit? Wait, did you bring it to me to see if I could tell it was a fake?"

"That's part of it." The man reaches into his bag for a pair of safety goggles. He slips them on.

The woman leans back, the jewel dropping against her chest on its chain. Her eyebrows draw together in curiosity and confusion. "Part of it?"

"Oh yes. We have to test the thing. It's just a small part of a much larger plan. As are you."

"Me? What do I have to do with your plan? If you want me to betray the king, it's going to cost you a lot more than what you've already paid me."

"Oh no," the man replies with a small, amused smile. He pulls a tiny device, no larger than a car fob, from the bag. "It isn't your cooperation we need."

"What then?" The woman scrunches her mouth to the side in irritation. "And you look ridiculous. Why are you wearing those goggles?"

The man stands, takes a few steps back and presses the button. "Safety first."

The jewel explodes.

A loud bang and bright flash direct the explosion's percussive force out from the necklace's setting up into its unique crystalline structure. The sapphire shatters into dozens of sharp, sparkling daggers, directed almost entirely at the woman wearing it. Shards of blue death blossom from her chest and face, a few escaping with enough force to embed themselves into the armchair she's sitting in. But she doesn't feel any of them. The explosion already did enough damage that she'll never feel anything again.

The man brushes sparkling blue crumbs from his grey shirt, slips off the goggles, and puts them back into his doctor's bag as he lifts it from the chair.

"We need you out of the picture." He tells what remains of the woman as her body slumps back into the chair. Then he carefully removes the chain and what's left of the necklace from her. "But I can't leave this lying around, now can I? Don't want anyone figuring things out too soon."

The woman, of course, doesn't answer.

Without a backwards glance, the man takes his bag and walks back out onto the sweaty, colorful street. He closes the door behind him with a satisfying click, and strides away.

Continue reading:
Sarah and Simon, Book 2:
The Seven Carat Conundrum

IF YOU ENJOYED THIS BOOK, PLEASE LEAVE A REVIEW!

An honest, written review-even just a few quick words-is the best way to support an author.

Thank you for leaving a Star-Rating or Written Review for The Phoenix Plan.

Click Here

ABOUT THE AUTHOR

Terri Selting David

Terri's career spanned more than a decade in 3D character animation for video games, films, television shows, and even a comic book (but mostly video games) encompassed character animation, art direction, writing, and story development. Then she had children, which tends to change one's view of what's truly important in life. She retired from the crazy world of video game development and, in 2015, co-founded the Renegade Girls Tinkering Club, a hands-on summer camp. Since then, she's created dozens of curricula, including more than 230 individual projects aimed at growing a solid foundation in STEM. But she doesn't always write about science. She turned her storytelling talents to fiction and continues to write books for smart readers who love great characters and exciting plots, blending smart comedy, action, and heart. She published her first book in 2020, and continues to create for kids and adults who think reading should be a pleasure.

She lives in San Francisco with 2 rowdy children, 2 cat overlords, and a fabulous, brilliant husband who brings her tea every night.

BOOKS BY THIS AUTHOR

Terri's Author Page

Check out a complete and constantly updating list of all Terri's books, including the Sarah & Simon, Teen Spies series.

The Renegade Spy Project

Wren is impulsive, curious, and always in trouble. Can her flaws become her greatest asset?

"It's The Babysitter's Club meets MacGyver!"

Build your own GADGETS! Instructions included in these charming story about friendship, middle school, and the Engineering Design Process, finding your place, and being a good leader for kids ages 8-12.

Renegade Style

Will Amber choose to stand out, or stand up for what's right?

The Renegade Success Plan

What is Ivy willing to sacrifice for success?

Learn about electricity and circuits while building DIY PROJECTS along with the Renegades in this interactive adventure proving STEM is for everyone. Instructions included for hands-on science and building projects.

TERRI SELTING DAVID

For a complete listing of books and to sign up for the mailing list for the latest news, please visit Terri's website at:

www.TerriSeltingDavid.com

Or visit her Amazon Author page at:
https://www.amazon.com/stores/author/B08F7JRGBM

Made in the USA
Columbia, SC
13 April 2025

56562142R00190